PIMPINAN

by

John Cooper

Dedication

For Rebecca, Clara and Henry

Acknowledgements

The author would like to thank Wikipedia, without which he would have had to get off his arse a lot more often, to find things out. A suitable donation has been made.

Thanks are also due to ConocoPhillips Indonesia Inc. Ltd., in whose paid employ much of the first few chapters of Pimpinan were written.

Self-aggrandising but Irrelevant Quotation

If you had a face like mine, you'd punch me right on the nose, and I'm just the fella to do it
- Stan Laurel

Prologue

Alan Jones, whose real name was Joe Gouder, was having nightmares again, and this time Mr and Mrs Jackman decided they had had enough of being woken by his muffled sounds of panic.

It was only six weeks since this strange, secretive man had showed up at the Jackmans' fittingly named Prince of Paupers public house, hidden away in the dingy backstreets behind Great Yarmouth's plastic and neon Golden Mile, and offered to work behind the bar in return for a bed and board and a few pounds spending money. Although not impolite, he seemed unwilling or unable to hold any kind of conversation, and some of the few regular customers of the Prince of Paupers had expressed a dislike for the sullen new barman who drank most of his weekly wages in supermarket vodka and eyed everyone in the room with a mixture of fear and suspicion.

Mr and Mrs Jackman resolved to let Alan Jones go the following morning for the sake of their own peace of mind, as a result of which Alan would wander the seafront aimlessly for three more months in increasingly dirty and foul-smelling clothes, begging passers-by for change and scrounging from the hot-dog stalls, always sleeping in a cheap alcohol-induced stupor under the pier until the night he finally fell asleep forever.

Joe Gouder's circumstances had not always been so bleak; in fact life in some of the gang-infested parts of east London had been peachy for a small-time gangster like Joe in the days before he had heard of Pimpinan, until one day the unseen, unknown Pimpinan had made Joe end his beloved twin brother Jack's life with the thoughtfully provided railway iron and flee in numb horror on the first intercity train out of London, never daring to go back home even for a moment and leaving a scene so appallingly shocking that Detective Constable Robbins subsequently spent weeks on sick leave having trauma counselling and, by coincidence, only returned to work on the morning Alan Jones got fired.

Chapter 1 - Detective Constable Robbins

Ron Robbins' career was not all it could have been, but over the years since he made detective with the Tower Hamlets Borough Police division of the Metropolitan Police, based at Bethnal Green, he had been making a concerted effort to get it back on track so that when he retired, he would be able to look back with at least some satisfaction on a job well done. At fifty-one years of age, Detective Constable Robbins was not one of life's winners, although Detective Constable Robbins had to admit that finding Jack Gouder hanging by his femoral condyles in the derelict railway shed was a stroke of luck that had led to his life taking a turn for the better, once he had finished milking trauma-leave for all it was worth. He was shy and awkward in the company of women, and had never really been able to come to terms with the young female officers who regularly overtook him on the career ladder with effortless rapidity, which he attributed to a secret policy of positive discrimination designed to hold back better detectives such as himself so as not to pose a threat to the positions of the senior officers. Detective Constable Robbins had been married once, many years ago, and his brief union had left him scarred; Lucinda was an outgoing, gregarious girl who loved to party and mix it up with the Beautiful People, and very quickly became bored with her husband's irregular working hours and staid personality. Within nine months she had left him, having had a string of casual affairs culminating in a cringe-making scene in the street outside the marital home when Police Constable Robbins, as he was known at the time, discovered his wife half drunk and half undressed in a twenty-year-old Mercedes with a nineteen-year-old member of the local Sunday League football team, and although Detective Constable Robbins craved the company of women and the comforts it promised, his dating activity ever since the break-up never lived up to his expectations. Women avoided Detective Constable Robbins, finding him nervous, clingy and dull.

In the nineteen-eighties, Police Constable Robbins' career was still with Thames Valley Police and had seemed promising enough. Nearly six years had seen him move from station duties to mobile response, attending break-ins and domestic disturbances, to motorway patrol within the Thames Valley jurisdiction of the M4 motorway heading west out of London. Finally he had been placed on fast patrol, driving a Police Range Rover in the days when many patrol officers worked unaccompanied, in which he had stopped speeding and erratic drivers, but he also was the main focus point for motorway surveillance. Constable Robbins' primary job had been to partially conceal his Range Rover in a special Police roadside lay-by and watch the traffic leaving London in the direction of Wales, looking out for whatever make and model of car had been reported to him as fleeing the scene of some crime or other, or known to be carrying someone wanted for something. In practice this meant hour after hour of sitting in a stationary car reading passing vehicle number plates, and although his colleagues regarded this as the most soul-destroying, wrist-slitting work in the entire force, Constable Robbins quite enjoyed it. On the rare occasions he spotted a target, he was expected to radio in and give chase, bringing the vehicle down if safe to do so. His Range Rover was powered by a 3.9 litre V8 race tuned engine specially produced for Police Range

Rovers, and was capable of up to 135 miles per hour, more than enough to outrun most standard saloon cars, however Constable Robbins was not expected to stop cars containing known felons alone, and he was rarely sure of what type of crime they were wanted for. He would give chase, constantly radioing in his position, and in theory another mobile unit of up to four officers would intercept the target from ahead, bringing the target up in a "sandwich" operation to the side of the motorway where the suspects would be cuffed and taken away.

Constable Robbins was a keen and fairly competent shooter and gun club member, and although he was always unarmed when on patrol, Constable Robbins dreamed of one day becoming a member of the Tactical Firearms Unit. His experiences representing the London Boroughs Gun Club team at Practical Pistol competitions all over the country had brought him into contact with many competitors who were serving Firearms Unit officers, most of whom Constable Robbins regarded as such poor shots that the safest place to be while they were on the shooting line was directly in front of the targets. Constable Robbins felt he would make a good Tactical Firearms Unit team member, and might possibly graduate to a Police firearms trainer; his superiors thought he was not the most physically fit or, as demonstrated by the infamous canteen Kit-Kat fight, the most stable of men and secretly wished they could find an excuse to take away the bastard's firearms certificate.

Ron Robbins' favourite gun was his Brno .22 rifle. While by no means the most powerful or expensive gun he owned, it was a beautifully crafted Czechoslovakian bolt-action rifle with a polished American rosewood stock which he had fitted with a good variable power telescopic sight, which he owned legally, and secretly had fitted with a detachable commercial silencer, which he did not. Ron Robbins could drive in a drawing pin with it at a distance of 75 yards, and with the silencer attached and using special subsonic ammunition it made no more noise than a man of questionable manners spitting out an orange pip. Ron Robbins and his Brno spent many happy hours stalking rabbits west of the M25 London orbital motorway in fields belonging to farmers who let him shoot there, and he often spent his working hours on the side of the M4 watching the rabbits gambolling in the fields instead of watching the cars barrelling along the motorway.

One day Constable Robbins stopped at his terraced house in his Police Range Rover and took the Brno with him, in its carrying case covered with a car rug to avoid the attention of prying neighbours. He also took an empty black plastic rubbish bin liner in his pocket for his rabbits, and set off for his assigned position a few miles past Heathrow airport on the westbound carriageway of the M4. It made Constable Robbins nervous to know that if he was discovered with a rifle in his patrol car he would face serious disciplinary proceedings, though in such an event he planned not to deny his guilt but to say in his defence that he intended to drop the rifle at the nearby Maidenhead house of a friend and fellow member of the London Boroughs Gun Club who was a skilled amateur gunsmith, for some attention to the trigger pull. He resolved to hide the bag with any rabbits behind the hedge if he was called off anywhere, and in any case it had been more than a year since anyone else had been inside the patrol car with him. Constable Robbins found that with the front passenger window open around six inches and by leaning on the seat back and the driver's door, he could keep the rifle entirely within the car and still get a perfect steady shot at any rabbit out to around one hundred and fifty yards away in the field next to the motorway, with very little chance of being seen from the road. The field was filled with recently cut wheat stubble, and he decided to make a note of where each rabbit fell and run out at the end of the day to collect them all in one go, to minimise the amount of time members of the public might be able to spot a uniformed copper plodding around in a field with a bin bag picking things up. Over the course of four hours motorway patrol, Constable Robbins managed to pot five rabbits, which he collected in the bin liner and dropped off at home together with his Brno before going off duty. Later that evening, Ron Robbins skinned and cleaned the rabbits and braised the meat in a homemade chicken stock with a little white wine, garlic and shallots and baked the mixture in three family-sized pie dishes with short-crust pastry toppings. Ron Robbins enjoyed the pies for the next few days, and pretty soon rabbit pie began to feature prominently in his diet until the day in nineteen ninety-seven when three plain clothes officers from the Metropolitan Police Flying Squad together with six uniformed Thames Valley officers battered Ron Robbins' front door in at four o'clock in the morning and led him away wearing only a pair of briefs, a blanket and a pair of handcuffs, and effectively froze his career for the next fifteen years and his penchant for rabbit pie for good.

Constable Robbins had been discovered in the act of sighting his rifle on a rabbit by an elderly gentleman named Harold Hines, who had been walking with his English Springer spaniel, Buster, along the edge of the field and who had silently appeared from behind the hedge as suddenly as it is possible for an eighty-seven-year old arthritic gentleman to appear from behind a hedge, and who had walked directly into Constable Robbins' line of fire, startling Constable Robbins so badly that any attempt to nonchalantly pass off the event was rendered futile. Harold Hines had shouted at Constable Robbins, as he rightly suspected he had narrowly avoided 'having me ruddy 'ead blown off', and later telephoned the Thames Valley Police station at Reading to report that he had had a narrow scrape with a uniformed copper with a 'shotgun' who was aiming the gun through the patrol car window in his direction. The car was quickly linked to Constable Robbins, and later that evening when Constable Robbins had finished his shift and gone off duty, waiting Forensics technicians fine-toothed the Range Rover to see if a firearm had been discharged recently in or near the vehicle, and were shocked to find significant firearm discharge residue covering every internal surface of the car and ingrained in all of the carpeting and upholstery, which the Forensics technicians reported to be consistent with the aftermath of a minor war. They also discovered traces of dried blood in the rear baggage area, and a warrant was immediately issued for Constable Robbins' arrest and detention, pending analysis and typing of the blood.

It took a full four days of investigation and intense interrogation of Constable Robbins before the Metropolitan Police Special Branch and then Thames Valley Police were able to satisfy themselves that Constable Robbins had not in fact been, as was at first suspected, involved in the planning or commissioning of Terrorism offences, Murder or Attempted Murder associated with Drugs Supply, Threatening Behaviour and/or Gang Warfare, Treason, Reckless Public

Endangerment, Illegal Arms Trading, Disorderly Behaviour with Intent to cause Harassment, Alarm or Distress or any other real or supposed offence involving capitalised words, and that the traces of blood discovered in the rear of Constable Robbins' Range Rover had not emanated from human victims but had actually belonged to a rabbit or rabbits unknown, which was a lucky thing because Deputy Chief Constable Bryant, who was in charge of the investigation once it had been passed back to Thames Valley Police, had somehow managed to keep the arrest of a serving uniformed Police officer on suspicion of terrorism activities and firearms violations off the media radar. By his own admission, Constable Robbins was, however, guilty of a wide range of other various offences and misdemeanours associated with the shooting of rabbits on private land without permission while on duty, utilising a marked Police patrol car and probably whilst claiming overtime and therefore was in much deeper shit than anybody had at first thought. Deputy Chief Constable Bryant considered that fiddling overtime and conducting personal business on force time, especially enjoyable, fun personal business, was an even more grave offence than actually engaging in terrorism-related activity, for the simple reason that if a copper spent his time shooting rabbits while he was supposed to be looking out for hot car registration number plates, he had no chance at all of intercepting any real terrorist being sought on the westbound carriageway of the M4 motorway at that time, leaving the said real terrorist free to proceed with the commissioning of mayhem and causing the deaths of countless innocent victims which, being so close to the busiest international airport in the world, was not a Good Thing and would make Constable Robbins individually and Thames Valley

Police collectively just as culpable in the resulting carnage as the real terrorist or terrorists that Constable Robbins may have inadvertently let slip through the net. Deputy Chief Constable Bryant resolved to throw the book at the little bastard for making him look bad in the Chief Constable's eyes, and proceeded to draw up a list of criminal, civil and disciplinary offences to discuss with the Chief Constable, who in view of the seriousness of the situation and the possibility of adverse publicity which would be certain to draw the attention of the Home Secretary and might therefore affect the Chief Constable's service record and likelihood of receiving another award to add to his knighthood in the Queen's Birthday Honours, had decreed that his authorisation was required prior to any decision being made about how Constable Robbins was to be dealt with. Deputy Chief Constable Bryant was also secretly sure that Constable Robbins' unforgivable transgressions were a carefully planned segment of a much wider plot to discredit Deputy Chief Constable Bryant in the eyes of the Chief Constable being hatched by his minions, his neighbours, the Round Table, the Conservative Club and probably the Freemasons, the latter of which Deputy Chief Constable Bryant had been trying unsuccessfully to be introduced to formally for longer than he could remember. The world was out to get him, and Deputy Chief Constable Bryant would not go down without a fight.

On a brand new lined yellow Legal pad, Deputy Chief Constable Bryant wrote at the top of the first page:

Constable 4582 Ronald Robbins – Offences for discussion.
13-Aug-1997

Motivated, he mulled ideas in his mind over lunch, and returning to his office at 1.30 pm sharp, he followed up with as many angles as he could think of.

1. Rabbits: stealing of (check with DPP who owns wild rabbits). Criminal.

2. Unlawful possession and use of an unlicensed sound moderator (silencer) contrary to (check section of firearms act with DPP). Criminal.

3. Failing to follow orders while on duty because conducting private business, i.e. shooting rabbits. Disciplinary and see 1 above. Also check if overtime claims connect with rabbits – spurious overtime claims = dismissal? Prosecution?

4. Causing noxious substances to be spread all over TVP patrol car, i.e. rabbit blood and gun crud (check proper term with forens.)

5. Discharging firearm on a public highway (check with DPP if TVP patrol lay-by constitutes public highway). Criminal / civil.

6. Using authorised firearm certified for range use in unauthorised location. ?? Plus unauthorised carrying of privately owned firearm in patrol car.

7. Nearly shooting Mr Hines – must be something there, reckless negligence, public endangerment etc??

8. Check prior record (still waiting - chase Cindy if not rec'd by tomorrow 9 am).

9. WHAT WOULD THE CHIEF DO????

Deputy Chief Constable Bryant decided to prepare an informal report to the Chief Constable (or a 'discussion paper', as he usually tried to spin it in order to avoid having to personally commit to any opinion. Not committing to any opinion until he knew the Chief Constable's opinion was the one political device Deputy Chief Constable Bryant excelled at). This was an important one, and failure was not an option unless Deputy Chief Constable Bryant was willing to be made to look a fool in the eyes of the Chief Constable. Deputy Chief Constable Bryant spent almost every working moment looking for ways to make a good impression on his superior officer, and spent his few remaining working moments plotting vengeance against any subordinate whom Deputy Chief Constable Bryant suspected of trying to undermine his authority and thereby sabotage his reputation in the eyes of the Chief Constable. The eyes of the Chief Constable were very important eyes to be seen in a good light in, and Deputy Chief Constable Bryant's constant focus was centred on maximising his time being seen in a good light in the Chief Constable's eyes, and never allowing the Chief Constable's eyes to view Deputy Chief Constable Bryant in a bad light. This strategy was meeting with only moderate success, due to the scheming and plotting of the many traitorous factions who were out to get him.

Deputy Chief Constable Bryant had a secret weapon up his sleeve which allowed him to always project an authoritative impression of himself as a brilliant, educated, erudite mind with a deep understanding of etymology, and Deputy Chief Constable Bryant was confident that his distinction as a wordsmith would result in *The Many Few* being a literary award-winning, runaway success. Deputy Chief Constable Bryant was a self-taught master of the art of articulate business and quasi-legal formal writing, having pioneered, perfected and pretended to register as a trademark The Single Most Effective Secret® for producing polished memos, reports, statements, policy papers and the like, which so far nobody else had discovered or learned to emulate despite Deputy Chief Constable Bryant's skill frequently being demonstrated to devastating effect. Recipients of his magnificent penmanship usually were at a complete loss to find words of response, and therefore often didn't bother to try. The Single Most Effective Secret® basically was this: Deputy Chief Constable Bryant would first draft out the article in rough copy; then underline every noun, adjective and verb and anything else that took his fancy, and then finally – the masterstroke – using a copy of Roget's Thesaurus, pick a synonym at random for every third underlined word on the draft, and replace that word with its synonym, taking care not to accidentally pick the antonym at the end of the list. Deputy Chief Constable Bryant didn't much care for antonyms, for in Deputy Chief Constable Bryant's experience he quite often found they seemed to mean the exact opposite of whichever word he was seeking to embellish, and he failed to see the purpose of including antonyms in an otherwise useful thesaurus where they would lurk like treacherous little stumbling blocks, lying in wait to trip one up. Deputy Chief

Constable Bryant had a personal key performance indicator by which he measured the success of The Single Most Effective Secret®, which was to force each recipient of every memo, report, statement or policy paper to refer to the dictionary at least three times to find out or confirm what his prose meant, and his personal best (as far as he could tell) was six.

It was thus that Deputy Chief Constable Bryant had found himself in an unmarked, chauffeur-driven Thames Valley Police car on the way to the office of the Chief Constable in order to receive the Chief Constable's decision following his evaluation of Deputy Chief Constable Bryant's informal report (headed "Discussion Paper" in Arial 14-point bold font) on the Robbins affair. Deputy Chief Constable Bryant's informal report on the Robbins affair was, in Deputy Chief Constable Bryant's opinion, a masterpiece without precedent, but the Chief Constable was a fearsome nut to crack, and Deputy Chief Constable Bryant was suffering from butterflies in his tummy and a noticeably elevated pulse and blood pressure which seemed to be escalating as he got closer to his destination. The Chief Constable was a political master with a photographic memory and an unerring eye for detail who did not beat about the bush and did not suffer fools gladly, but while no-one could rightly call Deputy Chief Constable Bryant a fool as far as he knew, his burning desire to impress the Chief Constable and live up to expectations had become an obsession which ate into Deputy Chief Constable Bryant's psyche and kept him awake at night, plotting and planning. Deputy Chief Constable Bryant and the Chief Constable had an unspoken special relationship which was underlined by the fact that while, traditionally, chief constables and their deputies had always addressed each other on a first names basis, Deputy Chief Constable

Bryant and the Chief Constable dispensed with such forced camaraderie and called each other "Chief Constable" or "Sir" and "Bryant" respectively. Deputy Chief Constable Bryant held the utmost respect for the Chief Constable that frequently morphed into abject fear and awe and led to periods of paranoid self-examination, while the Chief Constable gladly reciprocated by nurturing heartfelt contempt for Deputy Chief Constable Bryant, whom he considered to be one of the most inept human beings he knew, who had just happened to become a senior officer of Thames Valley Police thanks to the enigmatic entry on his curriculum vitae which nobody would admit to not understanding for fear of appearing foolish and unsophisticated, and whom the Chief Constable could not fire because that would mean everybody from Home Secretary level down would have to admit that they had sanctioned Deputy Chief Constable Bryant's appointment in the first place and then tolerated his ineptitude for years. The Chief Constable regarded Deputy Chief Constable Bryant's existence in much the same way that a haemorrhoid sufferer might regard their affliction: by recognising the need for keeping up a cheerful disposition, never publicly acknowledging the problem despite being constantly aware of its unwelcome presence, and never losing hope of finding a miracle cure that gets rid of it without involving further pain or unnecessary embarrassment.

Deputy Chief Constable Bryant strode purposefully into the Chief Constable's enormous but functional office clutching a copy of his masterful informal report (headed "Discussion Paper" in Arial 14-point bold font), acutely aware of the need to appear self-assured and confident. Deputy Chief Constable Bryant mustered all the self-assurance of a pet cat that had accidentally found itself in a dark alley smelling of fresh dog-piss, and when the Chief Constable barked "Sit, Bryant", Deputy Chief Constable Bryant sat immediately, and authoritatively began to fiddle with the crease in his trousers as he awaited the Chief Constable's attention in silence.

"What," began the Chief Constable a moment later as he slid a sheet of paper across the polished leather desk top towards Deputy Chief Constable Bryant without glancing up, "does this mean?"

Deputy Chief Constable Bryant's heart skipped a beat as he recognised the first page of his Discussion Paper, and realised with joy that he was about to be given the opportunity to demonstrate his outstanding command of the English language by gently guiding his superior officer through the intricacies of such a high-level document. Deputy Chief Constable Bryant recalled the sheet by heart in a flash:

Executive Summary

The Chief Constable and the Deputy Chief Constable presume to confer and consent on an apposite course of action with regard to adjusting and gruelling the incumbent Constable 4582 Ronald Robbins. It is held that the parties associated are before time familiar with the fundamental intelligence of the case.

The instance was accounted to elucidation by a member of the commune who reported intently escaping being fortuitously shot by the indicted whilst in the proceeding of commissioning a thievery of certain wildlife in the watch medium of conveyance, at a time when the incumbent applicant was hypothetically in the process of discovering vehicular transportation holding suspects sought after for interviewing and back-up with apprehension thereof.

As the facts and the culmination of the illustration portrayed in detail in this Discussion Paper will represent, it is for the Chief Constable and the Deputy Chief Constable to settle on by common treaty between two attainable progressions of action:

1. *The dishonourable relief of Constable Robbins from the Thames Valley Police Force with pasting of all pension privileges, consequentially the disqualification of the lately Mr Robbins from being adequate to hold a firearm certificate (FAC), and the ensuing inauguration of criminal measures with regard to theft, illicit firearm use in a municipal place, and inattentive endangerment of life and chattels, or*

2. *Some erstwhile course of action which the Chief Constable and the Deputy Chief Constable sagaciously come to a decision would be a just and pertinent castigation under the state of affairs.*

"Well, Chief Constable, Sir, the executive summary is a summary for the executive addressees to gain an..."

"No, Bryant", interrupted the Chief Constable. "What I am asking you; what I would like to know is: what on earth does any of this drivel mean? What is it you are completely and utterly failing to convey in these – eleven, is it? Yes, eleven pages, these eleven pages of disjointed and incoherent verbiage? Are you expressing some sort of opinion, or making a suggestion of any kind? Are you proffering information, or a recommendation? I completely fail to grasp one single point from it. You might just as well have written to me in Chinese".

Deputy Chief Constable Bryant's joy metamorphosed instantly into anxious trepidation as he suddenly realised, too late, that he had once again overestimated the Chief Constable's English language proficiency and that he would require all of his diplomatic dexterity to subtly steer the Chief Constable's understanding in the right direction without being patronising, or giving the appearance he was talking to a child. To be patronising toward the Chief Constable or to give the appearance he was talking to a child would almost certainly diminish his standing in the eyes of the Chief Constable or harm his annual performance review, and as much as Deputy Chief Constable Bryant did not appreciate being spoken to as though he were a nincompoop, he had to tread carefully, as he did not want to undo months or even years of intensive Chief Constable esteem-building. Deputy Chief Constable Bryant's mind screamed and raced desperately to find a starting point from which to calmly commence the tutorial, at which point, as if on cue, his inner turmoil was betrayed and increased by an order of magnitude by the rapid tick that suddenly began rapidly ticking away just underneath his left eye.

"This is what will happen, and what will not happen," said the Chief Constable without waiting for Deputy Chief Constable Bryant to respond. "I shall not risk the Press getting hold of this. There will be no sacking of Robbins. There will be no initiation of criminal or civil proceedings against Robbins. There will be no disciplinary hearing, and no announcement. This matter shall not be spoken of outside this room. No attempt shall be made to scotch any rumours among the troops about Robbins' recent absence, or activities that led to it. Rumours shall be neither confirmed nor denied, nor even commented upon, and shall remain simply rumours".

Deputy Chief Constable Bryant felt the air being crushed from his lungs as the enormity of the Chief Constable's pronouncement descended on him. The Chief Constable had not even considered Deputy Chief Constable Bryant's professional and eminently sensible reasoning and advice, but simply dismissed it like some gossip-rag tat while that bastard Robbins was getting away with making a fool of him by somehow making sure the Chief Constable sympathised with and subscribed to Robbins' treachery. It was too much to bear, and Deputy Chief Constable Bryant resolved there and then to do something spontaneous, drastic and certain to have the Chief Constable regretting his actions for the rest of his career.

"Chief Constable, Sir, I will NOT be overridden and ... and DISMISSED, dismissed without so much as a..." pleaded the Deputy Chief Constable, his chin starting to twitch and tears beginning to well up in his eyes. "Er, as a ... well, I hereby advise you..."

"Shut up, Bryant, and hear me out. I have spoken to the Commissioner of the Metropolitan Police on this matter, and Sir Alan and I agree that a high degree of diplomacy is required to prevent yet another round of tabloid publicity criticising the Police generally and further tarnishing the public perception of both the Met's and Thames Valley's professional capabilities in particular. We have therefore determined that a complete restructuring of the offending party's status as a Police officer is required involving the cooperation of two Services at the highest level. I am relying on you, Bryant, personally to put this plan into action and to manage and oversee this very delicate matter".

The Chief Constable leaned forward conspiratorially. "Can I count on your utmost discretion and loyalty at this time of crisis?"

"W..."

"Good", continued the Chief Constable, "because I want you to write in your inimitable style to Constable Robbins, in strictest confidence, informing him of these three salient points: number one, he has been found guilty by a top level internal review panel of gross misconduct and dereliction of duty, and accordingly is formally issued with a written warning stating that if his conduct deviates from the exemplary at any time during the effective period of the written warning, he may be dismissed from duty forthwith without the requirement for further disciplinary proceedings; number two, as a condition of this written warning Constable Robbins is to be transferred with immediate effect to the Metropolitan Police stationed at Bethnal Green with no loss of service, and number three, the effective period of this written warning is three years from the date of issue, following which, in the absence of any further disciplinary misdemeanours, it will automatically be removed from his file and deleted from Police personnel records.

"Robbins' immediate superiors will be advised that Robbins has been granted a transfer to the Met for personal reasons. So you see, Bryant, we have found a solution to our problem, and the problem has gone away with absolutely no ringing of alarm bells or need of press conferences. Robbins will move to the Met at Bethnal Green to avoid the prospect of his certain dismissal from Thames Valley, oblivious to the fact that Thames Valley could not possibly dismiss Robbins because to do so would unleash a firestorm of negative media publicity damaging all of our careers and probably resulting in further dismissals or sanctions higher up the ladder. Robbins will commute to his new place of work on the other side of London every day until he gets his career back on track, or as is more likely, he will become disillusioned due to the overwhelming amount of commuting, find another avenue of employment, and will leave the Force of his own accord".

Deputy Chief Constable Bryant's emotional roller-coaster reached a new apex with the realisation that he had contributed to such a brilliant strategy.

"Sir", he beamed, "this is exactly the sort of thing I was implicitly proposing between the lines in my Discussion Paper, if you would allow me to..."

"There is more, Bryant", continued the Chief Constable with barely a pause, "because of course such a damage limitation exercise is fraught with risk. We need someone capable and high-level to be on hand day and night taking control of the situation from within. What would happen if Robbins made some kind of cock-up and his disciplinary record was pulled? We cannot risk the spectre of a serving Policeman being dismissed in consequence of a minor disciplinary offence due to previous charges involving personal firearms on duty and near misses with the general public. It would smack of a cover-up the first time around, and the publicity simply doesn't bear thinking about.

"That is why I have arranged for you, Bryant, to be seconded to the Met on a special assignment until the three years is up or Robbins departs the force, whichever is the sooner. Don't worry, you won't need to venture over to Bethnal Green all the time; you will probably spend most of your time based at Paddington or somewhere central. Your role will ostensibly be to troubleshoot special projects, and your official secondary remit will be to facilitate close liaison and cooperation between the task forces of the Met and Thames Valley. However, and this strictly between you and me, your secret secondary remit will be to monitor all aspects of Robbins' performance and report them directly to me by secure means, and be ready to jump in at a moment's notice in the event of any occurrence that is likely to result in any form of disciplinary action against Robbins. We will have frequent, regular meetings on the rare occasions when I call them. You will be appointed to the position of Special Commander of the Metropolitan Police, which is, as the name implies, a specially created role at the rank of Commander. Congratulations, Bryant, this really is the front line of policing for you, and you cannot fail to make a big impression where it matters. The sky, as they say, is the limit".

Special Commander! Deputy Chief Constable Bryant felt so proud he might burst at the seams, and that elated feeling lasted unabated until later the same evening when Mrs Bryant pointed out to him that the position of Commander within the Met was a fifth tier position, junior to several handfuls of people, whilst her husband's present position was second tier with only one superior, namely the Chief Constable himself. Mrs Bryant's negativity and general lack of understanding of the complicated machinations of top-flight policing irked Deputy Chief Constable Bryant at times, and never more so than when she also pointed out that because her husband was being seconded from Thames Valley Police, his new role would not attract any inner London salary benefits or additional transportation cost allowances despite the additional two to three hours a day travelling time he would now have to get used to. But by then, it was too late. Meanwhile, about fifteen miles away at Chez Jacques, Sir Stephen and Lady Chief Constable were concluding their celebration of the Chief Constable's double stroke of genius with the last of a bottle of good Pinot Gris and some rather fine, well-ripened Camembert with oat biscuits. The Chief Constable had, he concluded, found the metaphorical magic ointment for his metaphorical haemorrhoid and could now metaphorically and literally sit comfortably once again.

— o —

Unlike Special Commander Bryant, who had found out on the third day into his three year stint at the Met that Thames Valley Police had wasted no time in installing a new Acting Deputy Chief Constable, Constable Robbins actually enjoyed his new Metropolitan Police life at Bethnal Green, with its opportunities to start afresh and to make new friends who were blissfully unaware of his previous reputation as a bit of a tosser, and had worked hard to portray himself as 'one of the boys' and a keen team player. He had even found some measure of success at pretending female officers were his equals and liking football, and his carefully cultivated, slightly indifferent disposition towards both had had the effect of causing his social life, particularly where women were concerned, to develop beyond being the reluctantly tolerated member of whatever group he was hanging on to. Constable Robbins had discovered from watching an episode of 'Whatever Happened to the Likely Lads' that the way to attract women was to appear aloof and apathetic.

"Treat 'em mean, keep 'em keen," the short one had said, "The more you try, the less you will succeed. Ignore them completely while carrying on with your interesting manly activities; eventually they will begin to think something's wrong with them and will come over and drop subtle hints about asking them out on dates, to reassure themselves. Women hate not being the centre of attention".

Once Constable Robbins had overcome the hurdle of only managing to appear aloof and apathetic in much the same way as a spider on its web or a serial rapist appears aloof and apathetic, the women in his new environs seemed to be more comfortable about being around Ron Robbins until he happened to mention that his friends called him "Rockin' Robbins", which nobody ever did. Without family to consider or happy memories to tie him to his old haunts, Constable Robbins had soon moved into a flat in Bethnal Green to be closer to his work, and was grateful for his fresh start. Constable Robbins partnered for several years with a younger officer named Sergeant Alicia Weston who taught him how to better relate to women, such as by never making jokes involving bazoomas, and good things had been said about him in the right circles. A few years before the Big Pow-Wow, Constable Robbins had been moved to the Criminal Investigation Department to become Detective Constable Robbins and had had to re-evaluate and upgrade his wardrobe with Alicia's help. Tank-tops and flared trousers were not becoming of a detective-in-training, apparently, and anyway the C.I.D. had very strict dress-code rules which ensured that its officers were smart and semi-formal in style with their off-the-peg polyester / wool mix suits and clip-on ties and plastic-soled shiny shoes and therefore looked like only trainee supermarket managers and Policemen who were trying very hard not to look like Policemen looked. Detective Constable Robbins was a little miffed at having to spend more than his allowance would cover on apparel so far removed from his own personality, and recalled with fondness the wide-lapelled, slightly-too-small brown suits worn with fist-sized tie knots and jumbo shirt collars by Jack Regan in 'The Sweeney' in the seventies, as he charged all over London in his Ford Consul arresting villains and yelling 'Get yer trousers on, you're nicked!' at everyone. They all knew Detective Inspector Jack Regan was a proper copper of the old school, in the days before the Metropolitan Police Force became the Metropolitan Police Service and stopped catching criminals in favour of writing reports and before political correctness put an end to topless girlie calendars on the canteen walls and the saucy banter with the WPcs when they still *were* WPcs and not just Police persons who happened to be of a gender allowed to wear stud earrings on duty, who was shown respect by Police and villains alike. Such respect would not have happened if Jack had been forced to dress like he was about to offer you a crazy two-for-one deal on packets of Persil at any moment, and Detective Constable Robbins wished he had been a detective in the Jack Regan days and could shout 'Get yer trousers on, you're nicked!' at people without being dragged before a disciplinary committee that would recommend he attend a Diversity and Inclusivity Refresher Course that would stain his career sheet forever.

— o —

Detective Constable Robbins had had a favourable performance review earlier that morning at which Detective Chief Inspector Maynard said that he would be recommending Detective Constable Robbins be promoted to the position of Detective Sergeant as soon as a slot came up and the section Superintendent had signed off on it. That meant that provided the section Superintendent agreed, which was almost a given, Detective Constable Robbins would be promoted within the next year or so, and Detective Constable Robbins bought the coffees for Detective Sergeant Ramsee and himself to celebrate. The good news and the coffee combined to give Detective Constable Robbins a buzz of euphoria which was still affecting him when he and Detective Sergeant Ramsee were on the road to the railway sidings close to Bethnal Green to attend the top priority callout that had plucked them from the relative comfort of the station and had them racing through the wet streets with Ramsee at the wheel. Detective Constable Robbins had the incident page up on the computer and read it out to Ramsee, but it made hardly any sense due to the limited information available, and as usual, Detective Constable Robbins called in with his cell-phone to the Crime Scene Investigation Office.

"CSIO, its D.C. Robbins, what's the story at the sidings?"

"Ron, hi, this is John. You got time for the full story, or the Reader's Digest version?"

"All you've got please John; we're completely in the dark here".

"Okay, well at 09.12 this morning an M.O.P. called in to say he's seen a white male, estimated mid forties to early fifties, exit the railway lines through a missing fence panel on Dimlington Street and return to a parked Jaguar. He was reported as being in a highly agitated state, not thought to be intoxicated but shaking noticeably, and vomited on the pavement before opening the vehicle. The M.O.P. reported he was acting like you would think twice about approaching him, very jumpy and unpredictable like. Before entering the vehicle he spent several moments pacing around the car and crying out frantically. Then he got in the car and drove off at speed, clipping a parked car as he went.

"The Jaguar is registered to one Joseph Bartholomew Gouder. Joe Gouder and his twin brother Jack are well known to Serious and Organised Crime, and are nasty pieces of work. Basically they fancy themselves as modern day Kray Twins – got form for extortion with menaces, actual bodily harm, you name it. Suspected involvement in the disappearance of several other local low-lifes but nothing proved. They fund their affluent lifestyles through good old protection of known drug supply establishments - pubs, clubs and the like in their patch in parts around Tower Hamlets and outlying areas. Also they're known to be involved in the building and refurbishment trade as unwelcome advisors, if you get my drift. Both done time, but nothing like what they are due.

"The M.O.P. identified himself and is available for questioning later if anything comes of it. He's a security guard at Duckham Electronics, some small firm nearby but he was off duty and on his way to work when he saw the incident. Made himself invisible, as you can imagine.

"We've sent Uniform in High Vis over to secure the perimeter with instructions not to enter anywhere or go near anything suspicious or unusual and just wait for you guys. No-one else is going yet, and we need you to call in and let us know once you've eyeballed the area. Let us know either way, if it's nothing or not nothing, so to speak. The Gouder twins are pretty high on the bosses' wish list by all accounts".

By the time Detective Constable Robbins had finished updating Ramsee, they already had the bright yellow high visibility jackets of the uniformed Police waiting for them in sight. Identifying themselves to the constables, Detective Constable Robbins and Detective Sergeant Ramsee entered the railway sidings through the fence and found themselves in a huge area of spaghetti-like criss-crossing tracks that glided down from the elevated section closer to the City and fanned out like river tributaries. It was not like Detective Constable Robbins remembered the area to be years before when he had occasionally ridden through from London Liverpool Street in the direction of East Anglia – most of the rusting disused branches of track had been removed or were in the process of being pulled up, and gone were all the numerous pipe-yards, oil tanks, abandoned wagons, shacks and parked railway machines that never seemed to move. New offices and apartment buildings had sprung up all around, surrounded by walls made of those dark red, glazed bricks everything seemed to be built from lately. A few lines branched away northwards and disappeared into the distance – these were shunting lines, as evidenced by the relatively winding layout not suitable for high speed passenger trains. Still others had not been used for a long time, as shown by the lack of a shiny silver bare-steel strip atop the darker rusted body of the line, and sets of bogeys and pairs of wheels were laid out on some. Looking around, Detective Constable Robbins could see nothing looking out of place or unusual other than a single remaining brick and tile shack between a fork in a line about two hundred yards distant. This was probably the last of many such shacks used by the rail gangs of old to shelter and drink tea and get warm by the coal-fired cast iron range. There were many tiles broken and missing from the roof and a busy rhododendron growing out of the top, and it struck both detectives as odd that a single tea shack had been left standing.

As they got close to the shack, taking with them two of the uniformed officers, it became apparent how large it was. It had probably not been a shelter for the rail crew after all; it was large enough to have housed some major machinery or a big generator of some kind. The double end doors were barred by a wide steel strap fastened with two huge brass padlocks. Around one side, they found a single door which had been forced open and hung awkwardly off a single hinge at the top. Despite the graffiti and spray-painted signature tags that covered most objects along all railway lines everywhere, it didn't appear as though anyone had been here or used the building recently. Peering through the door into the darkness, Detective Constable Robbins noticed the unmistakeable odour of human excrement. Faint light came in through a bank of windows covered by years of dust and grime on the opposite side, but it was too dim to make out anything. Detective Sergeant Ramsee found a panel of light switches on the inside wall to the right of the doorway, and not expecting any response, ran his hand down the switches, flicking them down – around a dozen sodium lamps popped on in rows hanging from the roof, and the building was lit up.

There were three timber support columns along the centre of the building holding up the roof trusses, each around a foot thick, and

Detective Constable Robbins' heart jumped as he saw that a nearly naked man clung to the far one with his legs on either side and his arms wrapped around it. The man was hanging limply but, curiously, he was also supporting his weight without falling. The man's head lolled to his right side and he was not moving.

"Police! Stay where you are!" shouted Detective Sergeant Ramsee, all the while knowing the order to be somewhat redundant, as both detectives walked briskly towards the man, taking care not to disturb anything on the ground. As they drew nearer the rising stench threatened to overpower them and a feeling of foreboding rose within them as the picture slowly came together, like a photograph reveals itself as it's downloaded over a slow internet connection, until the truth of the scene dawned on them both at once in the face-burning, heart-stopping realisation that the ability of human beings to feel empathy, to imagine oneself in the shoes of another, is both a blessing and a curse.

The man was hanging off the ground by his knees, which had been nailed through the knobbly ends of his thigh-bones to either side of the timber column. His arms were wrapped around the upright and fastened together at the wrists by a plastic cable-tie. The strange polygonal shape of his grasp on the pillar suggested that both arms had been broken both above and below the elbows. Protruding about a quarter of an inch from his bare left shoulder blade was a round headed nail which despite the surreal desperation of the situation, looked oddly out of place. On the right side of the man's head, extending from the right temple almost to the centre of the back of his head, was an indentation about an inch wide that was so severe it had breached the skin and the skull and almost removed the top of the cranium in a single piece, revealing the dull pink scrambled-egg-like mass that was the man's brain. The man was clothed only in a pair of soiled white briefs; he had excreted surprisingly copious quantities of both urine and faeces during the time he had been hanging on the pillar.

Both detectives fought desperately to keep control of themselves. Detective Constable Robbins had the presence of mind to discover that the body was still warm, and to look around and try to note the surroundings as they lay, while Detective Sergeant Ramsee rushed to the door to demand the uniformed officers get on the radio and call in the crime scene crew, forensics, the photographer and a hell of a lot of strong coffee. Detective Constable Robbins just had time to note the torn playing card, the tall bar-stool, the metre-long piece of square steel bar, and the discarded lump hammer near the far wall before the horror of the images in his mind overwhelmed him and began to shut his brain down, and Detective Constable Robbins' world turned somersaults around him.

Chapter 2 - Ravi the Postmaster

Postmaster Ravi Singh was acutely aware of the prestige of his position in the Essex village of Barmley. Ravi knew that in an age when village life all over England was being dismantled by the forced closure of local post offices, causing untold misery to pensioners and the unemployed who now had to somehow travel miles further to collect their pensions and benefits payments, Ravi's post office was the thriving hub of the community due only to his charisma, good standing with The Powers That Be, shrewd entrepreneurial acumen and sheer hard work.

Barmley was a picturesque community centred on a pretty village green and a duck pond, with a church, a pub and a community centre, but it had expanded over the decades due to its position well within the magic two hours commuting time from London by train, and subsequently was surrounded by newer, boxy residential estates with countrified names like Bramble Avenue and Skylark Heights that seemed identical to boxy estates of the same period everywhere. Many residents drove to Colchester and caught the train to London in the mornings, and returned home in the evenings. In the twenty-five years since Ravi had attained this lofty and distinguished position, his post office had expanded from a small one-room outlet that simply issued car tax discs, pensions and stamps, delivered letters and sold a few newspapers, into a bustling hub of commerce from where every kind of merchandise and service could be obtained and where every problem could be solved. People came from villages and towns for miles around to get their supplies and services from Ravi. From lawn mower repairs to chimney sweeps, from emergency baby-sitters and haircuts and carpet cleaning services to a guaranteed supply of fishing bait, everybody knew that Ravi was the man to consult to get what you needed cheaper and more quickly than anywhere else. Ravi delivered grocery orders for elderly customers in an age when personal service had all but disappeared, arranged transport to hospital for sick and disabled friends, helped little old ladies across the road and was kind to animals. He never spoke ill of the dead, never bit the hand that fed him and always looked on the bright side of life. Many people thought he was a sycophantic weasel, but never dared to say so, and everyone was careful not to notice Ravi's hair plugs.

Ravi was an honest man who got along in life by being likeable and friendly, and everybody knew Ravi was not a man to cross. He was a powerful man; Ravi was a magistrate sitting at Colchester, a member of the Round Table, and the Community Centre quiz champion for three years running, but most significantly of all Ravi was the Postmaster of Barmley and had developed that privilege into a position that shaped people's futures without them ever being aware of the fact. People who upset Ravi tended to suffer an extraordinary number of infuriating problems in life, and people whom Ravi favoured often received unexpected pleasant surprises.

Twenty five years ago, Ravi knew that being the kind of Postmaster who pilfered birthday cards sent to his customers' children in the hope of finding an enclosed five pound note was the road to ruin. It seemed logical to Ravi that when parcels mysteriously don't arrive at their destinations; when greetings cards disappear; when the collection box for the Guide Dogs for the Blind charity vanishes from the Post Office counter, or when the Jubilee Commemorative Plate being returned to the warehouse due to looking nothing like the picture in the Sunday supplement never makes it back, the common denominator was always the Post Office, and there was never smoke without fire. Ravi had never been the victim of an attempted robbery, and in Ravi's world, armed robberies at other, lesser post offices almost always turned out to be an inside job.

Ravi was ruthless with any errant postal delivery workers, and when once Ravi discovered that a Christmas card expected by eleven year old Jimmy Small had failed to arrive from Jimmy's dear old grandma, the delivery man responsible had been made to issue a public apology in the next Barmley and District Chronicle and Property Digest, admitting his negligence and promising compensation. To show his customers Ravi was a fair and upright chap who could forgive his fellow man and give credit where credit was due, when the missing card turned up from *Barnsley* three weeks later due to the unfortunate addressing error by dear old grandma, Ravi had magnanimously published another notice exonerating the man with an unblemished service record. Ever since the emergency operation on Mrs McTavish's West Highland Terrier recovered more than forty rubber bands from the dog's stomach, which Mrs McTavish blamed on her postman, Ravi had required his postmen to count back every rubber band they went out with, to prevent his customers being annoyed by discarded litter lying in their driveways, and losing a crocodile clip was a disciplinary offence.

Ravi's inexorable rise to prominence had all begun on Tuesday the fourteenth of April nineteen eighty-seven, with what Ravi construed as a racially motivated discourtesy as he enjoyed a quiet drink in the Three Feathers with his charming wife, Nessa. The landlord had referred to Ravi as 'that gentleman' when asking his staff to serve Ravi, without looking in Ravi's direction. Ravi took that as a personal affront, and was sure that if it were not for his visibly Asian appearance, the man might have behaved more courteously. He was even more sure when the landlord nodded at another, white, customer sometime later.

"I'll be with you in a moment, Sir", he had said.

Nessa Singh had tried to assure her husband that there had been no disrespect intended, but for Ravi the seed of a man slighted had been planted. He stewed about it all night, and stewed about it the next morning. He stewed about it for several days afterward, and had nearly stopped stewing about it by the following Monday afternoon when an electricity bill addressed to The Three Feathers arrived in his sorting office.

Ravi was tempted to throw the bill away, but was reminded by his philosophy concerning smoke and fire that to do so might arouse suspicion in the future. So Ravi carefully opened the bill, all the while his heart racing because he was committing probably the first criminal offence of his life, and read it. It was for £563.37. Ravi marked a tiny tick on the top left corner of the back of the enclosed pre-addressed payment reply envelope, resealed it neatly, and placed it in the sorting bin. A week later a water bill arrived for the Three Feathers, and he repeated the same process, and this time his heart did not race quite so much. A plan had been born.

Over the next few weeks, Ravi's sorting office processed dozens of identical payment envelopes addressed to the various utility companies, and Ravi diligently studied the backs of each one until finally, his tiny tick reappeared. Ravi simply tore the enclosed cheque for the sum of £563.37 into tiny pieces and sent the payment slip on its way, safe in the knowledge that as the Three Feathers had not lost any money, and as Ravi had not gained anything from it, nothing could possibly be traced back to him. He enjoyed a surge of euphoria every time he contemplated the way he had instigated what could possibly become a tide of misunderstandings and ping-ponging correspondence, and laughed to himself as he imagined the chaos that might ensue between the Three Feathers and the anonymous army of incompetent and disinterested clerks at the electricity board. The rush of empowerment felt so good.

Soon, other errant customers began to be included in what was to become Ravi's mission to make disrespectful people suffer inconvenience and frustration. That surly man who demanded a book of first class stamps with no please or thank you, that awful scruffy woman who made use of a four letter word when he didn't have the right kind of wrapping paper in stock, then people who's faces Ravi simply didn't like all started becoming the objects of Ravi's campaign for good manners and respect. Pretty soon Ravi was starting to lose track, and realised he needed a system to keep tabs on who was being sanctioned for what, so he bought a colourless felt-tipped pen which wrote with ink that was only visible under ultra-violet light, and one of those lamps used for checking for counterfeit banknotes. He developed a clever system of three digits which he marked on the return envelopes in ultra-violet pen, and efficiently kept detailed records in a secret book against the three digit codes. Sometimes Ravi enjoyed the challenge of 'running blind', which was when no pre-addressed envelope was provided by the sender and Ravi would be tested to identify the response when it arrived, not by his code but by the presence of clues anticipated and noted in his secret book, using clever sleuthing and logical detective work. When the landlord's handwriting appeared on a letter to the Finance Manager of the electricity board, he was immediately able to tell without even consulting his secret book that it was a response from the Three Feathers to the electricity board's fourth letter demanding payment, which had threatened to cut the power within ten days if payment was not received forthwith. Ravi was pleased to find the envelope contained not a last minute payment, as demanded, but an irate letter from the landlord pointing out the numerous times he had advised them by mail and by telephone that cheque number 78639122 for £563.37 had been issued some thirteen weeks ago, and would they please get their bloody acts together and sort this mess out and actually reply this time. Ravi simply Tipp-exed over "78639122" and "£563.37", then scrawled "Not verified" and signed it "Elizabeth R." on the top with a flourish in green ink and sent it on its way. Two weeks later during a busy lunchtime session, the power was abruptly cut to the Three Feathers. The beer stopped flowing, the ice machines started thawing, the ventilation shut down and the whole place took on the dimly lit atmosphere of a dingy drinking den. People were complaining loudly and demanding their money back, and one man who had been enjoying a two-hour liquid lunch threatened to punch the landlord's lights out because the electric cash registers remained firmly shut. It was not until eight o'clock that night following numerous phone calls by the landlord and an emergency trip to the electricity board with a replacement cheque, including an additional £53.00 reconnection fee, that the power came back on and the Three Feathers could admit customers again. Ravi was ecstatic, and even more so when, the following week, the water supply to the Three Feathers was cut off at one o'clock in the afternoon, causing the plates and glasses to go unwashed all night and the lavatories to become strongly inadvisable. The Three Feathers had suffered the penalty, and Ravi graciously would now allow them to go back to normal.

A petition was raised by some of the more vociferous villagers against the incompetent utility companies who kept misplacing payments, sending legal notifications and arbitrarily disconnecting customers' supplies, and Ravi duly signed it. A community open letter was written to the local Member of Parliament, a certain Ken Lommet, and Ravi followed suit with a letter of his own and posted Mr Lommet's reply on the community notice board to show what an upstanding member of the neighbourhood he was. Ravi was quoted by the Barmley and District Chronicle and Property Digest as saying that although he hadn't been personally affected, he was appalled by the stories his customers were telling him about their mistreatment, and suggesting that the utility companies in question were waging a vendetta against the citizens of Barmley. The electricity board apologised, blaming the computer, and promised a comprehensive retraining programme for its clerical staff.

Meanwhile, certain villagers began to become seriously in arrears with their credit card bills, and the worst offenders suffered the embarrassment of reduced credit limits and unexplained rejected transactions. On one occasion Ravi had the sweet pleasure of reluctantly cutting into two pieces, at the instruction by telephone of the Visa card verifications office, the credit card of poisonous old Jack Ecclestone who made no secret of his views to anyone within earshot that all non-Anglo Saxons unable to demonstrate their family existence in England back to the end of the last ice age were immigrants who should be deported back to the place whence they came.

Ravi decided to cool things down for a while in all but the cases of the most serious offences; however he soon found himself getting restless. He had noticed that utilities and credit card payment slips bore the instruction "DO NOT FOLD OR STAPLE", and "DO NOT WRITE BELOW THIS LINE", so in the interest of scientific research he tried folding a payment cheque and slip from Mrs Blenkinsop in half and banging two industrial strength staples smack through the middle of the envelope, cheque and payment slip and all. Sure enough, a red bill followed for Mrs Blenkinsop, and Ravi wondered whether the envelope had jammed the automatic letter opening machines, or the machines had merely shredded the envelope and everything in it. Actually the staples in the letter had been detected by a humourless metal-detecting scanner and routed to a seventeen year old clerk named Amanda Jones for manual attention; Amanda Jones had tried unsuccessfully to prise the staples open and cut her thumb in the process, and then surreptitiously binned the envelope. Ravi wrote *Thank You Very Much!!* across the bar code area of a water bill payment from 67 Peewit Drive, and was slightly peeved to find it was processed normally.

One day Ravi took his social management duties along a slightly different avenue, and intercepted a bill payment from a nice old lady called Mrs Pertwee who always chatted to Ravi when she came to collect her pension. Mrs Pertwee was a kindly widow who could hardly make ends meet, and Ravi often used to slip an extra tin of corned beef or mint humbugs into her meagre shopping. Mrs Pertwee always came back apologising profusely and telling Ravi that she must have accidentally pilfered these items and offering to pay, but Ravi would simply smile and tell her that would not be necessary, and Mrs Pertwee loved Ravi for what she knew was his unspoken kindness. Ravi took the payment cheque from a wealthy and arrogant villager named Paul Kingston, put it in Mrs Pertwee's payment envelope, and tore Mrs Pertwee's cheque up. Mrs Pertwee was subsequently surprised to find that not only was her money still in her bank account, but her half yearly water rates had been cleared and her account was also in credit, almost to the tune of a further year. The matter was subsequently resolved for Paul Kingston, but Mrs Pertwee was never contacted by the water board as the beneficiary of Kingston's payment, and enjoyed a whole eighteen months of free water as a result.

Ravi started helping people he took a shine to in earnest, with mixed results, and at the very least he succeeded in temporarily robbing the rich and putting off the day of reckoning for the poor, and the utility companies were under investigation by the various regulators for their appallingly inept handling of payments into the correct accounts in the vicinity of Barmley. Ravi's position as a magistrate at Colchester Magistrates Court also enabled him to disallow with a flick of his wrist or a flamboyant wave of his hand, applications by the utility companies to send in the bailiffs to their defaulting customers, or his *flock* as he had become accustomed to calling them, on the occasions they were accused of failing to pay for services rendered for periods in excess of six months, on the spurious grounds that the whole mess was probably caused by the utility companies themselves being so incompetent as to not know who had paid, and who had not. On the rare occasions Ravi was asked by his peers whether he knew the defaulting party personally on the even rarer occasions one them actually showed up at court to hear the proceedings, Ravi would simply claim he wasn't sure.

"I may have seen him in one of my shops once or twice, I don't know;" Ravi would say, "they all look the same to me".

Ravi didn't care much for the Right Honourable Ken Lommet, MP, feeling that his socialist views and liberal ideals were contrary to Ravi's belief, as a successful entrepreneur, in high reward for hard work and sharp business acumen, and Ravi would have been much happier with the alternative parliamentary candidate whose name he couldn't recall but whom he had seen on television with his nice suit, neat hair and good teeth. Ravi was always meticulous in his tax affairs, despite resenting having to fund the government's tax-and-spend policies, and felt that a change of government would result in a far more reasonable and understanding approach to the taxation issues of an honest part public servant, part self employed businessman such as himself. Additionally, despite Ravi's occasional representations to Mr Lommet requesting action from Mr Lommet over the statistically much higher than average incidence of erroneous bill processing by the utility and credit card companies for the Barmley area, Ravi felt that Mr Lommet was failing to address the issue satisfactorily, and suspected he was far more interested in living the high life in Colchester and his London residence whilst leaving the simple village folk to fend for themselves.

Ravi decided to go into politics.

Ravi purchased a top-of-the-range personal computer with desktop publishing facilities and a photo-quality scanner and printer, ostensibly to produce pamphlets and public notices to distribute with the mail in his position as Chairman of the Barmley Community Centre Elderly Welfare Action Committee. Ravi knew from Mr Lommet's non-committal replies that, when at his London residence, he sent out his constituency letters on House of Commons headed paper, but when living in his constituency he used Basildon Bond A5 cartridge paper printed with his local office address. In both instances he used House of Commons envelopes. It was an easy task to reproduce Mr Lommet's home stationery, however Ravi decided the risk of hidden security measures in real House of Commons paper was too great.

Mr Lommet also printed his letters using Arial 10 point font on a laser printer, and wrote the "top-and-tail" greetings and signature by hand using a medium-nibbed fountain pen with Waterman Florida blue ink, which he had on occasion purchased from Ravi's own Art and Calligraphy Materials department when attending his monthly rural clinic at Barmley Community Centre.

Ravi set about searching for the perfect political tool with which to begin the due democratic process by examining the contents of the House of Commons envelopes that trickled in to Barmley through his sorting office every few days. After a couple of weeks, he found a letter addressed on Mr Lommet's own stationery to Mrs Vera Huntley, a widowed fellow magistrate and member of the parish council with a face, Ravi contemplated, like a bulldog chewing a wasp, and with a sense of humour to match.

It read:

Dear Mrs Huntley,

Thank you for your letter of the 10th inst.

I share your concerns over the lack of transparency concerning the funds generated by trial speed cameras in your parish. I will endeavour to determine the Department of Transport policy for proportional allocation of funds from temporary installations to the originating locations, and will revert in due course.

Yours faithfully

Ken Lommet, MP

Ravi considered Mr Lommet's prose style was out of date and a touch over-formal, and would benefit from a few exclamation marks and a lighter tone to convey jollity and honesty. It was obvious that it would be far more agreeable to Mrs Huntley to receive a letter with a bit of warmth and sincerity to it, so Ravi set about helping Mr Lommet by creating a suitable improvement.

Dear Vera,

Thanks for the recent letter, my dear.

I agree it is a bit of a cheek! As you can see I am home at the moment, so why don't we get together to discuss the matter over a spot of candlelit dinner, say at 7 on Tuesday? I will send the Jaguar over to pick you up!! Wear something fetching, as I will be fetching you at 6 pm sharp!

Can't wait to get to grips with issues, if you get my drift!

Kenny

Ravi was glowing with pride at his acute political savoir-faire as he expertly resealed the letter and popped it into the pigeon-hole, so much so that ten minutes later Nessa asked him what he was smirking at over dinner.

It was therefore a bit of an anticlimax for Ravi when he didn't read on the front page of Friday's Barmley and District Chronicle and Property Guide about Ken Lommet MP being arrested for stalking members of the parish council, or being deselected by his peers for bringing the party into disrepute, or even being mildly rebuked for his temporary lapse of moral judgement, and he was positively glum when he didn't read the same things the following Friday. Ravi wondered whether Mrs Huntley might have been open to a little *extra-curricular activity* after all; something he had completely failed to consider. He would have to think carefully about his next political manoeuvre and not make a similar mistake.

However, one afternoon soon afterwards, while Ravi was helping a young lady find a lid for a china casserole in his Discount Cookware department, Ravi overheard a couple of old men gossiping in the adjacent Fishing Tackle and Outdoor section.

"Screamin' like a couple of old fishwives, so they say, posh old Mrs Huntley yellin' "you jolly well keep that philandering husband of yours under control" an' Mrs Lommet shoutin' "I'll call the Police if you don't get off my property right now, you insane woman!", chuckled the first man.

"No way!" exclaimed the other, "he couldn't be that desperate, 'eck, nobody could, old ma Huntley, who told you that?"

"Smiffy knows some chap who's got a mate in Colchester Parks Department who heard the whole thing, so they say, and old ma Huntley wavin' this letter he wrote her apparently, and Mrs Lommet went straight to the station to go down London and sort 'im out", said the first man.

"Of course!" muttered Ravi under his breath. "Rumours! It always starts with rumours!"

"You what?" the young lady in the Discount Cookware department said. "You got a lid for this, or what?"

Soon the affair was the talk of the constituency, and Ken Lommet MP appeared three days later on local television to deny reports to the effect that he had been attempting to instigate an extra-marital affair with a widowed lady despite his "back to basics" platform on morality and family values, which proved his guilt beyond a shadow of a doubt. When the Colchester Gazette published verbatim the contents of a letter received from an anonymous source which Ravi had kindly sent them without a covering letter in a plain envelope bearing a Colchester postmark, in which Ken Lommet invited the widowed Mrs Vera Huntley out on a dinner date in very familiar terms, and which invitation the Colchester Gazette made clear Mrs Huntley had turned down flat, Ken Lommet was exposed as the liar, predator and serial womaniser he presumably was. Mr Lommet's credibility was shot to pieces at a stroke, and following an ugly procedure involving a vote of no confidence, Mr Lommet's summary de-selection and a swift by-election, the man with the nice suit, neat hair and good teeth became

Ravi's Member of Parliament, and Ravi wondered why everybody thought politics so complicated.

With the advent of internet banking and the declining use of personal cheques for payment of bills in favour of payment by direct debit or bank transfer that came in the nineties and early noughties, Ravi's opportunities for dispensing justice and helping the less fortunate of his flock such as the late Mrs Pertwee by the traditional methods diminished somewhat, but by then Ravi was deeply involved in monitoring and helping with the personal income tax affairs of many of the wealthier members of the community. It was surprising how many of them forgot to declare obvious sources of income or accidentally claimed foreign holidays as international business travel expenses, and Ravi churned out heartfelt declarations of innocence in response to accusations that had not yet been made by the dozen, inviting audits "to clear my good name" and offering paltry sums in full and final settlement. Ravi also occasionally appointed himself as arbiter in legal proceedings, particularly divorces which Ravi enjoyed immensely, pointing out to the guilty party's wife's solicitors that the husband's relationship with his secretary was simply a companionable one between 'just good friends', as demonstrated by the sharing of a room at the Changes and Chances conference at the Leeds Holiday Inn, which was a good example of symbiotic cost-saving economics in these financially austere times.

Ravi had also accidentally become a pioneer of 'micro-marketing', a new paradigm of corporate sales strategy whereby major consumer goods manufacturers eschew expensive national newspaper, magazine and television advertising in favour of "community embedded" targeted advertising in the local free newspapers and parish magazines, and on flyers composed and printed at the point of distribution (Ravi the Postmaster) and submitted individually to entire communities with their deliveries. Not only did the Three Feathers indirectly contribute to Ravi's retirement fund due to the spectacular rise in their custom, in particular the overwhelming demand for hot gourmet Cornish pasties with chips and salad garnish as a result of a recent micro-marketing campaign, but also Ravi was credited as a great visionary in Gavin Soames's bestselling book "Micro-marketing – a New Paradigm of Corporate Sales Strategy" which made Gavin Soames an overnight millionaire shortly before he resigned his position as Head of Marketing at Colton Fine Foods, wholesale purveyors of gourmet Cornish pasties to the catering trade.

Ravi owed it to his flock to keep them on the straight and narrow in his self-appointed position of guardian of public decency, or as he liked to call himself without a trace of irony, 'pillow of society'. The keystroke loggers Ravi installed on his public internet access terminals proved invaluable for this purpose, and he had even managed to save the reputation of sixteen year old Diane Parsons, daughter of the appropriately named Reverend Alfred Parsons, minister of St. Peter's and St. Paul's Church, Barmley, by deleting the explicit nude photographs of her which boyfriend Phil Clarke had uploaded onto his MySpace page before anyone could see them, after first making copies for his own private records and without even distributing them to his friends. Ravi didn't much care for Reverend Parsons, and suspected him of being a closet Catholic, but it was a measure of Ravi's impartial nature that he had defended Reverend Parson's daughter's honour just the same, and Ravi never peeked at anyone's bank account unless he was able to. Ravi's DVD rental business was becoming a big success, and the explosion in mail order DVD sales meant that Ravi was able to intercept and perfectly duplicate all of the latest titles and many X-rated ones, replacing the original with the copy and consigning the original to his own shelves with scanned and copied sleeve jackets. All of his best customers received free membership of his DVD club, although anyone known by Ravi to buy mail-order gay pornography never received their membership cards, because Ravi publicly disapproved of pornography and privately disapproved of homosexuality. On many occasions, home shot DVDs gave Ravi the chance to catch up on family holidays and birthday parties of friends and faraway relatives of his flock, and very occasionally attractive ladies he didn't know would send footage of themselves posing and frolicking unencumbered by clothing, which Ravi would religiously copy onto his hard drive for future reference in case any of the ladies in question ever became famous or linked romantically to a politician or a minor celebrity.

On July the twenty first of his twenty-seventh year as Postmaster of Barmley, Ravi received the package that would be the last he ever surreptitiously opened; the package that would make him lose the will to be Postmaster for more than a minute longer. It was a small, innocent-looking padded envelope addressed to the enigmatic Paul Kingston, and it contained a mini-DVD of the kind that fit directly into some older types of video camera, which Ravi decided to check out on his computer that evening after dinner. The disc contained a handful of video files, which Ravi opened, and the scene began with a bored-looking middle aged man wearing a tweed jacket with leather elbow patches and dark green corduroy trousers standing at the far side of a plain room, holding what looked like a remote control unit which he placed on a table beside him. Ravi thought the man looked like a teacher in the nineteen-seventies, and when the man started walking towards the camera, Ravi almost decided it was too uninteresting to watch. The man pulled a piece of paper out of his jacket pocket, unfolded it and held it up to the camera. It read:

KINGSTON, PAUL A.

I KNOW WHAT YOU DO. YOUR BUSINESS HURTS DECENT PEOPLE. THIS IS YOUR FIRST AND ONLY WARNING – STOP DOING IT. IF YOU DO NOT STOP, I WILL PERMANENTLY STOP YOU SOON. REMEMBER THIS.

PIMPINAN

Behind the paper, the man's voice said in a slightly bored tone, "You remember getting this note? You took no notice of it. Perhaps you thought it was a joke, or an idle threat. You were warned. This is what I will do to you unless you leave now, right now, and never come back".

The video stopped momentarily as the player switched to the next file, and then resumed, auto-focussing briefly before becoming sharp. Ravi smiled at the amateurish attempt at home movie editing; he had seen some poor efforts in his time, but this was one of the worst. The scene was now a small room entirely tiled in white, completely empty apart from a man sitting on a high-backed wooden armchair slightly offset to the right. The man was wearing only undershorts, and he was strapped to the chair with silver-grey tape around his forearms, calves, chest and biceps and head so that he was unable to move anything except his eyes, fingers and toes. A strip of tape was secured over his mouth, and he was straining and mumbling what Ravi guessed were probably expletives. Superimposed on the bottom left hand corner of the picture was the date and time in red, which had not been set properly. It read *2001-01-01 11-32*.

Ravi's amusement turned to curiosity and trepidation; he had never seen anything like this before. He wondered where this was leading. The man in the chair looked angry and he struggled in vain against the tape. After a few seconds, the sound of a door opening and closing, and the man glaring to the right of the camera with rage in his eyes. The same bored-looking man, now wearing brown corduroy trousers, appeared from the right and walked up to the man in the chair, and stood beside him facing the camera.

What Ravi saw next turned the blood running through his veins to ice-water; his face blanched as white as a sheet, and his legs started shaking visibly in disbelief of the utter horror of what he was witnessing.

The man reached into his jacket and pulled out a heavy ball-peen hammer. With what seemed to be a disinterested sigh, he nonchalantly positioned the hammer in his hand with the ball side downward, then swung it viciously at the man's left knee, shattering the kneecap with a sickening *Pock!*; the man's eyes bulged with shock and surprise momentarily before he convulsed in constrained agony as the bored-looking man slowly delivered three heavy blows to the outside of his left knee-joint, before strolling round behind the man in the chair to the man's right side. The bored-looking man smashed the man in the chair's right knee cap – *Pock!* – and meticulously worked on the outside of his right knee joint in exactly the same way as the left. The man in the chair was struggling to breathe and screaming and bellowing through his nose like a speared bull and straining against the tapes with all his might, tears and snot running down his face.

The bored-looking man studied the man in the chair's eyes for a moment as he replaced the hammer inside his jacket, then he reached forward and ripped off the tape covering the man in the chair's mouth, and the room exploded with a scream of such intensity and sheer panic that the camera momentarily shut the sound off before readjusting to the new noise level, making every hair on Ravi's body stand up and giving Ravi nightmares for the rest of his life. Without saying a word, the bored-looking man ambled past the camera, and after a few seconds the camera shut down and the picture went black.

Ravi's ears were ringing and he was numb to his bones; he knew he wanted to stop the film, but his hand refused to obey his command. He tried to remember where the computer's mouse was and how to shut down the video player program, but somewhere between half a millisecond and twenty years later the picture resumed and the man in the chair was still screaming but it was different now; it was a pleading, begging scream of unbearable pain which did not preoccupy the man in the chair quite enough to not notice the bored-looking man amble back into the room and over to the man in the chair, taking out the hammer from inside his jacket as he walked. The man in the chair had pure terror in his eyes and he managed to get his first words out through the pain – *please, no, no, please* – and the camera clock said *2001-01-01 12.29*, which Ravi was almost too distressed to note meant a whole hour had passed since the man in the chair had permanently lost the ability to walk. Ravi gave up desperately fumbling with the mouse and pressed the computer's OFF button hard, but in the four seconds it took for the computer to cut its power and shut down the bored-looking man blasted the man in the chair's left shoulder joint with the hammer, splintering it as the screams went up an octave, the man in the chair sitting there erect and unmoving like a half naked bus passenger with his knees like purple footballs, and the jolt of realisation that the nightmare had gone when the computer suddenly shut down brought Ravi no relief at all.

Ravi stared at the blank screen, all the while his brain refusing to believe what his eyes had just seen. Questions raced through Ravi's mind – who were these men? Why was this happening? Ravi guessed that the man in the chair did not survive, but how long did it take; how much did he suffer before death relieved him of his agony? It was not something Ravi could imagine, nor bring himself to find out by watching the video a moment longer.

"What the hell do I do about this," Ravi said aloud, "and what the hell has Kingston done?"

Ravi knew he simply must get the DVD to the Police, but at the same time he knew Paul Kingston was in grave danger. Being caught betraying public trust by illegally opening mail no longer seemed to matter a jot, but Ravi was scared half to death of what would happen if he blundered into a world of murder and shocking violence. So once he had composed himself, he copied the disk onto the only DVD he had, a full size disk, and sent the copy on to Paul Kingston. The original mini DVD he posted to Essex Police C.I.D. at Colchester without a note of any sort, and Ravi scrawled VERY URGENT on the envelope.

That night Ravi went to bed hungry and had nightmares about a bored-looking man with leather elbow-patches and a hammer, and Nessa Singh decided the stress of being the Postmaster of Barmley was no longer good for her ageing husband.

Chapter 3 - The Many Few

Like Mrs Malaprop, Special Commander Bryant had a knack of securing the undivided attention of any audience listening to his orations in breathless anticipation of another of his famous gems of eloquence. Special Commander Bryant put this down to having a reputation for original, witty and spur-of-the-moment observations and one-liners which people would remember and quote later, and he spent a good deal of the day looking for memorable ones on Google, and waiting for opportunities to spontaneously come out with them.

'Drawing on my fine command of the English language, I decline to comment' was one of Special Commander Bryant's favourite sayings, and when he would add something of his own, like 'so let's pull up the weeds under our bridges' or 'we need to get all our ducks in the road', people would murmur appreciatively and start jotting down notes.

And like most other distinguished authors before him, Special Commander Bryant knew that one of the keys to writing great fiction was possession of well-developed powers of observation combined with an ability to relate real experiences, in ways that the reader could vividly imagine and identify with. Readers of fiction generally did not like to have to reach for their dictionaries every few minutes, so Special Commander Bryant did not make use of The Single Most Effective Secret® in his fiction composition. No, fiction should flow smoothly in the reader's mind as it conjured up images and painted pictures based on the author's own experiences and imaginings, and who better to relate exciting experiences than a senior Police officer such as Special

Commander Bryant. Well-chosen words were brush strokes upon paintings in the imagination, thought Special Commander Bryant, and Special Commander Bryant's laptop computer was his canvas, or possibly his easel, although Special Commander Bryant didn't have time to spare for thinking about similes or metaphors or which ones were which. Special Commander Bryant's policy on split infinitives was that they are generally acceptable for modern English usage, in moderation, which was a well-judged position because he was not entirely sure what an infinitive is, or how one might split it, and was thus careful to subtly avoid discussion of the subject.

Special Commander Bryant also knew that probably the most important sentence in a book of fiction is the very first one. This was known to authors such as Special Commander Bryant as a hook, and a skilfully crafted hook would tease and intrigue the curious reader to the point that he or she was simply unable to put the book back on the shelf, unread, and walk away.

And so it was that Special Commander Bryant sat and stared at the perfect hook on his screen for an hour, wondering where to go from there. Special Commander Bryant had written and rejected many hooks over the last thirty or so years:

'*It was a dark and stormy night*' had seemed a good bet until Special Commander Bryant found out that some charlatan had beaten him to it, as had:

'*Senior Policeman turned top private investigator Doug Wholes enjoyed one of the few moments of relaxation in his busy schedule after satisfying himself that arch criminal Jack "The Pigs" Jackson was securely cuffed and would never again feed his enemies to his hungry pigs, thereby confounding all but the finest criminally investigative minds with the absence of cadavers to testify to Jack "The Pigs's" crimes'* until Special Commander Bryant decided that the hook should be crisp and brief and not spoil too many of the plots and secrets of the following story. Special Commander Bryant had also quite liked:

'*There comes a time in every man's life when he fancies a bit on the side*', however it had occurred to Special Commander Bryant that this one might not be such an effective hook with women, and the radical feminists in particular with their peculiar, humourless outlook on such things, and women's and radical feminists' glowing reviews and royalty money were just as important as anyone else's according to Special Commander Bryant.

— o —

The Many Few

By [good pseudonym here]

Chapter 1

It was an amazing coincidence.

— o —

Now all Special Commander Bryant needed to do was to think of a huge coincidence with a vague connection to some kind of story that was so amazing the curious reader, having picked up a copy of *The*

Many Few and flicked to the first page in the railway station branch of W H Smith bookshop, would not want to get on the train without it. After an hour of racking his brain, nothing had leapt out of the wild blue yonder, but still, Special Commander Bryant had a cool title and the perfect hook and at least he was making progress. Special Commander Bryant had started writing rough drafts of *The Many Few* back in his Thames Valley Police days when all the secretarial stuff was done by the civilian girls in the typing pool on typewriters with either a "golf ball mechanism" or the superseding "daisy wheel mechanism", both of which moved electrically far faster than the eye could see and neither of which mechanisms suited him at the time because he couldn't use them without looking conspicuous, and besides, he didn't know how to undo his many typing and grammatical errors. On joining the Metropolitan Police on secondment, Special Commander Bryant had been issued with a laptop computer on which he was expected to do all his 'work' and store 'files' in 'folders' on 'servers' and send 'mail' and did not need to 'print' his 'documents' until he actually needed them and could then batch-print them *all at once,* which was the greatest breakthrough since carbon paper, which didn't seem to be readily available any longer. Special Commander Bryant had begun to think more seriously about *The Many Few* in recent years, and had utilised a lot of his not inconsiderable spare time hatching plots, and noting down literary gems that occurred to him late at night while he couldn't sleep, although ironically one of the recent reasons he often couldn't sleep also happened to be the thing that threatened to cut down his spare time following the Big Pow-Wow, as the troops liked to call it, namely Operation Krakatoa with all its pressures and intrigues and frightening videos to watch. Operation Krakatoa had begun a few weeks into the fifteenth year of Special Commander Bryant's three year secondment at the Met, and had been the first real opportunity for genuine, proper work that had come up for Special Commander Bryant since he had become a commander of the special sort. Special Commander Bryant's first role on Operation Krakatoa was to find out why the old film title *Krakatoa – East of Java* was geographically inaccurate *and* spelt wrongly (*Krakatau*, as Special Commander Bryant now knew, was always (and what's left of it is still) situated off the *west* coast of Java, which is in Indonesia), and then to pass information and orders from Operation Krakatoa's mysterious, senior front-line detectives to the rank-and-file detectives and keep copious notes about everything to use for producing Special Commander Bryant's famous reports later on. It was critical work which could only be handled by a senior Policeman of the utmost integrity and erudite capability and Special Commander Bryant was clearly the man for the job. No other officer was considered when Commander Unwin needed a senior representative of Scotland Yard to travel to Jakarta to establish relations with POLRI, the Indonesian National Police, and despite some hiccups such as failing to meet the British Ambassador as planned, feedback from Tarzan was positive.

Despite the Thames Valley Chief Constable's assurances to ex-Deputy Chief Constable Bryant on his last day at Thames Valley Police that the Chief Constable and Special Commander Bryant would liaise closely in the future and hold regular high-level strategy meetings, Special Commander Bryant never heard from the Chief Constable again. Despite constant efforts to make contact and to ensure his secret dispatches to the office of the Chief Constable were getting through, the only time Special Commander Bryant succeeded in speaking to the Chief Constable's office at all was some seven years later, when he had a twenty minute conversation with a Personal Assistant to the Chief Constable before it dawned on them both at the same time that they were actually talking about completely different Chief Constables, Special Commander Bryant's Chief Constable having retired the previous year. Special Commander Bryant had long ago resigned himself to spending what remained of his working life with the Metropolitan Police, so his ex-Chief Constable's retirement from Thames Valley Police did not really matter. Special Commander Bryant had long suspected that his ex-Chief Constable had fabricated the special duties and secret assignments given to him simply as a means of fobbing him off onto the Metropolitan Police and getting him out of the way, especially when he found out that the file on Constable Robbins, the careful handling of which was supposedly Special Commander Bryant's entire *raison d'être* as a Thames Valley Police insider at the Met, contained no mention at all about Constable Robbins' treasonous escapades with a rifle on the M4 motorway, or the disciplinary sanctions imposed upon him in consequence, and it never had. The only disciplinary record on Constable Robin's file had concerned a formal oral warning issued following the infamous canteen Kit-Kat fight, when Constable Robbins and a Constable Smith had come to blows in the basement canteen after each heatedly accusing the other of helping himself without permission to fingers of their Kit-Kat bar. It had transpired that each man had separately purchased a Kit-Kat, as claimed, and sat together to read their Sun newspapers. At one point one of the men broke off and ate a finger of Kit-Kat, at which the other man wordlessly but glaringly ate a finger of the same Kit-Kat. It was only when the Kit-Kat was finished that an argument ensued concerning who had bought and owned the Kit-Kat, which rapidly escalated to insults being traded and then fists being swung. It was recorded that after the brouhaha had subsided, a second Kit-Kat had been found under the table, and each man had wrongly assumed the other had been deliberately provocative in eating fingers of his Kit-Kat without asking. Only in the middle classes, thought Special Commander Bryant, could a reluctance to complain (which is itself so peculiarly middle-class) build up to a point where it boils over and two grown men get into a fist fight at work over something as trivial as a chocolate bar. Nevertheless, lack of a record of personal firearms discharged in a Police Range Rover notwithstanding, this was proof that Special Commander Bryant had been right all along about Constable Robbins' instability and treachery but, not one to hold a grudge, Special Commander Bryant vowed to let bygones be bygones by getting Robbins back one day for causing that vague uncomfortable feeling of not being entirely in control of one's own destiny.

Special Commander Bryant decided the Chief Constable had clearly been worried about the threat to his position posed by so politically capable a deputy; one able single-handedly to achieve great feats of teamwork, and Special Commander Bryant was philosophical about the whole affair, regarding his days at a provincial *shopping carts and car parks* policing facility such as Thames Valley as a stepping-stone to greater things. The Chief Constable had contrived to present him with a Hobson's Choice (or perhaps it was a Morton's Fork; whichever it was, however, it was clear he had not been a victim of his own indecision, like Buridan's Ass. Decisions came easily to Special Commander Bryant, particularly when there was only one option). He had rocketed up the ladder at Thames Valley, becoming the youngest Deputy Chief Constable in the force's history, and having outgrown Thames Valley in record time, had been discreetly inserted into the grandest Police Service of them all, responsible for every aspect of policing of the Capital and known the world over as Scotland Yard, protector of Londoners and Parliament and even Her Majesty the Queen and the Royal Family, not merely as a common-or-garden Commander, but a *Special* Commander! Mr Bryant, as he was known at one time, had joined Thames Valley Police by way of a graduate trainee fast track development initiative at the age of twenty-four with a law degree, and had immediately been sent on a residential seven-month career planning and development course for potential high-fliers at which he had learned the value and importance of (1) being seen to be doing something; (2) producing high profile results, and (3) thereby getting noticed and making a name for oneself. Superintendent Bryant, as he was known at one time, identified and exploited a career-enhancing niche by establishing a transparent and accountable system for recording and publishing (some suggested 'advertising') Police operational expenditure, with particular emphasis on senior Police officer's expense claims and detailed analyses thereof, up to and including Chief Constable / Commissioner level, in a way which would not seek to sweep the issues uncovered under the carpet, as had traditionally been the case, but would admit that the elephant in the room existed, and would look the elephant in the room squarely in the jaw, grasp the nettle by the horns and call a spade a spade. By the time Chief Superintendent Bryant, as he was known at one time, was identifying and establishing his niche, he was already deeply involved in developing The Single Most Effective Secret® and was therefore able to churn out complex, unsolicited reports to the various Home Office departments dealing with such matters, and back them up with landslides of requests from fictitious members of the public for information concerning Police Force spending of public money on business and entertainment. Chief Superintendent Bryant's results were so high profile and got Chief Superintendent Bryant so keenly noticed and made such a name for him, that once it had become apparent that murder, threats or intimidation were not sensible options under the circumstances, for the rest of his career Bryant would be untouchable. But what really catapulted Chief Superintendent Bryant onto the stage was his mother's advice, given to him at every opportunity since the age of six, to always wear one's values on one's tunic. In other words, to always let your modesty, humility, deportment and commitment to fair play make it apparent to everyone around that you were a decent and upright chap, if that was what you indeed were. So when Chief Superintendent Bryant returned his curriculum vitae to the CVDesign Labs agent with all the lily-gilding and self-praise removed and simplified, according to his mother's advice, and the CVDesign Labs agent, who was slightly miffed by Chief Superintendent Bryant's cavalier editing, had then heard that Thames Valley was inviting applications for a newly vacant Deputy Chief Constable position and decided to submit Chief Superintendent Bryant's revised curriculum vitae as a cruel joke, it was all over bar the shouting. Chief Superintendent Bryant's amended curriculum vitae began like this:

Summary

A confident and polished professional, a career Police leader with an impeccable track record and strongly established political savoir-faire. Possessed of far reaching principles and an unshakeable business ethic at the core of his leadership skill, he is a quality-minded and active team player equally at home as a leader and a top level public servant. Diversity-aware and decisive under pressure; a valuable friend and colleague and a formidable opponent of crime.

I turn the lights off and close the door behind me.

Although Chief Superintendent Bryant didn't recall ever being invited to apply for the Deputy Chief Constable position, once the Home Secretary was in possession of his edited curriculum vitae there really was no other candidate worth considering. At his numerous interviews for the post, he would enter the room to find the panel looking as though they had just finished discussing matters of the utmost gravity but now had the opportunity to do something far more interesting instead, and everybody would stand up and deferentially shake his hand and smile knowingly and make cryptic comments like 'Well, with any luck we'll be turning the corner and bolting the doors today, eh?' that left Chief Superintendent Bryant wondering whether he was at the right meeting. Nobody ever enquired about the enigmatic Summary entry on his curriculum vitae. Junior level members of the Freemasons on the interview team assumed it was some kind of senior Lodge sign, and did not want to appear dull and unknowing among their superiors. The Home Office representative thought it showed a remarkable, poignant and concise insight into the brilliant mind of someone who does not dwell on the past but is in full control of his lot and looks always to shape his future, while subtly but steadfastly refusing to rule out recourse to events that occurred prior to turning off the lights and closing the door.

"The only other man I've heard of who was as forthright as this candidate in his life portfolio", said the Chairman of the panel afterwards in respectful, hushed tones, "went on to lead the country through the Second World War".

Special Commander Bryant spent most of his time prior to the Big Pow-Wow and Operation Krakatoa instigating cost-saving reviews, chairing strategic procedural and policy-making meetings, and writing directives as a result of his own strategic initiatives. Because he was in a unique position with a unique job-title that did not appear anywhere on the Metropolitan Police Service organisation charts, Special Commander Bryant had no direct reports, no peers and no superior officer, and was therefore not subject to performance targets or any form of performance measurement or evaluation, and could pretty much do as he liked. Nobody ever queried what Special Commander Bryant was working on lately, or what he spent all day doing, but they were sure it must be something of the utmost importance and top priority and probably something to do with the Joint Intelligence Committee and possibly in cahoots with the CIA. All of his fellow senior Police personnel assumed he was part of a high level strategic monitoring system reporting directly to the Home Secretary, and went out of their way to cooperate with him in case it got back to the Powers That Be that as they were not part of the solution, they must be part of the problem and would be therefore vulnerable to career-stalling sideways moves or even early retirement. He was, in short, viewed as a spy; a fly in the ointment or, as Chief Superintendent Watkins liked to say, a 'turd in the swimming pool' of harmonious Police life. Nobody was sure whether Special Commander Bryant was a man with an intellect far greater than those around him, as shown by his written communiqués that were comprehensible to everyone except anyone actually reading them, or a complete and utter clown, as shown by his written communiqués that were comprehensible to everyone except anyone actually reading them, and Special Commander Bryant was obviously a very dangerous man to find oneself on the wrong side of. This last point was once demonstrated in spectacular style when Special Commander Bryant had made an inspection of an equipment receipt depot in east London.

"What is that?" enquired Special Commander Bryant, pointing at a large plastic dome on a pallet.

"It's a transponder, Sir", the Store Manager had said.

"Ah, yes, indeed", Special Commander Bryant replied, and walked off.

The next day, Special Commander Bryant issued a flurry of memos and Stores Receipt and Materials Handling Procedures to all and sundry, in each of which the word 'transponder' appeared at least seven times, prompting the Store Manager to post a copy on the canteen wall with a note to the effect that when some management fool learns a new word, you had better expect that word to appear in everything he writes for the next six months. Later that afternoon, in connection with an entirely unrelated matter concerning the Store Manager's fraudulent stock keeping and mismanagement of outsourced maintenance services over a number of years for his own personal gain, the Store Manager was abruptly escorted from the equipment receipt depot premises by two well-built but apologetic security guards and never seen or heard of again, and Special Commander Bryant's clout and ruthlessness overnight became legendary among every individual of the whole of the Metropolitan Police, with the sole exception of Special Commander Bryant himself who remained blissfully ignorant of any part of the incident for the rest of his life.

The title of Special Commander Bryant's thirty-odd year old book project, *The Many Few*, was actually a mondegreen born sometime in the nineteen eighties in a cricket match beer tent at Maidenhead, where he had misheard someone behind him talking intoxicatedly through the noise about 'my nephew'. Many few! What a delicious, oxymoronic designation, he thought, for the legions of uneducated rabble that congregate in pubs and on street corners and at cricket match beer tents, talking with great gravitas about subjects they grasp only the rudiments of, such as the government's immigration policy or what West Ham United's manager *should* have done, as though the illustrious leaders of government and football clubs would do well to have a word with them to sort things out. Each with unwavering confidence in unflinching opinions on so many things, everyone seemingly so sure of himself or herself being on an equal or superior footing with the few captains in charge of such things – so many aspiring to so few. *The Many Few* – it would make a great name for a rock band, or title for a book. The basic idea behind *The Many Few* had come to Chief Superintendent Bryant, as he had been known at the time, during a sleepless, hot summer's night reverie. Chief Superintendent Bryant had grasped he was on to a winner immediately in a light-bulb moment, and went downstairs to make hot milk and sketch out a rough draft of his idea before it faded from his mind, like so many enjoyable dreams seemed to within seconds of his waking. Chief Superintendent Bryant's rough draft of his idea had been like this:

2 male <u>identical twins</u>, separated at birth for (??) reason. Both grow up in different towns with different families, unaware of the existence of the other.

* *Twin 1 – petty criminal always looking for an opportunity*
* *Twin 2 – high profile businessman / local council leader*
* *Twin 1 gets a visit from mysterious stranger, informing him of the existence / contact details of twin 2. Twin 2 doesn't know about twin 1*
* *Twin 1 doesn't contact twin 2, but observes and adopts twin 2's hair style / dress style – perfect to set up misdirection (identical twins!)*
* *Twin 1 commits (??) crime using name of twin 2 and looking exactly like him (security cameras)*
* *Twin 2 arrested but has cast iron alibi and Police haven't a clue what to do*
* *Relevance of The Many Few?*

Chief Superintendent Bryant and Deputy Chief Constable Bryant had spent innumerable working hours trying to tease a plausible story out of what he was convinced was a solid plot, but was never happy with any of his drafts. Frustrated, Deputy Chief Constable Bryant asked Mrs Bryant for her opinion of the storyline, in the hope she might come up with one of his brilliantly original ideas.

"It's been done a hundred times already", Mrs Bryant said, "It sounds remarkably similar to the premise behind 'The Man in the Iron Mask'".

Somewhat deflated, Deputy Chief Constable Bryant's face fell.

"I could understand your scepticism, my dear, if I was talking about rival identical twins that knew about each other, or were even in cahoots to fool other people. Are you doubtful simply because it involves identical twins where nobody had considered the possibility of a twin? Because, and this is the key, here we have separated identical twins and the only person in the world who knows there is another twin to either of the twins is one of the twins himself. Only one, that's the key bit".

"Partly the twins thing, and partly because it's an absurd plot which could never happen in real life. We have fingerprints nowadays, for example – you're a Policeman, for goodness sake!"

As usual, Mrs Bryant had completely failed to grasp the point, but at least she had highlighted the fact that drastic changes were needed, and as soon as Mrs Bryant had stepped into the shower, Deputy Chief Constable Bryant surreptitiously slipped the entire manuscript into the bottom of the dustbin. The detail of *The Many Few* was now as dead as a dildo, thought Deputy Chief Constable Bryant, although the basic concept was still as viable as ever. A fresh start was required.

The next day, Deputy Chief Constable Bryant rewrote the rough draft of his ageing idea, and added some new lines:

* *Turns out Twin 2 was the first to find out all about the other twin*
* *Twin 2 <u>sent</u> the mysterious stranger with the news to Twin 1, knowing he would probably exploit this opportunistically*
* *Now both twins know about the other, but only Twin 2 knows the other one knows. Twin 1 still thinks he's the only one that knows.*
* *Twin 2 commits a <u>huge</u> crime (??) with his identity on full display, and hides the loot.*
* *Twin 2 contrives to let the Police know about Twin 1 without letting the Police know <u>he</u> knows about Twin 1. (Could be tricky)*
* *Twin 2 is questioned and has a carefully set up alibi. Twin 1 is questioned and is found to know about Twin 2 and has adopted his exact likeness, so he is a prime suspect since he's keeping information about Twin 2 secret, which he's used to concoct <u>another</u> crime he planned to blame on Twin 2 as well*

Against his better judgement, Deputy Chief Constable Bryant ran the evolved idea past Mrs Bryant.

"Don't mention fingerprints; I've already got the issue of fingerprints covered", he lied.

"Well, you just have to hope the Police don't get any DNA samples from the crime scenes. They may be identical twins, but they still have different DNA".

"Aha! Yes they do, but the differences are so subtle that routine DNA testing would be more than enough to convict the wrong twin. The level of testing required to distinguish between identical twins is so protracted and expensive it would only be carried out if the Police were convinced that there was, in fact, an identical twin".

"As in the case you've just described", sighed Mrs Bryant. "One twin is found to know about another twin who apparently doesn't know about the first twin – how much more convinced do the Police need to be? Or perhaps your esteemed readers won't notice that minor detail".

Still, at least the amazing coincidence was now sorted out in Deputy Chief Constable Bryant's mind. Someone exiting a building would accidentally bump into a man wearing a carnation button-hole coming in, and minutes later as the man enters another building a few hundred yards across town, he would accidentally bump into the same man wearing a carnation button-hole coming out. It would take another couple of years for Special Commander Bryant, as he was then known, to figure out where both button-hole-wearing identical twins were going, and why, but it would be worth it – Special Commander Bryant knew that if the same thing happened to him, the surreal impossibility of it would have him aghast and doubting his own sanity for the rest of his life, and if he read about it in a railway station bookshop, he would be well and truly hooked.

Chapter 4 - The Red Light

Despite his sensations of giddiness and uncomprehending confusion, Paul 'Paulie' Kingston knew it was a very bad situation, and quickly recalled and immediately regretted ignoring the letter that had long sat niggling at him at the back of his mind, which probably had something to do with it. Paulie Kingston had let his bravado, which he had spent years cultivating in order simply to survive in his chosen world of drug supply with all its associated risks and dangers, get the better of his curiosity and trepidation when the letter warning him to stop "doing it" – whatever that meant – arrived on his doormat one morning, and had merely thrown it in the bin without later admitting to himself any of his frequent second thoughts. Now his bravado had popped like a child's party balloon and he was as scared as a lost puppy in a busy railway station.

Paulie Kingston tried to remember what had happened. It was as if he had woken from a bad dream to find himself in the middle of an even worse dream. He had materialised lying face down on the metal floor of a moving vehicle – a van of some kind, with his eyes and mouth bound by sticky tape. In his world of blackness, Paulie tried to remember what time of which day it was, and decided to buy some time by keeping very still and not attracting attention. He had no way of knowing who or how many people were with him and could see him. Paulie's left wrist was securely taped behind his back to his right ankle and his right wrist to his left ankle, causing an odd sensation of asymmetry which made struggling difficult to coordinate. Paulie could feel the painful hardness of the cold metal floor pressing into his ribcage, and the sharp tugging of the hairs on his legs sticking to the tape. Paulie had a splitting headache but could not remember anyone attacking him or hitting him or... but now it started to trickle back – he had made the exchange at Starbucks at Piccadilly Circus as planned, left the cafe with an attaché case identical to the one he had arrived with, and taken a taxi to his next meeting place in the car park at Hyde Park. The next thing he knew, he was in this damn van being driven to who knows where. Paulie had no idea how long they had been driving.

It didn't make sense. What had happened, and why? Paulie recalled waiting in the dark by the tree at the side of the car park – not many cars there, even fewer people – he was a little early – and then the hood – yes, a thick canvas hood had instantaneously snapped over his head and in one motion a stiff band had tightened and locked around his neck – not chokingly tight, but tight enough to stop the hood from being lifted off. No-one had spoken or touched him and he had not seen or heard anyone, but there he was, panicking and swaying on the grass wearing this hood which he had struggled in vain to pull off, shouting and swearing and kicking out blindly, and an instant later came the icy cold liquid which suddenly soaked the hood and stung his nostrils with a pungent overpowering smell of solvent that reminded him of school, followed immediately by the dizziness and the ringing in his ears which got louder and more intense, and his legs became unsteady and turned to jelly until his knees finally buckled and everything turned black and then – then there was this van. The whole thing had taken just a few seconds.

Shit. This was serious. Paulie had no idea – none – what fate intended for him. Could this be the Police? Paulie doubted it – this was not the way they did things, unless they were the Flying Squad or some kind of S.W.A.T. outfit, and Paulie was not a big enough fish to warrant that kind of attention. More likely some drugs gang whose turf Paulie had inadvertently walked into, or even just a mistake. Paulie suddenly wished he remembered how to pray. Thoughts raced through Paulie's mind – at best he knew he was about to get a severe kicking, and possibly might end up in a garbage bin or an alley with a terminal knife wound to the belly. Paulie needed a plan – he needed to communicate with the people in the van; he needed to convince them that he would not be a threat to them if they let him go. But for now, Paulie Kingston was utterly helpless. Salty fluid flowed into his mouth and he felt nauseous, making him swallow every second to keep himself from vomiting. Paulie did not want his life to end by choking and drowning on his own vomit. Emesis contains powerful stomach acids, and consequently it is a very unpleasant substance to drown in. It burns the airways and the lungs, causing intense pain, the final icing on the cake of a drowning person; something even a person in the throes of the terrifying process of giving up their life to half-digested Starbucks sandwiches would not fail to notice. Paulie, of course, did not know this, although he probably would have realised the truth of it had he thought about it for a moment, but right now he had more pressing things to think about, such as how to get himself out of this mess.

— o —

After another forty five minutes, which Paulie guessed was around three hours, the van slowed and turned and moved slowly up a gravel driveway. Paulie's heart raced as the van pulled to a halt and the driver got out, then moments later got back in and the van moved slowly forward. Paulie could tell from the sound that they had entered a building. The van pulled up again and the engine cut, and the driver again got out. Paulie heard doors being bolted behind the van, then silence. Only one person had exited the van – could it be that he had been alone with the driver all the time? It might be a trick. Paulie noticed the sudden quietness; there was no traffic noise, no people around, and he thought he heard an owl over the rushing sound of blood pumping in his ears. Minutes that lasted hours passed, until the rough metallic sound of a trolley rolling over concrete, like a warehouse pallet truck, approached the van and stopped. The back doors were flung open. Paulie gave up all efforts to appear unconscious, and made his first attempt at communication, a futile high-pitched mumbling noise that was supposed to sound like 'hey, what do you want?' but sounded more like a three year old girl protesting her innocence, which had no effect on the proceedings whatever.

Paulie heard the trolley-thing being pushed closer to the van and bang against the metal floor behind him, then felt a rope or a strop of some kind bunching together all four of his limbs behind his back. The trolley-thing was making a rhythmic pumping sound now; *one – two – three – four – five -* and with each stroke Paulie felt his ankles and wrists being bunched harder together and pulled upwards until most of his weight, but not all of it, was lifted from the floor of the van, and then his whole body was being tugged backwards and dragged along the floor until it finally fell from the back of the van, banging Paulie's cheekbone on the edge of the van floor, and Paulie was left swinging face-down by his wrists and ankles which hurt badly, and for the first time Paulie experienced feelings of utterly helpless humiliation like being a hog-tied animal, except this was worse because live hogs or rodeo-steers don't end up swinging beneath a trolley like inconsequential still-breathing meat waiting for someone to decide their fate. Through the cold fear, the first little spark of anger flashed in Paulie's psyche, and the trolley was being pushed along over concrete now as Paulie struggled and swung madly, completely disorienting him as a rumbling private rage began to build inside him.

The trolley stopped. Paulie shouted as fiercely as his taped mouth would let him, as his body made futile token strains and pulls at the tapes and rope holding all of his limbs together, despite the fact that if he had been successful in breaking free, he would simply have dropped straight onto the concrete, face-first. A hood suddenly covered his head and Paulie recoiled from it instinctively; it still had the residue smell of the cold liquid which made him feel sick, but he could not get free from it and then, as he knew it would, without warning the hood turned icy cold and wet again and although he fought it with every ounce of his strength, Paulie felt himself slipping quickly into the blackness once more.

— o —

In his horrible dream, Paulie had been sitting in a chair in the centre of an empty white room for an eternity, waiting for his death. He vaguely remembered dreams dreamed when he had been younger, when his life had depended upon being able to flee, to get away from something he knew was fatally dangerous but which he hadn't yet seen and didn't yet know, only to find that he was strangely immobilised and unable to run. This dream felt familiar, similar to the dreams of falling from a great height but never hitting the ground, and Paulie knew that it would end with a crescendo of fear culminating in a sudden wakening with a cry, heart pounding and mouth dry and bed-sheets damp in his familiar room where everything would be tauntingly normal and life would resume after a brief recovery. But this dream was also different and refused to go away, and despite Paulie's dogged insistence that the dream would end any second, the white room managed to invade his psyche and become real and clear on the wrong side of his dream-world.

For an hour, Paulie drifted in and out of consciousness, until he knew his situation was clearly not going away on its own and the stark white room demanded his undivided attention. Denial gave way to acceptance, and worldly damage limitation began to seem more and more urgent as reality finally stamped its uncontested authority onto Paulie's being with the warm flow of urine he could no longer hold back which flooded his thigh and soaked his bottom and which he could hear trickle softly onto the tiled floor. Paulie found himself thinking curious thoughts about his late mother with deep regret – thoughts about how, as her only child, he had filled the last years of her life with worry over his unannounced moving from London out to the sticks, or the source of his wealth; thoughts about how he had failed to take care of her or provide for her after his father had passed away, and how she had loved him unconditionally up to the end even though he had never shown her reciprocated love other than the occasional unannounced visit, or drunken late night telephone call when the latest girl had walked out on him. Paulie's mother had missed his father terribly, and Paulie had been an inconsiderate, absent son while his mother had been brave alone. Now Paulie knew how it felt to be utterly alone and left to face fate without help.

Paulie took stock. He remembered Hyde Park, and the hood. He had seen nothing between Hyde Park and the present in the white room, and in between them had lain a blur of surreal events and emotions in which imagined terrors had become real and real circumstances had been dismissed as imagined, in which time itself had become hopelessly distorted. He remembered the van, and the trolley, and the hood again, and the dream which wasn't, and pissing himself through fear or natural bodily function or both, and finally the white room which refused to go away.

The white room was the size of a small bedroom, tiled on all surfaces he could see except for the ceiling, which was painted white. There were no windows visible, and a single white door was directly in front of him. To the right of the door was the only other thing in the room; a compact video camera atop a tripod, aimed directly at him, with a single trailing cable leading under the door. A harsh light filled the room from what Paulie guessed was a bare bulb directly overhead, meaning he was unable to determine what time of day or night it was. Paulie was completely unable to move from his seated upright position on a hard, high-backed wooden chair with solid arm rests and what felt like a block foot-stool. He was wrapped in unyielding tape at key points around his head, chest, arms, legs and torso, but otherwise his body was bare and he appeared to have lost all his clothes except for the wet underwear he could feel but not see. His eyes were uncovered but his mouth was still taped, and the only movements he could make from his formal, upright seated position were wiggling his fingers and toes, and moving his eyes. He tried to jerk the chair to see if it was fixed to the floor, but couldn't muster enough movement to tell. He was aware he had not eaten or drunk for a long time, but felt strangely full and already his bladder was sending signals that it wouldn't be long until the next relief was needed. Paulie felt the anger returning; anger at the humiliation he was being subjected to as he, Paulie Kingston, sat half-naked in his own piss without a word of explanation or any chance of being able to account for himself or put up a fight, and the anger was a welcome diversion from the sheer panic which threatened to overwhelm him; panic at his helplessness magnified by the complete silence of the white room in which the only sounds were his laboured breathing and expectant heart beat. Suddenly the light went out in the white room, and the silence in the new blackness became deafening and overrode any hint of anger as Paulie shivered and wept pitifully in the dark.

— o —

Vivid hallucinations of danger punctuated Paulie's hours in the dark during which Paulie knew he was awake, but could not shake off the images. Enraged bulls and bears and other huge animals barrelled towards him out of control, dogs and lions snarled at his feet, flame-throwers took aim and fires burned all around while people scattered in terror and Paulie stood rooted to the ground in Hell. A Policeman sank a hand-axe into the face of a tied-down man just as the light came back on and Paulie struggled to suck enough air through his nostrils to stop his heart bursting. The light was blinding and was not a relief, for it announced reality, and reality was the unknown, which was no less frightening than the dreams.

After a few minutes, the door opened and a man in corduroy trousers entered, carrying a length of clear plastic hose-pipe with a funnel fitted to one end, and a plastic tub of liquid. The man didn't acknowledge Paulie or look him in the eye, but walked over with the air of a man for whom the whole thing is a bit of a chore, and put the tub of liquid on the floor by Paulie's side. He stood over Paulie in front of him, and briskly ripped the tape from Paulie's mouth – Paulie winced from the pain, but it didn't matter – and his heart pounded at the first opportunity to communicate with his abductor; Paulie's mouth opened to shout out, and in a flash the man plunged a thick plastic hook behind Paulie's lower teeth and pulled hard, yanking his jaw wide open and hurting his tongue and gums enough to make him cry out. The man inserted the plastic pipe into Paulie's throat and fed it down, making Paulie gag and panic and scream inside as he sat erect and unable to move a muscle, and then the man raised the funnel above Paulie's head and poured the contents of the tub into it, and Paulie felt the cold liquid pouring down his gut and his stomach expanding with the volume, terrified that he was being poisoned or drugged, until the tub was empty and the pipe pulled out and the tape replaced on his mouth before he could get out a single word of protest, and the man left the room as abruptly as he had arrived. Paulie's distended stomach hurt from the ridiculous volume of liquid suddenly filling it, and he could taste the residue, sweet like honey, and guessed that he was likely to sit in the chair for a long time, because why else would he be force-fed sugary water if not to keep him from dehydrating or dying of thirst, and to keep his blood sugar level up; not as an act of kindness, but to keep him alert and healthy and thus prolong the misery. To what end, Paulie could not bear to guess.

Paulie hadn't cried for years before the last twenty-four hours, and now it seemed he couldn't stop. Fear had given way to sadness and self-pity, and introspective shame at the mess he had made of his life. His mother had always had confident high hopes for her son, and Paulie had wasted everything – his education, his upbringing, and above all his mother's love. If he died in this chair today, nobody would miss him; nobody would grieve, nobody would mourn their loss. It was unlikely anyone had even noticed he was missing, or was looking for him. All Paulie could point to as typical features of his recent life was a string of disreputable lovers who despised him, even more disreputable friends and accomplices, violent confrontations, sordid deals to supply heartless drug dealers who lined their pockets with the money of the weak, and the trappings of wealth bought with the despair of others. Paulie knew that the unspeaking, bored-looking man who now controlled his destiny was somehow out to make him pay for his decadent life, and wished with all his heart that he could just speak to him, plead his case, admit his guilt, beg for mercy, vow to change his ways and make amends. And he would, too; Paulie had once considered himself a Christian, but for many years had not felt worthy of the name on the rare occasions he had even thought about it, and now he missed the feeling of being a Good

Man. In his heart, Paulie hoped that was what his predicament was all about – a big shock; a scare, a bit of a beating, perhaps; a metaphorical rap on the knuckles. A wake-up call to end all wake-up calls. An aversion therapy session that needed no follow-up. Always the optimist, a small glimmer of hope sprang to life inside Paulie just as there was the faintest of whirring sounds and the red light came on. The red light on that damned video camera – it just came on!

Eyes wide with fear, Paulie tried to look confident in the knowledge he was being observed, and a second later the door opened and the bored-looking man strolled back in. The bored-looking man was dressed in different, unfashionable corduroy trousers and a sport jacket, with an open-necked checked shirt and brown suede desert boots, and, more worryingly, a pair of latex surgical gloves. Paulie guessed the man was shorter than himself, but was muscular and self-assured and smelt strongly of cologne. The man walked to Paulie and bent to peer into his eyes, and Paulie realised this was the first time he had made eye contact with him. The man's eyes were soulless and devoid of emotion, and Paulie could tell he was actually looking *at* Paulie's eyes, not into them, and Paulie felt no connection with the man through this act at all. Adrenalin felt like fire in Paulie's belly, and the man turned to face the camera and pulled a pair of stout side-cutters from his jacket pocket, held them up to the camera momentarily, then pushed one cold hard steel blade into each of Paulie's nostrils and tightened them, severing the cartilage between his nostrils deep into his nose with an audible '*snap*' as a bright flash of pain lit up Paulie's vision and his face exploded into agony. The tape was again ripped from Paulie's mouth and the man walked unhurriedly out of the room and closed the door, leaving Paulie screaming and screaming.

Over the next eleven hours, the man visited Paulie at approximately hourly intervals, and each time his impending arrival was announced by the red light. Each time, the man stayed for between two and a half minutes (the time when he split each of Paulie's fingers in half lengthways from the tips of the nails to the second joints) and seven minutes (when he delicately snipped off both of Paulie's ears, one 3/8" equilateral triangle at a time). The man carried out his work briskly with the resignation of someone who would have preferred to be doing something more interesting, but was willing to make the effort under the circumstances, and did not seem to notice Paulie's agonised bellowing, screaming, bloody pleadings and begging for mercy as his body was systematically reduced to little pieces. During the interminable intervals between the visits of the man, through the red mist of pure unimaginable pain that reached into each of the trillions of cells of his body, what Paulie feared the most was the unstoppable appearance of that red light, until the time the red light killed him and the man walked in to find Paulie in the throes of a massive heart attack, his face blue and his eyes rolling and his body spasms producing odd gurgles through a mouth devoid of lips that announced the end of the torment for Paulie and the early conclusion of the man's labour.

Chapter 5 - The Big Pow-Wow

It was all Detective Sergeant Robbins could think about. The complete absence of visible panty lines under the attractive American woman's cream high-waist skirt had alerted Detective Sergeant Robbins and had him moving around the room in an attempt to position himself behind her inconspicuously in order to prove the matter to himself one way or the other, and there was no doubt. Detective Sergeant Robbins was an expert on such things, and knew that ninety-nine times out of a hundred, the illusion would be given away by a small triangle of fabric in the small of the lower back or a thin horizontal string of material above the hips, disclosing the presence of tiny panties. But this time he had hit the jackpot, and Detective Sergeant Robbins knew beyond doubt that underneath that cream material with its tantalising hint of translucence, the American woman was wearing nothing at all, and for that moment nothing else existed in Detective Sergeant Robbins' universe. He had read (or was it fantasised?) that American women aspiring to ever-higher positions of power used such tactics to distract their male competition, or to reinforce their 'out-of-your-league' status among the male underlings, but Detective Sergeant Robbins had never imagined the devastating effect someone's apparent personal and private state could have on him, or that everyone else in the room at the time would seemingly be completely oblivious to it.

Everyone was taking their seats now; the American woman, her American male colleague who looked like a stereotypical buzz-cut Marine in a good suit, and three senior uniformed officers were at a table at the front of the room behind name plates, and facing them were Detective Sergeant Robbins and around twenty or so other mainly plain-clothes detectives at desks arranged in classroom style. Detective Sergeant Robbins had strategically placed himself at the front of the class directly in front of the American woman, but for now his secret goal was being thwarted by a fabric tablecloth covering the top table and hanging down to the floor.

"Good morning, ladies and gentlemen", began one of the three senior officers without getting up, "Thank you all for coming. I trust you arrived with no trouble. This room will be the strategic control centre for Operation Krakatoa, on which you will have received preliminary briefing, from now on. Before we begin, I want to repeat the security provisions of the Operation that you have already been briefed on and accepted. You were asked to leave cell-phones and any other recording or transmitting devices at the door before you came in; this will be strict policy at all times in this room. All aspects of the Operation are highly classified and information will be shared on a need-to-know basis. There will be no leaks. You are not to discuss any aspect of the Operation with anyone outside this room, and results of your work are to be passed to your direct supervisor, and to him or her only. As far as anyone outside this room is concerned, Operation Krakatoa does not exist. Each of you was specifically selected for your involvement based on your track record with major operations and your history of confidential handling of cases. You have all signed operation-specific secrecy agreements. In some instances, some of you have had prior experience with events that have been amalgamated into this Operation, and these events are henceforth included in the specific secrecy provisions.

"My name is Commander Alan Unwin and I will be the commanding officer of Operation Krakatoa, reporting directly to the Commissioner. Traditional matrices of top level reporting will not apply to Operation Krakatoa, for reasons I hope will become apparent later. On my left is Superintendent Smith, to whom the lead detective of each of your groups will report. On the far right is Special Commander Bryant, who you can consider to be involved in an indirect capacity and who will facilitate much of what we require at, uh, a high level. Now, it is my pleasure to introduce Special Agent In Charge Emma Gajewski, who is here to help us for two months unless I can persuade her to stay longer. Special Agent In Charge Gajewski is with the Federal Bureau of Investigation; the FBI, based at San Ramon, California, and is one of their foremost forensic psychology experts specialising in anticipatory and interceptive profiling. Her services have been made available to us as a result of organisational cooperation at the very highest level. Listen to everything she tells you; she will be providing vital insights at this meeting and we are very lucky to have her expertise available".

Detective Sergeant Robbins was pleased to note Commander Unwin had completely ignored the suit-wearing baboon accompanying the American woman, whose name didn't sound anything like the way it was spelt on her name plate, and wondered briefly whether her mastery of psychology had enabled her mischievously to impose the inner turmoil which Detective Sergeant Robbins was continuing to suffer, or simply didn't know about it, before dismissing the question as a no-brainer. The woman is probably drunk on underhand self-empowerment, he guessed.

Detective Sergeant Robbins had a feeling he'd encountered the Special Commander before, as he started to flick through his copy of the Kick-off Briefing file that was placed on every desk and tried to get used to the fact the chair he was sitting on would be his home for the next two days. The Kick-off Briefing was thick and marked TASK FORCE SECRET – NOT TO BE REMOVED and would take time to read, despite being well endowed with photographs. Detective Sergeant Robbins found a section on Jack Gouder, whom he had seen and smelt at first hand clinging to the upright in the railway shed, and quickly learned some new facts which reawakened emotions and made him glad he wasn't aware of the facts at the time:

- It is estimated the victim hung alive on the support column for between ten and fourteen hours before death. Extensive rodent bites were inflicted, mainly on the fingers and toes, prior to death
- Victim had been force-fed water, probably in the form of glucose solution prior to hanging on the column. Dehydration was subsequently not a contributing factor to death
- The knees were drilled through before 210 millimetre x 7 millimetre nails were inserted. Bone shavings were found at the scene. Common, commercially manufactured nails, but nail points had been pre-sharpened by grinding

- Both arms were cleanly broken above and below the elbows, thought to have been by blunt force levered against a fulcrum, prior to hanging the victim on the column
- Death was caused by a single massive trauma to the head. Weapon left at the scene (length of 1" square x 26" tempered steel railway points bar, weight approx. 3.5 kg) had victim's brother Joseph Gouder's fingerprints on it
- A playing card is thought to have been nailed to the victim's left shoulder and probably torn off by Joseph Gouder. A round headed, three inch nail was embedded in the victim's left shoulder blade. A torn card (the three of diamonds) bearing Joseph Gouder's thumb print was found at the scene
- Joseph Gouder died in Great Yarmouth some fifteen weeks later. Cause of death: liver failure, attributed to alcohol abuse complications compounded with sudden dietary deterioration; Joseph Gouder was a recently-established vagrant at time of death. It is assumed Joseph Gouder found his brother alive and administered a mercy killing to end his suffering, and then went into hiding. Whereabouts between Jack Gouder's death and his own death unknown. Joseph Gouder not a suspect in his brother's abduction
- Joseph Gouder's telephone records reveal on the day of his brother's death, he received a four-minute call from a mobile telephone in Jakarta, Indonesia which is of utmost interest to the investigation
- Experiments with a test manikin show that with drilled knees and nails pre-inserted, a single male person would be easily capable

of mounting an unconscious victim onto an upright column in this way, with the help of a suitable seating cradle. A high backed bar stool of the type found at the crime scene would be ideal

"Detective Constable Robbins as he was then, now Detective Sergeant Robbins, attended the scene", said Superintendent Smith, bringing Detective Sergeant Robbins back into the room with a start, "so while these videos will be disturbing, being at an actual crime scene is a whole different ball game, as D.S. Robbins can attest.

"As a result of the positive DNA identification from the hair lodged in the shoulder wound, we arrested a suspect. While he was in custody, an identical DNA match to microscopic skin samples found under the fingernails of Victim Number 2 came to light. There were many other, discrete but unidentified, DNA types obtained from the fingernails of Victim Number 2, suggesting they were not lifted directly from the attacker. At that time, Victim 1 and Victim 2 were still separate investigations. Victims 1 and 2 did not know each other to our knowledge, and neither of them have any connection to the suspect that we can discover. So we have overwhelming forensic evidence against the suspect linking him to the two cases, and absolutely nothing else to connect him to either of them. This is a highly unusual scenario; unprecedented even. The suspect has a record of minor sexual offences; public indecency, soliciting, that kind of thing. In short, he enjoys engaging in consensual homosexual liaisons in public places and pestering horrified people that walk in on his activities, including minors, into joining in.

"Then there are the fingerprints. On each occasion, the perpetrator made no effort to wipe his fingerprints – on the contrary. Both times he left a full set of ten prints, arranged evenly spaced and in order as though he had been providing a ten-print set for a Police print record, in one of the first places we looked; along the back of the bar stool in the first case, and along the shaft of the bat above the handle in the second case. We have no record of them, and neither does Interpol. They are not from the suspect, who we have had to release. We maxed out the time we had him in custody, came nowhere near to having anything to charge him with, and let him go. He is not considered a flight risk and I just know we will be spending a lot of time with him in the near future, but frankly we are at a loss to understand how he is involved".

Special Commander Bryant was making notes now, since clues of this sort could be vital to solving the case in *The Many Few*. Special Commander Bryant had not yet spoken and felt a little out of his depth, but it was a mark of his seniority that he could sit there looking superior and composed in his immaculate uniform with its crossed tipstaves and let everyone assume he was more in his depth than anyone else was in their depths and anyway, he reminded himself, he had been hand-picked to go to Jakarta.

"Next there are the playing cards, on both occasions the three of diamonds nailed to the left shoulder. What is that telling us? Why is it done at all?" continued Superintendent Smith.

"I was thinking he could be telling us he drives a Mitsubishi, or maybe he's Japanese", said Detective Sergeant Bowlen, who as Detective Sergeant Robbins knew was wearing bikini style briefs.

Superintendent Smith looked blank.

"Mitsu bishi is Japanese for "three diamonds", she said apologetically. "My husband drives a Mitsubishi, so I know that. The logo on the front? It's three red diamonds arranged in a triangle, not the normal cut diamond shape but the playing card type".

"We'll record that in the register. We clearly need a lot more thought on this, but it's a good point. Now I want to summarise quickly where we are with the victims generally, and then move on to the second group, the video victims, before we watch the video evidence together. This is mandatory, and I have to warn you, it will be very distressing. I want everyone to look for common themes or anything that strikes you as unusual that may have been missed so far, bearing in mind the circumstances – does the perpetrator glance momentarily at someone or something out of shot? Does he show any emotion, however brief? Does he reveal a tattoo, or jewellery? Lunch will arrive at twelve, and we'll have a short break then and continue. After the videos, we will discuss, by which time it will be late afternoon and we'll then break for the day. Tomorrow we will ask Special Agent In Charge Gajewski to help us understand the type of man or group of men we are dealing with.

"Six victims, all male. All suffered horrific protracted deaths designed to cause maximum suffering for as long as possible. Two were left to die in remote but publicly accessible places, where they were found by accomplices, in one case by the twin brother. Four were torture-murdered in a white-tiled room where they were videoed being assaulted by the same man at roughly hourly intervals until their deaths.

The man assaulting the victims and the suspect we arrested for questioning based on the DNA typing are not the same man.

"Five victims were known to Police as predators, prone to varying degrees of violence, with a variety of criminal records, in several cases the subjects of ongoing Police surveillance and investigation. The sixth, a video victim, has not yet been formally identified. None of the video victims' bodies have been recovered. Make no mistake, folks, these were nasty people who we were doing our best to keep off the streets, and ironically now we have our wish.

"Additionally, three other people fitting the general profile of the victims have disappeared from our radar suddenly. In one case a note from the Pimpinan man or men and one of the videos was found at his home when we were attempting to make an arrest. It is not known whether he took the hint and cleared out, or he was taken by Pimpinan, and in the other two cases it is not yet established whether there are any connections which Operation Krakatoa should be concerned about. It must be stressed that all these are just the ones we know about; there may well be more.

"It is thought that a video of each killing is sent as a warning to the next potential victim or victims. If they take the hint, they are lucky; if they don't, they may become the star of the next video. Three of the four videos we have were found in victim's homes, in two cases in unopened mail. This suggests he doesn't waste time in carrying out his threat. The fourth was found in the missing person's house. If the missing person was indeed taken by Pimpinan and murdered in the same way, another video has presumably been sent to the next in the chain – who is it, and has he seen it? Is he another one of our recently disappeared friends?

"With one exception, each of the unopened videos included a three of diamonds playing card in the envelope. Curiously, the unopened video that did not include a three of diamonds playing card in the envelope was a copy of the original, the original having been received by mail at Essex Police in Colchester. By the time it got to us, all forensics had been destroyed and it was up to its neck in Essex coppers' fingerprints. Who copied the video and why? Who sent the original to Colchester? What happened to the card?

"Note the videos are all made on a camera or cameras recording directly to a mini DVD. These are not generally available any more, but many are still in circulation and are widely used. He never uses more modern hard disc drive or flash drive cameras, and we have no evidence to suggest he ever sends videos directly by email or indirectly by some form of cloud storage or internet drop-box service, which is a shame because our forensic internet capabilities are shit-hot, pardon my French.

"In short, Operation Krakatoa exists because what seemed like a handful of cases has merged to become a huge organised case that is unlike anything seen before. Serious and Organised Crime suddenly cannot cope; Scotland Yard as a whole is suddenly overwhelmed with possibilities and swimming in evidence which is freely offered by this Pimpinan entity on a regular basis, all of which lead absolutely nowhere. The Home Office is concerned that if and when the press pick this up and join the dots and the magnitude of the case becomes public, it will inspire copy-cat crimes that will interfere in our investigations, but just as importantly may stir a certain level of public sympathy for motives of the perpetrators, who might be seen to be achieving what many people would secretly like to do themselves, namely rid the community of violent criminals. Intelligence shows that the existence of Pimpinan is becoming known among certain categories of London's criminal fraternity. It seems to be spreading like an urban myth that has some grounding in fact, and they are becoming cautious. Street dealers are finding it harder to get supplies. Targets of protection gangs are getting fewer visits. These are things the general public would be likely to view favourably, so we have to tread carefully, and potential for our embarrassment is growing. I find it inconceivable that this is being carried out by anything other than a highly organised group. The level of research, planning and organisation required, not to mention the difficulty and danger of plucking dangerous, violent men from their comfort zones, makes the likelihood of this being a lone wolf practically non-existent. That is a personal opinion, however I know Special Agent In Charge Gajewski disagrees".

At seven fifteen that evening, having watched the four killing videos multiple times during which all five female officers and several of the male ones needed time out to compose themselves, and subsequently having discussed the killings to death, the entire team decamped via a laid-on bus to the nearby Hilton London Paddington for the night. They had been forbidden to go home or meet families or friends at the hotel, or to discuss any aspect of the case with the rest of the team other than in a hotel conference room that had been secured for the purpose and swept for listening devices.

Special Commander Bryant felt drained of all energy, and lay in a hot bath for almost an hour with a large Scotch. He had seen the videos before, but it was distressing to witness the effects that they had had on his juniors, and he was concerned enough to wonder whether a good crime writer could be convincing and successful without having to resort to such gory unpleasantness. After a while the Scotch and his eternal optimism combined to convince him that a writer of his calibre could do anything he pleased; after all the reason he was hand-picked to go to Jakarta was because this was such an extraordinary case unlike any that, say, Thames Valley Police would ever handle, and Special Commander Bryant was at once both an extraordinary leader and an everyman who happened to be a gifted writer. His Special Commander hat was an essential accessory to the case, but his crime writer hat would be put back on when the time was right, and a man should not try to wear two hats at the same time. Special Commander Bryant got dressed and went downstairs in search of food.

Detective Sergeant Robbins and a handful of other officers were sitting in the lounge with Special Agent In Charge Gajewski, who wanted to be called Emma outside the strategic control room, and Larry the suited baboon whose surname or rank nobody could remember, when Special Commander Bryant walked in. Special Commander Bryant did not normally mix with the rank-and-file on a social basis in case they felt intimidated by the presence of such a senior officer, but he headed in their direction, and Emma waved him over and he sat down and ordered a crème de menthe.

"It's French", explained Special Commander Bryant, "for 'cream of menthe'", and hoped no one would ask him what 'menthe' was. Special Commander Bryant knew that sipping a tiny glass of green liqueur would add sophistication and set him apart from the beer-drinkers, although he was a little concerned it might react with the Scotch and make him say something silly.

"We were just demonstrating the internal conflict between logic and emotion with a simple game", said Emma. "It's often said that women are driven by emotion and men are driven by logic, but that is a cliché. In reality, everyone is driven by both to different degrees, and we make a choice. Quite often we find ourselves being pushed in opposite directions by the two. Of course this is an oversimplification; many other drivers shape our processes and behaviour; but the game showed how differently each of us handles logic and emotion".

"If the world were a logical place, it would be men that ride side-saddle", said Special Commander Bryant, looking slightly puzzled and putting his phone back into his shirt pocket.

"Wow! Special Commander! How very ... deep! Who said that?" asked Emma.

"Well, I did", said Special Commander Bryant, his ears turning pink, "just then, as it happens ..."

"Okay ... I have a feeling Dr. Google said something similar." said Emma, "What we just did, I asked everyone to agree to write down, on a piece of paper, the next sentence I said, word-for-word, even if it was a lie, and sign it and pass it to the person on their left, and then discuss how we felt about it. Once everyone agreed, I said 'I hope my best friend dies in a car crash tomorrow'. One of us refused to do it, one of us crossed the words out before passing it on, most of us wanted the pieces of paper back afterwards, and all of us found it pretty uncomfortable.

"We all agreed logic dictates that nothing would happen to our best friends as a direct result of our game, but emotion told us the opposite – that we were tempting fate, or talking up trouble, and at best it was a nasty thing to write. A lot of us considered how terrible we would feel if something did happen to our best friends tomorrow, regardless of what logic told us. It was a powerful demonstration of logic and emotion battling it out inside us. We all tore up our papers afterwards".

"My best friend died in his sleep", grinned Special Commander Bryant, "unlike the three screaming passengers in his car at the time".

A stunned silence lasted for a few seconds, and then as if on cue a waitress appeared and said "Your table is ready, if you'd like to come through" and people started rising and drifting off towards the dining room, leaving Special Commander Bryant with Larry and Emma and Detective Sergeant Robbins, who was now host to a new wrestling match between logic ('go and have dinner') and emotion ('I'm horny, with no chance of scoring – stay where she is and suffer'). Special Commander Bryant noted the awkward choice of whether to stay in the lounge or join the others for dinner, and decided he would order room service.

"Larry, didn't you say you have something to do tonight?" Emma asked the baboon without smiling. Larry looked irritated but got up, said goodnight and left.

Special Commander Bryant sensed (wrongly, as it happens) he was about to be censured in front of a junior rank for his witty quip which seemed to have been mistaken for a social faux-pas, and pre-empted the situation by taking out a pen and scribbling on a scrap of paper while he said "Well, if you'll excuse me I have some calls to make. I'll see you in the morning", and handed Detective Sergeant Robbins a folded note.

"Here's that phone number you asked for", he said with a wink, "'night, all".

"That guy," said Emma after Special Commander Bryant was out of earshot "is a hundred-dollar haircut on a half dollar head. How insensitive; he seems completely devoid of social skills. And does he really think no-one suspects he found the side saddle thing on Google? Sorry to speak about your superior in that way".

"I never met him personally before", said Detective Sergeant Robbins, "I don't think of him as my superior, since he's up in the stratosphere compared to me, like the Duke of Cambridge. I have a feeling he was the Deputy Chief Constable at Thames Valley Police when I was there, years ago". Detective Sergeant Robbins peeked at the note, and his eyes widened.

"Isn't Deputy Chief Constable senior to Special Commander? What is a Special Commander actually? It isn't something we've ever heard of".

"I think the emphasis is on the *Special* part. We don't actually have a rank of Special Commander, and Bryant doesn't show up on any organisation plans. It's like he's a ghost, or a spy or something. People talk about him like he's one step up from the Commissioner".

"Then you'd think he'd display more social awareness and be in possession of better refined leadership skills", replied Emma, "which means his clumsy demeanour is a sham. No-one gets to such a position without being pin-sharp and way ahead of the game, not even in Britain. I hate to admit, but if that's the case he certainly fooled me".

"Or, perhaps he's intimidated by you, being a psychology expert and everything. It can make you feel a little uncomfortable, knowing someone you're talking to can look into your soul, maybe even read your mind or make your mind go in a certain direction".

"Let me tell you something about psychology. What you just described; it doesn't exist. That's a product of your own making; you've seen movies and got this image of forensic psychology as some kind of dark art that you don't understand and that's stronger than you. I'm not a stage magician or a hypnotist – I can't see anything anyone else cannot see, or manipulate people like Hannibal Lecter; all I can do is figure out what makes people do what they do", said Emma, and Detective Sergeant Robbins didn't believe a word of it.

"But if I *could* read your mind and look into your soul, what would I see?"

Detective Sergeant Robbins blushed. "I don't know, why don't you tell me?" he said, knowing as the words tumbled out of his mouth that it was a mistake.

"Okay, then; let's give it a stab", she said, leaning forward slightly and making eye contact with him like a dentist's drill makes contact with your teeth.

"I have known you for about a day, so this is just the surface, but I see a man who is unfair to himself. You have sadness in your eyes, even when you are smiling, and you feel you have not been a success in any area of your life. You blame yourself for it and are trying not to let mistakes shape your life any longer. You are ambitious but realistic – you do not covet, say, Special Commander Bryant's position, but you very much want to be recognised as a successful detective and a good friend and boyfriend or husband. You are not confident you can be any of these. I suspect you have had unsuccessful relationships and painful break-ups, and your self-esteem has been hit. You set yourself goals but knowingly allow yourself to be distracted from them".

Detective Sergeant Robbins' cheeks were burning now. It was like being told a truth he had always known but had never been aware he had known, and now his instincts were telling him to change the subject and divert attention away from his private self, and with a jolt of embarrassment Detective Sergeant Robbins realised that while his conscious mind was searching for something to say, his subconscious mind had been staring at the long, smooth expanse of thigh showing through the split in the skirt covering Emma's crossed legs, a shiny maroon above-the-knee skirt now.

"The look on your face tells me I'm very warm. Let me tell you some things I see when I look at you, which maybe you don't know. You are a kind, decent, genuine man. You have what it takes to be a good detective and a good friend and boyfriend or husband. People do like you. You have an issue with self-esteem, which I feel counselling could help with. You have an issue with sexual frustration, which you do not deal with well and blame on the mistaken assumption that you appear unlikeable to women. Again, counselling might help. Life may have dealt you a few bad hands, which have left scars, but let me tell you this – I know for sure you have what it takes. You will prove to be a fine detective, even though you've left it a bit late in life to make your mark. Just don't keep allowing yourself to be distracted".

"Distracted? How do you mean?"

"Well, for example, you spent a good deal of the day today checking out my ass and trying to engineer situations and think of ways to look up my skirt. We both know it, and it's okay. I'm not flattered by it and I'm not offended by it; it's called testosterone and it makes men act like idiots. But if you channel your detective energies into finding a suspect instead of figuring out what women are wearing underneath, think how much better a detective you'll be".

Detective Sergeant Robbins' face was scarlet now, but he had a strange impression of a slate being wiped clean, like a guilty kid who's caught pilfering in a sweetshop and let off with a stern but kindly word of warning.

"And with that, my friend, I too am away to do some work before bed". Emma leaned over and picked the note which Special Commander

Bryant had given Detective Sergeant Robbins out of his hand, and as he quickly moved to protest, kissed him lightly on the cheek, then leaned into his ear and whispered "And no, I'm still not wearing any. I very rarely do, for reasons that are not your concern. Now ask yourself this: what do you do with this information, and how does it benefit you in the slightest?", and with that she stood up with a smile and strode off, and despite the utter humiliation he was feeling Detective Sergeant Robbins could not stop himself from checking out her shiny maroon ass.

Detective Sergeant Robbins felt like something enormous had just happened but had no idea what exactly it was, other than that he had just been comprehensively mind-fucked by a true expert, and now she had that bloody note, and Detective Sergeant Robbins decided he needed a very large gin and tonic before bed if he was to have any chance of sleeping at all.

— o —

At eight thirty the next morning, everyone was assembled in the strategic control room except Special Commander Bryant, who was conspicuous by his absence. Detective Sergeant Robbins had actually slept like a baby, and had loaded up at the breakfast buffet so as not to need a large lunch, which seemed a good idea if yesterday's dismal lukewarm pizza lunch was anything to go by. Special Agent In Charge Gajewski was standing with a microphone in her hand.

"Before we begin", began Special Agent In Charge Gajewski, "I'd like to introduce Special Agent Larry Donaldson. Agent Donaldson is a gifted agent whom the FBI has assigned to shadow me as a final part of his secondary career development process. He will someday in the future be assigned to forensic psychology roles in the same way as I currently am, and he is presently assisting me in my assignments and learning from doing so. That is his role, and apart from that he has no direct involvement in assisting Operation Krakatoa. The FBI has seen fit to loan our services to the Metropolitan Police at this time, and to pick up all costs involved.

"Last night at the Hilton, something happened which leads me to question the level of appreciation of this initiative in some quarters. I have spoken to Commander Unwin about it, and he has agreed that it would be appropriate for me to mention it".

Detective Sergeant Robbins froze; his face turned white, in contrast with Commander Unwin's shiny-domed head which was the colour of beetroot as he stared at the table, massaging his temples.

"I discovered a note which had been passed in the lounge, where Agent Donaldson and I were talking with some team members". She held up the note. "It reads: '*You can tell who wears the testicles in that partnership*'. I can see you're shocked by that. Whoever wrote this rude and offensive note was not very complimentary to either Agent Donaldson or me, and both of us are pretty upset about it. Now, I apologise if my talking about this has made you feel uncomfortable, but let me tell you I know who the author of this note was, and it wasn't any of you. I do believe the recipient of the note is not a party to the misogynistic sentiments expressed in it. Further, Agent Donaldson assures me his testicles remain firmly attached and are adequate in most respects, and I can guarantee to you I have no interest in verifying that claim or removing them from his control".

The room erupted into laughter; Agent Donaldson gave an embarrassed thumbs-up sign, and Detective Sergeant Robbins realised he had been holding his breath for thirty seconds and could now breathe again. Special Commander Bryant clearly had been fingered for an appalling error of judgement by Special Agent In Charge Gajewski without even mentioning his name, and now he was somewhere else.

"But seriously, folks, let's view this as a lesson learned. If you hold dinosaur-like opinions about the role of women in positions of leadership or professional excellence, it is best to keep them to yourself, although nobody is saying you cannot hold whatever opinions you like. For my part, I do not believe that possession of testicles is a prerequisite or even relevant in any way to my job, and neither incidentally does Agent Donaldson. If we can all agree on that, we can go forward a stronger and more cohesive team and nail this case shut together".

While the applause died down, Special Agent In Charge Gajewski checked the connection between her laptop and the projector.

"Now, I want you all to assume for now that Pimpinan is a single operative. I know this is the subject of debate, but everything I say from now on applies to a single operative or to the leader of a group of operatives in equal measure. I am not categorically stating that this is the work of one man; that is to be established later, but I will be talking in the singular and I will be assuming that the man we saw yesterday in the videos is the man in question.

"Pimpinan is the name he has chosen for himself, and as we have heard, it is a Malay word meaning 'leadership'. If you Google 'pimpinan', you will find mostly Malaysian and Indonesian sites appear. Malaysian and Indonesian are two distinct languages heavily borrowing from Malay. In conjunction with other evidence, it is apparent he chose 'Pimpinan' to tell us there is an Indonesian connection here. Why is he helping us in this way? More to the point, what does it tell us about the man that he *doesn't* want us to know?

"To answer that, it's important to understand the word itself. It's pronounced 'pim-pin-an', spoken as in 'bam-bam-bam-pim-pin-an', without inflection on any syllable. Like many Indonesian words, it has many subtleties of meaning – it does indeed mean 'leadership', but depending on the context can also mean 'management' or 'manager', 'director', 'directorate', 'guidance', or 'superior' when used as a noun. It is a word he knew would have us reaching for our computers to find its meaning. It is a word which demonstrates that he sees himself in a prominent position of governance, guiding and driving the governed. It has no sinister overtones, suggesting he sees his role as valid and managerial. He clearly thinks he is a force for good. He has appointed himself to a position of authority.

"Now, serial killer – that is a term everyone has in their minds. I have a lot of experience with serial killers, and they don't pre-announce themselves to potential victims. They don't try to warn potential victims. They don't offer them chances, or provide powerful incentives to avoid further attention, as Pimpinan does. Insofar as Pimpinan has killed, and we think will continue to kill, a series of victims, he is a serial killer. But that is where the similarity all but ends. I want you to look at serial killers generally and think about how they compare with Pimpinan. Slide please, Larry"

Special Agent In Charge Gajewski used a remote control to dim the lights in the room, and stepped out to one side.

"Serial killers are almost always, but not always, white men. This may surprise you. So far so good; the videos we saw featured a white man. Rose West and Myra Hindley were women, but they are rare exceptions who were accomplices of men; who were under the strong influence of men. There have been a handful of female serial killers working alone, and some notable serial killers from other races, particularly in America, but we do not need to be concerned with these. Slide please, Larry.

"Serial killers almost always, but not always, prey on their own race. There is a notable exception to this rule: that of female prostitute victims, particularly street-walkers, where the public display of the sexual nature of the victim's occupation overrides any issue of race. Now we depart from the model somewhat; none of the victims were female or street-walkers, yet two of the victims we know about so far were black, the rest were white. Slide please, Larry.

"Serial killers are often loners and are almost always unremarkable. This probably does not surprise you. When we think of Peter Sutcliffe, or Harold Shipman or Fred West, we can see how it would be possible to live next door to them and never suspect a thing. No close friends, a bit of an odd-ball perhaps, but nothing that sets alarm bells ringing. They are often sophisticated, charming and persuasive. We don't know who Pimpinan associates with or how many friends he has, but the man killing victims in the videos we watched together wouldn't look out of place working in a library. Slide, Larry.

"Serial killers are cowardly, opportunistic individuals. Does this surprise you? Many people imagine serial killers as being typically mysterious individuals most notable for the daring with which they put their repugnant fantasies into reality. That is a false perception. Without exception in my experience, serial killers prey on those they perceive as the weakest or most vulnerable that fit the mould for their rage. Examples of victims are commonly prostitutes, female or male, whose work makes them vulnerable and places them alone with strangers on a regular basis, or lonely men and women who have been taken into the confidence of the killer, or who have been attacked and killed while alone in their own homes. This case is a striking departure from the serial killer model; this killer preys on men, and so far only men, who are themselves predators of the worst sort; people regular citizens fear and avoid. He does not concern himself with the crack dealer on the street; he goes after the man who controls or supplies the crack dealer on the street, not the hired thug; but the man who the hired thug works for and is afraid of. Cowardice is not an attribute of this man. He doesn't lure with money or promises; on the contrary, he threatens and if that fails, attacks. He doesn't wait for opportunities, he doesn't pick victims based on weakness, he researches and nominates a target others fear and avoid and if his threats go unheeded, he goes and gets. Slide.

"Serial killers are always driven by a sexual motive. Now, this is a complicated one, and one which surprises most people. I'm not just talking about serial rapists who kill, whose primary motivation is rape and who kill as a secondary feature. Many serial killers were badly abused as children, sometimes by their mothers or other women, physically or mentally or both, either sexually, non-sexually or both, leading to aberrations in their sexual development as adolescents. Some that go on to kill do so without apparent sexual motivation, but it is always there. You may recall the movie *Manhunter*, which introduced us to Hannibal Lecter, and which featured a serial killer with a facial disfigurement whose grandmother had taunted him about it as a small boy, and had repeatedly threatened to cut off his 'disgusting little thing' whenever he wet the bed. He became a hopeless sexual inadequate with a deep, sexually-driven hatred of women, and preyed on happy-family mothers with no apparent sexual molestation of the victims – this is a work of fiction, but is an entirely plausible representation of a genuine theme. Boys who were frequently beaten in a manner with sexual overtones, or were beaten and taunted for trying on their mothers' clothes, or were sexually abused by stepfathers while their mothers watched and laughed, or were forced to sleep in their prostitute-mothers' bedroom while the mothers suffered sexual violence at the hands of male clients are typical of what we find when we delve into the background of what makes a serial killer tick. Pimpinan, on the other hand, displays absolutely none of these markers. We have seen him in action, in minute detail and on several occasions, which is in itself unheard of. He does not molest his victims; in fact he appears to be careful not to have any intimate contact with them at all. They are never fully naked in his presence that we have seen. He does not gloat. He does not flaunt or seem to relish his power. He does not engage with them at all. He does not appear to take pleasure in what he does. He is in no hurry – there is no urgency to his actions. He is not driven by lust or rage or emotion – on the contrary, he appears to find the whole thing tedious. I would bet his blood pressure and pulse rate do not increase significantly.

"Never in my career have I encountered a serial killer without some kind of sexual driver; even Shipman had one which my profession never got the chance to fully understand, but in this case I am willing to admit I have an open mind. What this all means is we have to stop thinking of this man as a serial killer in the traditional sense; the sense we understand. If he has not been twisted by sexual factors, something equally powerful is driving him. If we can find out what, we have a chance of understanding his motives, anticipating his moves and intercepting him. Last slide now please, Larry.

"Serial killers leave a calling card at every event. Now we risk diving into the deep of the psychological profiler's art, but I'll try to keep this simple. By a calling card, we mean clear sight to the identity. Physical clues, such as fingerprints or DNA or dropped objects will be picked up by the crime scene guys. But he will also leave behind equally clear sight to his psychological state and thus what is driving him and ultimately who he is, which will be much less obvious. This part of the calling card is hidden in the way he executes his crime. You can think of it in two parts: the modus operandi or MO, and what we call the signature.

"The MO, as the name implies, is what a killer does when he kills and where, how and when he does it. The killer is conscious of this, he may choose to change it, or it may evolve over time. For example, he may break into doors to gain access for a while, and then find that a glass cutter and a window is quieter and more effective. He may switch from younger to older victims if he feels they are less capable of putting up a strong fight. He may at first attack at night, and then decide the early hours of the morning, or mid-afternoon, give him less chance of disturbance. He will often deliberately change his MO to try to throw us off the scent, or insert diversions or red herrings. It is relatively easy to profile his MO and detect changes and red herrings.

"The signature, on the other hand, is constant or develops gradually over time. It cannot be changed by the killer and he is generally unaware of it. It is not something he chooses or can hide. It is the psychological fingerprint left by the killer which reveals his needs and how he satisfies them in committing the crime. Serial killers are driven by obsession, and obtain sexual gratification from the act of killing, sometimes at the time but very often later, in another place as they remember the process. They are invariably consumed by anger, rage, and lust for revenge. This means that simply ending a life is usually not enough – they may require to torture the victim, or make them call him by a particular name, or mutilate the body after death, or arrange it in a particular way. They may take specific souvenirs from their victims, to help relive the killing later – photographs, a lock of hair, an article of clothing, underwear. The killing is not complete without it. They may only be interested in targets with a certain hair colour, or of a certain height or weight, or that bear a physical resemblance to a particular celebrity or person that has affected their past. Like any addict, they follow a repetitive pattern and tend to be uninterested in alternatives. Decoding and unravelling the signature is a very complex process involving examining in minute detail, every facet of the psychological activity associated with the killing, and that means, basically, re-enactment of the entire thought process by the psychological profiler and asking 'why did I do that? what makes me feel better about it? who made me so angry? why did I choose this victim? '

"Pimpinan changes his MO on every occasion, yet also keeps constants. In the white room he has used the same total restraint of the victim each time, the regular-as-clockwork visits to slowly end life in an agonising way. In the videos, he has begun the process with the victim gagged each time, then immediately removed the gag once the killing has commenced, and recorded the screams. But the method of killing has been different each time, yet equally terrifying; hammer, side-cutter snipping tool, knife, saw. One method per victim. We have no indication yet of a repetition. Outside the white room, both deaths involved nailing the victim to an object and leaving him to be found, but in very different places and in different ways. Both victims were left so that they would likely not be found until an associate showed up, making it almost certain he tipped off the associate about the victim's whereabouts. At the time of discovery, two things would be apparent to the associate: number one, immediate action would be required if the victim's suffering was to be ended, and number two: it would be impossible to remove the victim quickly from his predicament without inflicting further massive, probably fatal trauma. This presents the associate with an impossible dilemma, and I believe was designed to inflict maximum stress and trauma on the associate. On both occasions, we believe, the associate killed the victim, to put him out of his misery, to coin a phrase. It is likely the victims begged the associates for death.

"Now the signature: Pimpinan's signature does not fit any pattern that I've come across. Pimpinan obviously knows a lot about our thought processes in hunting down his psychological make-up, and is very adept at misdirecting the investigation. He knows that the most effective way to mislead a hunt for his character is to offer it on a plate, mixed with an avalanche of red herrings and irrelevances so that each has to be thoroughly investigated and discounted. So, he blurs the distinction between dropped objects and psychological pointers. He knows we are looking for his calling card, so he leaves a ton of physical clues which may or may not have a link to his psychological make-up – his fingerprints, DNA from as-yet unconnected persons, the hammer, the stool, the bat, the book of matches from a nightclub in Johannesburg that closed down in 1981, even – get this – an actual card. The three of diamonds. The hammer, the stool and the bat were obvious tools used in the execution of the crime. The rest may be misdirection; a way of wasting our time thinking about an irrelevance, or each may be a vital piece of the puzzle, or simply his way of saying 'I know you're looking for my calling card; I'm way ahead of you. Will this do?' Every one of these requires painstaking investigation. We have crime scene DNA evidence from suspects who may be completely uninvolved, or may unknowingly be key to the enquiry. He knows without doubt that no records exist of the fingerprints; otherwise we would likely have caught him by now – how could anyone be certain of such a thing? Are they his fingerprints, or does he obtain them from someone who he knows has never been fingerprinted or has never dropped prints anywhere they might have been picked up? Again, how could anyone be certain of such a thing? Either way, the fact of the fingerprints shows either that he is utterly confident that the owner of the prints, whether the owner is him or someone else, will never be called on to provide print records or randomly drop them at an unrelated crime scene, or that he is utterly confident the owner of the prints is immaterial to his cause – in other words, that if the owner's identity is discovered, it will not lead to Pimpinan. So we don't yet know how he is sure no record exists of the fingerprints, or whether they are his, or how he obtains them if they are not his, but we do know of his utter confidence in the fact that his providing the fingerprints to us will not help us find him. There is no thought in his mind that leaving fingerprints might be a bad idea. He is a supremely confident individual. Confidence and arrogance often go hand in hand, and arrogance sometimes leads to risk-taking, but there is no evidence so far that he is arrogant to the point of taking risks.

"We can corroborate this in the way he displays a complete lack of rage or anger or drive or urgency – too much so to be faked, in my opinion, but we don't know. To us, he is not saying catch me if you can; he is saying 'here I am, this is me: try to stop me if you like, but we will play by my rules'. He is playing to an audience, the audience being potential future victims, and of course, now, us. He seems to be aware of our forensic internet analysis capabilities – he makes DVDs and puts them in the mail, for heaven's sakes. That is not how video files are generally exchanged these days, but it is a lot more anonymous than uploading over the internet.

"He seems to have access to the structure of informal criminal organisations – he seems to be picking victims through intelligence, not through impulse. In short, he is unlike any killer I have ever come across before. He is ruthlessly cruel but displays no signs whatever of being a sadist – of being sexually aroused by the cruelty, or enjoying it in any way. But there is one aspect he has in common with all others, which is a good starting point – he is pathologically devoid of mercy, or compassion. He is a psychopath, and he therefore does not consider he is committing a crime or doing wrong. He will continue to kill until we stop him, and like all repeat killers, eventually he will make a fatal mistake.

"To summarise, Pimpinan is not a serial killer in the sense of any existing definition. He is not driven by sexual urges or sexual hatred. He does not kill to satisfy an uncontrollable compulsion. He is in control of his situation, and is not controlled by it. Which all leaves us with very little from which to build up our understanding of his motives. His signature is very faint. So what does he do, and why does he do it? One word – vigilante. We need to learn, to teach ourselves, about the completely different signature of a vigilante killer compared to a serial killer signature. The two things could not be more dissimilar, and the former is much rarer and greatly more difficult to unravel and understand than the latter. The only common factor is the broad concept of revenge.

"Before coffee, I would like to quickly go back to the issue of single or multiple perpetrators. It is extremely rare for a man inclined to commit serial murder to find a like-minded individual to team up with, although it has happened. In almost every case, it has been a spouse or a sexual partner – someone who already shares intimacy with the killer. It is extremely rare for an accomplice to be an outsider - the chance of a killer's discovery increases by an order of magnitude when he approaches someone else or involves someone else, and it's not the kind of thing you can advertise for in the local newspaper. So far, the only thing that points to more than one individual is the sheer logistical mountain of organisation and muscle needed to carry out these murders, which seem too much for one man alone. We must not forget to consider what attributes, skills and resources one lone man would need, what sources of intelligence, training, equipment, and identify what, if any, type of man could do it alone and why he would do it, before we dismiss the idea. Alternatively, if this is a gang of men or some kind of firm, we need to consider how they are organised and disciplined and how the existence of every other identity has until now been successfully hidden from view. After coffee, we'll look at what else we already know about Pimpinan, what we can safely assume and what we need to find out".

Detective Sergeant Robbins felt giddy with admiration for this woman, and for the first time since he could remember felt no distractions from the task of getting on with the job, which was a welcome relief.

Outside the strategic control room, Special Agent In Charge Gajewski retrieved her cell phone from the holding desk and saw she had a missed call. She was about to call the number when her phone vibrated, and she checked the caller name and answered without speaking.

"I'm in the Singapore Airlines business class lounge", said Special Commander Bryant, "I brought the flight forward. How did Larry's testicles go down?"

"Like a team-building dream. Set them up for guilt by association, then give them an immediate way out. Appal them, and then make them laugh. Commander Unwin says it was better than a day out at the seaside, and a lot quicker and cheaper. Remember – not a word to anyone for now. They all assume you've been bounced".

Chapter 6 - Tarzan

There was no way Commander Unwin could spare his time, or that of any of his top officers on Operation Krakatoa, to travel to Jakarta for a courtesy visit with his Indonesian counterparts for the best part of a week. The main purpose of a trip to Jakarta was to seek the Indonesian National Police (or POLRI) co-operation in investigating the source of the phone call from an Indonesian telephone to Joseph Gouder, and pull the suspect in for questioning before they could be alerted to the net closing around them. It was a key part of the investigation that could shed light on the Indonesian connection and help them understand the background of Pimpinan, and might lead directly to Pimpinan himself. However, Indonesian culture was a complex subject of great delicacy which dictated that before any such actions could take place, top level introductions had to be made personally, gifts exchanged, dinners attended, lashings of mutual respect traded and friendships made before the business of the day could be commanded of the minions. So while the actual Police business could easily have been quickly undertaken by any detective with a modicum of experience, it would require someone with the authority and position befitting a minor state occasion to get the wheels turning. Since sending two people was out of the question, what Commander Unwin needed was someone with a grand title who was not important enough to be missed by the Operation, to go and shake a lot of hands and compliment a lot of people, before not screwing the work up and then returning to London with good news. Commander Unwin decided these criteria fit Special Commander

Bryant to a tee, although he had a little trepidation about the 'not screwing the work up' bit, but when Commander Unwin approached Special Commander Bryant about it he immediately had second thoughts about his decision when Special Commander Bryant suggested combining it with a courtesy visit to the British Ambassador in his spare time.

— o —

Special Commander Bryant didn't get where he was today by falling for childish practical jokes. A couple of hours into the flight on the Singapore Airlines Airbus A380, Special Commander Bryant had finished a splendid lunch, had another glass of champagne and settled down to brief himself on his visit. His itinerary told him that he would arrive in Singapore at eight a.m. local time the next day, and four hours later fly on a short hop to Jakarta and be met at the airport by a POLRI driver holding a sign. He was to get a visa-on-arrival at Jakarta which would cost thirty-five US Dollars, which he had in cash in an envelope marked 'Visa', and be driven straight to the palatial Hotel Mulia Senayan where he would recover from the journey and relax for the rest of the afternoon. At nine o'clock the following morning, the same driver would be standing by in the hotel lobby ready to take him to POLRI headquarters where he would meet Grand Commissioner Tarzan. Except, as Special Commander Bryant knew, he would not be meeting anyone called Tarzan, especially not one even grander than a Commissioner, and even now Special Commander Bryant could picture his treacherous underlings giggling at the prospect of him wandering around a foreign Police station looking for Tarzan, ready to mess up his crucial assignment before it even started. Heads would roll, and although Special Commander Bryant had never been called on to dismiss anyone from service until now and would not actually fire anyone until the day he fired Calamity Jane at the Shangri-La, it occurred to him that stellenbosching or firing someone might lead the minions to think twice before viewing him as a soft touch for a practical joke.

Special Commander Bryant was enjoying his flight, with the comfortable seat and the champagne and the pretty stewardesses who treated him like the important person he was, so unlike the staff at home, thought Special Commander Bryant, and despite his watch telling him it was only three thirty in the afternoon, he decided to take a nap, and pressed the button to turn his seat into a bed. The last thing Special Commander Bryant saw before he fell asleep was a pretty Singaporean girl's smiling face as she spread a blanket over him and tucked it under his chin, and Special Commander Bryant thanked his lucky stars that British Airways had been fully booked before he fell into a deep sleep and dreamed of his mother.

Special Commander Bryant was woken by the cabin lights slowly coming on, and pushed the button to turn his bed into a beach lounger. The crew were quietly but efficiently busy taking orders for breakfast and laying out starched white table cloths and silver cutlery onto the tables. It took a few seconds to realise he had slept through almost the entire flight, and for a moment he wondered where he was and why his watch was telling him it was ten p.m. at breakfast time. Special

124

Commander Bryant decided to embrace the local culture by foregoing his usual omelette and going for nasi goreng with prawns, topped with a fried egg and served with a couple of skewers of chicken satay and a giant prawn cracker, and gradually his fellow travellers came to and became active and before he knew it, everyone was wide awake and chatty and he was feeling satisfied and refreshed and they were descending into Singapore.

Changi was not like any other airport he had encountered. He arrived in a vast expanse of plushly-carpeted, cappuccino-sipping un-hurriedness where upmarket shops competed with cafes and restaurants and children's playgrounds as far as the eye could see, and people were ambling along and pointing out the real palm trees and fountains. Smiling first-class passengers were being whisked to the gates on long electric golf carts, and Special Commander Bryant wished Mrs Bryant could see this. He bought a skinny latte and headed for 'the tropical zone' where he sat amid the giant tropical plants and listened to the water trickling thirty feet down a realistic rock-face wall into a pond full of bright yellow fish, and just stopped himself from calling Mrs Bryant, whom he knew would not appreciate an enthusiastic call at one o'clock in the morning. After an hour, he took a two-minute journey on the Sky Train to Terminal 3, where after a lot more leisurely looking around he boarded another Singapore Airlines flight, a Boeing 777 this time, to Jakarta.

— o —

The journey so far had gone swimmingly well. Special Commander Bryant had his visa-on-arrival stuck in his passport, and had cleared Immigration and retrieved his suitcase and put the one million Rupiah (one million!) pocket money in his wallet, when he was a little surprised to notice that the Customs people were asking passengers to put their baggage through an x-ray scanner at the exit. This meant a slight delay to queue up of about five minutes, the first delay of his journey, but it didn't matter, although when the Customs man at the other end of the X-ray machine placed Special Commander Bryant's suitcase on a separate bench and beckoned him over to open it, he felt a tiny pang of anxiety. The Customs man pulled out his three black half-litre bottles of extra virgin olive oil which Special Commander Bryant had been told to use as gifts for his driver and anyone else who helped him during his visit, and used one to gesticulate drinking from the bottle, then held up a leaflet in English that explained that the duty-free limit was one bottle of wine, shaking his head all the time.

"No, it's not wine", explained Special Commander Bryant, "it's olive oil. Oil! From olives!"

"No, no oil, wine", said the Customs man. "You come to office".

"Look, it's plainly not wine. Look at the label; it will say 'olive oil' on it".

The Customs man turned the bottle over in his hand several times, studying it, and Special Commander Bryant noticed that the label was written entirely in Italian and didn't say 'olive oil' anywhere, but it did say 'Tuscany' in red letters, and Special Commander Bryant thought this was not going as well as he'd hoped.

"Is problem", said the Customs man gravely, rubbing his chin, and then a great idea seemed to hit him and he lowered his voice and said "I help you, you give me something?"

"Help me what? And what do you want me to give you?"

"Up to you, boss".

"Now look, I'm Special Commander Bryant of the Metropolitan Police in London", said Special Commander Bryant, pulling out his identification card, "so if you're asking me for a bribe you're asking the wrong man. This is not wine and I have no need of your help".

The Customs man's eyes popped when he saw the photograph of Special Commander Bryant in his important-looking cap under the words 'METROPOLITAN POLICE' in blue, and now he was grinning embarrassedly and saying 'is okay boss, is good, is good', and helping Special Commander Bryant to zip up his suitcase. Special Commander Bryant had a feeling the plotting underlings had chosen Italian olive oil specially to get him into trouble, but it hadn't worked. He wheeled his suitcase out of the double door in the frosted glass wall into the arrivals hall, and found immediately he had to make a choice between turning left or turning right, in each case to walk along a row of money changer stalls and taxi kiosks full of people frantically trying to attract his attention, towards throngs of waiting people crushed against stainless steel barriers. After a pause, Special Commander Bryant chose the right and approached the crowd, looking out for a POLRI sign and finding only Hotel Shangri-La and InterContinental Hotel signs and hand-written signs with foreign-sounding names, and slowed down as he got closer and, seeing no sign of POLRI, began to turn round and go the other way but a uniformed security man the size of a ten year old moved to stop him, so he exited into the crowd and a dozen men seemed to zoom in on him calling 'Taxi, Mister? Taxi?" Ignoring the taxi touts, Special Commander Bryant pushed his way around the back of the money changer stalls to the opposite end of the exit, and looked around for a POLRI sign, but again there was none. He can't have given up waiting so soon, thought Special Commander Bryant; the flight was on time and I was hardly delayed at all. What to do? He noticed the arrivals hall was less crowded away from the exit barriers and, unlike at the arrivals area at Heathrow, there was plentiful seating provided, so he decided to go and sit for a while and compose his thoughts, all the while looking out for a POLRI sign being held aloft.

He hadn't been sitting for more than a minute when a furtive looking man approached him and said "Hello Mister! Rolex?" and held up a gold watch. Special Commander Bryant shook his head and looked away, but the man was persistent and kept holding the watch in front of his face and saying "only two million, only two million" before pausing and saying "is very good, one point eight", and Special Commander Bryant noticed that another man had quietly sidled up to the man with the Rolex and was patiently waiting his turn, clutching a pair of fake Mont Blanc pens. Special Commander Bryant had been trained for this situation in his foreign travel briefing and knew that in Indonesia, the last thing you should do is lose your temper or raise your voice, as to do so would draw a lot of unwanted attention and make everyone around view you with contempt. He also knew that hawkers of counterfeit goods were commonplace, but Jakarta was generally a safe place if you kept out of trouble, so he went into 'broken record' mode and started repeating 'no thank you, I have a watch, no thank you, I don't want a watch, no thank you, I have a pen', over and over again until the sellers went away. Ten or fifteen minutes had now passed, during which time, Special Commander Bryant realised, he had been distracted from looking out for a POLRI sign, and now a scruffy young boy was standing in front of him holding a shoe brush and timidly pointing at his shoes, which were looking dusty and tired after the journey.

"You want to shine my shoes? How much?" asked Special Commander Bryant.

"Yes!" smiled the boy, and stood stiffly in front of him, still pointing at his shoes. Special Commander Bryant was not one to encourage child labour or hawkers generally, but things probably worked differently here and he admired this boy's enterprise, so he took off his shoes and passed them to the boy, who turned and walked off with them, leaving Special Commander Bryant feeling conspicuous and hoping people weren't laughing at his stupidity. He'll be back soon, thought Special Commander Bryant.

Another fifteen minutes passed, during which time Special Commander Bryant alternately looked for a POLRI sign and wondered how he could have found himself abandoned in an airport on the other side of the world with his shoes stolen, when the boy returned, and Special Commander Bryant was stunned at how jet black and immaculate and shiny his shoes were. They looked better than brand new.

"This is an excellent job, just excellent!" he said, "How much do I owe you?" and the boy just smiled uncomprehendingly, so Special Commander Bryant took out a single fifty thousand Rupiah note from his wallet and offered it to the boy, hoping he wouldn't be insulted if it was not enough, but the boy looked as delighted as if all his birthdays had suddenly arrived at once and took the money and backed away, bowing all the time and saying 'Terima kasih Mister! Terima kasih Mister!", which unmistakably meant 'thank-you'.

Special Commander Bryant went outside to investigate ways to make his own way to the hotel. He didn't know what could have gone wrong, but would have his office contact POLRI to explain he hadn't been picked up as planned, and was at the hotel and would look for the driver in the lobby in the morning. Special Commander Bryant realised this was the first time he had been in the open air since London, and boy, was it hot and humid. He was at a car pick-up strip running the entire length of the airport terminal, but there was no sign of busses or trains. He noticed an area to his right where people were queuing and there were taxi signs, and he got into a long queue at the Silver Bird Executive Taxi stand, where smart uniformed girls with walkie-talkies were speaking to customers and looking along the road for cars, of which there were none presently available. Eventually, a black Mercedes E-class with a 'Silver Bird' light on the roof arrived, and a lady at the front of the queue got in and left.

"Where are you going, Sir?" asked one of the taxi girls, and Special Commander Bryant showed her his booking confirmation from the Hotel Mulia Senayan. "It will be about fifty minutes or one hour", she said. "I'm sorry, we're very busy today".

Special Commander Bryant felt almost unable to hide his frustration. He was feeling suddenly tired now, having been travelling for the best part of a day, and the journey was far from over, so when he felt a slight tug on his sleeve and heard a hushed "Taxi, Mister?' he turned and looked the man in the eye.

"Five hundred", said the man, holding up five fingers. Special Commander Bryant did a quick calculation in his head and decided he must be talking about five hundred thousand Rupiah, which was around thirty one pounds, which seemed reasonable.

"Okay, let's do that", and the man strode off with Special Commander Bryant's suitcase while Special Commander Bryant trotted behind, carrying his cabin bag and trying not to sweat. They got to a rank of about eight battered-up old cars of various colours and makes, and the man approached a metallic green one with a 'Selebriti Taksi' sticker that looked as if the suspension had collapsed, and held out his hand for money. Special Commander Bryant smelled a rat.

"I'm not sure I want to risk getting into this", he said.

"Five hundred", said the man, holding up five fingers.

"Absolutely not. I'll give you two hundred now", he said, handing the man two hundred thousand Rupiah bills, "and the rest when we get there". He pointed to the direction he guessed the city was.

"Okay, okay" said the man, and creaked open the boot and put the suitcase inside. Special Commander Bryant got in the back, and noticed the missing window handle and the wisps of green spray paint on the yellow paint inside the door. The car smelled of stale cigarette smoke, but the engine started first time and after they had left the airport, they started driving down a long straight dual carriageway through mangrove and marshland past gigantic advertising billboards. The car did not have air conditioning and Special Commander Bryant was sweating profusely now, and there was no handle on the window and only a hot breeze from the driver's open window in front. He was hoping no-one would notice him arriving at a five-star hotel in this old wreck, but beggars can't be choosers, he thought, and at least he would soon be able to have a shower and unwind. He looked at his watch and saw it was now eight a.m. in England, and decided to call Mrs Bryant as soon as he got in, just as the engine stopped and the car began to rapidly slow to the side of the road.

Special Commander Bryant couldn't take it any longer. "What the hell is happening now?" he shouted, noticing his voice had betrayed a slight feeling of panic. "Can we get this thing moving?" and the man got out and looked under the bonnet momentarily, then got back in and turned the engine over, seeming confident that a quick glance at the motor might have fixed the problem. It turned strongly but did not fire at all. The man tried again. "Sorry, sorry", he said, and babbled something in Indonesian while pointing at Special Commander Bryant with his thumb, then he went to the back of the car and began to push. Special Commander Bryant got out, although he did not like the way this was turning out.

"No, no, you can't push as well. You have to get in the seat and put it in gear. Let me try to push; I simply have to get to the hotel. I expect at least a third off the fare for this".

The man said 'oh yes, please, thank you Mister' and got back in, and the instant Special Commander Bryant's hands touched the back of the car the engine burst into life and the car sped off, leaving Special Commander Bryant standing on the side of the road with his mouth wide open in disbelief. It took a few seconds for the gut-wrenching realisation to set in that the man wasn't looking for a place to turn round and come back for him, and Special Commander Bryant had been tricked, and he was miles from anywhere in a foreign land with only the clothes he was standing up in and his phone – thank God he still had his phone, but what was still in the car? His suitcase containing his clothes and olive oil and – oh no, his dress uniform for the meeting tomorrow, and – what else – his cabin bag – his leather folio with his *itinerary*, and contact numbers for POLRI and the hotel and – oh NO, his *passport*. Special Commander Bryant felt like crying, and sat down on the verge as the cars sped past, and noticed again how clean and shiny his shoes were. "There's nothing worth stealing, no money", he screamed aloud, "but it's all my stuff, you little bastard!"

Special Commander Bryant did not have any of his useful Jakarta numbers programmed into his phone, and the only solution was to call Commander Unwin and have him get in touch with POLRI. Luckily Commander Unwin would be awake, and he braced himself for the call, and dialled. After explaining what happened and how he got into his situation (leaving out the part about his passport, and having his shoes shined), while Commander Unwin listened and said 'uh-huh' a dozen times, Special Commander Bryant waited to hear what Commander Unwin would do.

"I don't understand; why are you there so early? I thought you'd still be on the way".

"Well, after I had to disappear for the second day owing to Larry's testicles, I brought the flight forward to around lunch time. It meant arriving at a more agreeable hour".

"Did you let POLRI know about your change of plans? I can't imagine they just wouldn't show up".

"Your office made the arrangements, Alan, and while I didn't specifically ask them to rearrange my airport pick-up, I assumed someone would be bright enough to realise it would be necessary".

Commander Unwin's hackles rose. "But why didn't you call POLRI from the airport? What possessed you to get into some taxi bandit's car? Your transportation is taken care of for the whole trip. You should have no need of taking taxis at all".

"I did call, Alan", he lied, "but I couldn't make myself understood. I thought it quicker and easier to make my own way to the hotel".

"Well, that plan worked like a dream, didn't it? Right, stay there and don't move, Bryant, and try not to fuck anything else up in the meantime. I'll call and get you picked up. Have you any idea how embarrassing this is for me? I'm the commanding officer of a major operation requiring discreet international cooperation, and I have to call my Indonesian counterparts and tell them that one of my senior officers, whom they've been expecting and are probably looking for as we speak, has been in the country for ten seconds and got lost in the airport, and now he's been robbed and is standing on the side of the road, and could they please pick him up. You're there as a senior ambassador of the Metropolitan Police to facilitate co-operation between the Forces, for heaven's sake, to open doors, and you're acting like some clueless tourist who doesn't know what day of the week it is".

Special Commander Bryant didn't care for Commander Unwin's tone and felt like pointing out that as he was the *special* commander he should be treated with the respect befitting the senior officer of the two, but under the circumstances decided to bite his lip and let it go, and about forty five minutes later Special Commander Bryant was picked up, shirt soaked and sticking to his torso and wet hair plastered to his forehead, by a convoy of five *Polisi* cars and two huge Yamaha motorcycles with lights flashing and sirens blaring. Special Commander Bryant sat in the middle car with the officer who spoke good English, and they took him directly to the Hotel Mulia Senayan where they would ask him questions so the thief will be catch and put it in the prison chop chop, while the traffic parted to let them through. The officer who spoke good English kept apologising for the terrible thing, you very important man, so many thief in Jakarta, especially the taxi because we can't stop them if they don't have the licence.

"But I was expecting a POLRI driver with a sign", said Special Commander Bryant, "and he wasn't there. There were lots of people with signs, but none of them from POLRI".

"He there", replied the officer who spoke good English, "but of course POLRI cannot wait in the public area with a POLRI sign. We are POLRI, not the travelling agent. So, he waiting in the office. With the sign".

'Well, how the hell was I supposed to know that, and anyhow what use was a sign if he was sitting in an office somewhere?' thought Special

Commander Bryant as his systolic blood pressure rose a couple of millimetres, but said nothing, and they both sat in silence for the rest of the journey, and they only killed the sirens after they had startled the life out of all the guests milling around as they pulled up outside the opulent Hotel Mulia Senayan.

When he was finally alone, Special Commander Bryant looked around his room and wondered what was next. The officer who spoke good English had said his boss would visit Special Commander Bryant and discuss the arrangements for tomorrow, which would not be as previously planned, and Special Commander Bryant decided he would not risk another misunderstanding by leaving his room even for a moment until then. He took a bottle of chilled Equil sparkling water from the cold-tray, and thought about which television to watch – the big one in the lounge, or the smaller one in his separate bedroom. This really was a fine room, he thought; actually four rooms in total if you counted the small toilet marked *powder room* in gold letters, with its plentiful Bvlgari toiletries and thick white towels. He was thinking of calling Mrs Bryant when there was a faint tap on the door, and he opened it to find a small skinny man in a drab, dark brown POLRI uniform wearing an embroidered badge that said *Kombespol Tarzan* who nearly made Special Commander Bryant choke on his Equil when he announced 'Hello, I'm Tarzan' with a grin, looking exactly like Johnny Weissmuller never did.

Kombespol is not my first name, explained Tarzan, who had walked into the room with a lit cigarette and who, like many Indonesians, only had one name; it is a short form of 'Komisar Besar Polisi' or Police Grand

Commissioner. Special Commander Bryant thought that if the Kombespol hadn't looked at all like a Tarzan should look, he looked even less like a Grand Commissioner, but was too polite to say so. Tarzan was very upbeat about the prospect of finding the rogue taxi driver and getting Special Commander Bryant's possessions back, but his passport might be a different matter, and for now Special Commander Bryant should concentrate on getting a replacement. He would be loaned a dedicated car and driver and would go to the British Consulate General in the morning to obtain an emergency replacement, from which time he would have twenty four hours to leave the country. He would have to fly to Singapore and visit the Indonesian embassy to get a business visa, and when he got back, business would commence.

"Strictly speaking, you shouldn't have come in with a visa-on-arrival; they're for tourists and social visitors", explained Tarzan, "it would have been fine if you'd brought someone with you for the work, and yours was purely a social visit. But as you'll need to sign some forms, probably, that is classed as doing business, which must have a business visa". To be on the safe side, Special Commander Bryant should arrange to stay overnight in Singapore, and Tarzan would need to accompany him as his sponsor, provided, of course, Special Commander Bryant picked up the tab for his hotel and airfare and paid for dinner. Next, Tarzan dialled from the room phone and spoke in Indonesian and a minute later, the General Manager of the hotel was with them.

"I had asked for a good room for my friend", said Tarzan in English, "but this one is a little ... small, and it smells of cigarettes". A blue layer of smoke still hung in the air. "My friend will check out early tomorrow morning and return in the evening the next day, and we hope you can give him something a little better, for the same price".

— o —

Special Commander Bryant spent most of the day in Singapore hanging around Orchard Road feeling jet-lagged and drinking coffees while Tarzan shopped for his wife. Tarzan had arranged for a formalities agent to collect Special Commander Bryant's new emergency passport from the hotel as soon as they had arrived, and neither of them had needed to go to the Indonesian embassy, which made Special Commander Bryant suspect that Tarzan had simply fancied and all-expenses paid couple of days out in Singapore, and when he arrived back at the Grand Hyatt that evening and his passport complete with visa was waiting for him, meaning they need not have stayed overnight at all, Special Commander Bryant was sure of it. He was not looking forward to presenting Commander Unwin with an expense claim for two extra business class airfares and hotel rooms in Singapore, but he would argue that this had been all part of a fast-track relationship-building and planning exercise which had shaved a day or two from the overall timeline. That night, over fine postprandial brandy and cigars, Special Commander Bryant and Tarzan became close colleagues and friends who had a plan and were fired up for affirmative action, and the next evening in Jakarta Special Commander Bryant did not need to queue up at Immigration, or look for a POLRI sign, or get his shoes shined.

"Oh, and by the way", said Tarzan as they raced along the brightly-lit toll road into Jakarta with the huge Yamahas front and rear, "tomorrow you will see your taxi driver again. And your things. Passport, too".

Chapter 7 - Suparman

It was Special Commander Bryant's fourth day since arriving in Jakarta, and he still had not done a thing towards solving the case, but instead had incurred unplanned additional expenditure of six times the amount of his entertainment budget of three hundred and fifty pounds. At nine o'clock, he sat in Tarzan's scruffy office while Tarzan smoked and drank sweet coffee and explained that the mobile phone number was from ExelComindo, one of the top three mobile service providers in Indonesia, and that his friend was ExelComindo's head of corporate governance.

"He will be able to get all the information we need quickly", said Tarzan, "probably this week. You will go with one of my men. He can speak English very good, he was at school in Australia".

Special Commander Bryant didn't think 'probably this week' sounded quickly at all. "What is his name, your man? Batman, by any chance?" he asked wryly, failing to convincingly hide a smirk.

"Batman? No, of course not, no-one is called Batman. It's Suparman. Inspector Suparman".

Special Commander Bryant knew it would be very rude to laugh at the absurdity of investigating a case with Tarzan and Suparman, and was only saved from letting out a giggle by a Policeman coming in and talking in Indonesian with Tarzan. The Policeman had an ugly bulbous melanoma the size of a coin on the side of his top lip, from which sprouted half a dozen two-inch long black hairs, which made Special

Commander Bryant glad that neither of them were looking at him and wonder how he would be able to resist staring at it, or snipping the hairs off.

"This man will show you your taxi driver and your things", said Tarzan, "and you must tell us if anything is missing. He will ask you to forgive him. It's up to you, of course, but I suggest you do not make a decision immediately. If you forgive him we will let him go in maybe two weeks. Anyway, we don't really want him in the prison, since he has no money".

Special Commander Bryant followed the Policeman through endless corridors and open areas with people sleeping and eating and working at manual typewriters under wobbling ceiling fans that threatened to fly off and decapitate someone at any moment, to a small table with his belongings laid out on it. Everything was there except the olive oil and the cellophane wrapping that had covered his dress uniform, and the Policeman handed him his passport. "It's all here", he said, feeling slightly uncomfortable that his neatly ironed and folded underpants were on full display to the sniggering Policewomen.

Any feelings of wanting revenge that Special Commander Bryant harboured evaporated when he entered the windowless room and saw the taxi driver. It was unmistakably him, but now he was dressed in threadbare knee length shorts and worn out tee shirt, shoeless, and was squatting on his heels until Special Commander Bryant entered the room. His face had several angry bruises and reddened areas visible, and when he saw Special Commander Bryant he began wailing loudly and sat on the floor cowering in front of him, sobbing 'I sorry Mister, I sorry' and kept glancing up fearfully at the Policeman.

"He denied it at first, but he failed the lie detector test, and now he has admitted his crime", grinned the Policeman. "He admits he pretended the car was broken, and tricked you to stealing your baggage. We are very diligent to catching the thief".

"You have lie detectors? Polygraphs, and such like?" asked Special Commander Bryant, who had not seen anything more technologically advanced than a floppy disk drive in the entire station.

"This is our lie detector", said the Policeman, handing him a heavy black leather glove that had pouches filled with flat lead bars over each finger, covering the knuckles and extending to the second joints. "It never makes a mistake. Would you like to try?"

Special Commander Bryant felt awful. He had heard that such things happened in some parts of the world, but this was his first experience of being associated with open Police brutality, and he did not like it. The taxi driver had caused him enormous stress and heartache, but now he pitied him.

"Shall I make him dance for you?" suggested the Policeman.

"No – no, no. I want you to interpret for me, if he doesn't understand what I say", he replied, and then addressed the taxi driver. "What you did was wrong, and foolish. You knew I was a visitor to your country, and you stole from me. You took everything I had and left me alone in a dangerous situation, in a strange place. I need to know if you regret what you did, or if you only regret being caught".

"He says he has no money to give you. He says if you forgive him, his wife will work for you without payment for as long as you want, and if he goes to prison his family will starve. He says he is sorry. It sounds like bullshit to me".

"Tell him to take care of his family. Tell him I forgive him".

"He would have killed you if it had been easier", said the Policeman. "He hates infidels, probably, especially rich ones", and then told the man he had been forgiven, and the taxi driver burst into uncontrollable tears, making Special Commander Bryant feel wretched for the rest of the week.

— o —

Inspector Suparman looked about sixteen years old. He wore a long mullet swept back into a pony tail and home-made tattoos, and was dressed in a knock-off Manchester United shirt which he had bought specially to impress Special Commander Bryant, and blue jeans and Nike sneakers.

Special Commander Bryant was supposed to be actively investigating with Suparman, but was in effect following him around while Suparman figured things out and decided what to do and where to go next, and this joint initiative was making steaming progress. The phone was currently active in the Senayan area of Jakarta, probably not far from Special Commander Bryant's hotel, although they could not pin it down to less than an area of a few city blocks. The phone account was registered on April seventeenth four years previously, on a ProXL post-paid plan, to an expatriate named Russell Waite, at an address in Kemang. Russell Waite was British and had provided ExelComindo with a copy of his KITAS, or semi-permanent residence permit, showing he was employed by an agency specialising in providing expatriate expertise to the oil and gas companies. Russell Waite was still employed by the agency and was found by Inspector Suparman without difficulty. When interviewed informally, he confirmed that the phone previously belonged to him, but claimed it had been lost or stolen in November a couple of years previously, at which time he had terminated his account with ExelComindo and now used a pay-as-you-go phone card from another provider. Except, ExelComindo still had the account operating and active in his name. Suparman had suggested they shouldn't take Russell Waite in for formal questioning at this stage, since he seemed to be telling the truth, and keeping him in normal circulation might prevent any alerts being picked up by whoever had stolen the phone.

Further enquiries with ExelComindo revealed that the customer had indeed terminated his account two years ago last November, but had visited the Mega Kuningan offices of ExelComindo the same day and reported the phone found, withdrawn his termination, and reinstated the number. At the same time, he had signed up to e-mail billing, ending his monthly statements by post in favour of bills sent by email to a Yahoo email address. Two other interesting facts came to light from ExelComindo: first, from that date, the account stopped being paid by automatic credit card charge under the name of Russell Waite and began being paid, customer present, in cash. Second, from that date the usage changed from being mainly local outgoing calls and texts with occasional international calls to Singapore, Thailand and the UK, to being entirely call-free months, or months with one or two calls which were entirely international, to the UK, and no texts at all. ExelComindo allowed email billing not associated with a postal address provided they had a valid credit card charging authority. They would charge the bill to Russell Waite's card on the due date if it had not already been paid by other means, but since the termination and immediate reinstatement in November two years previously, it had always been paid within three days of the statement being issued by email, in cash, at the Mega Kuningan office.

Special Commander Bryant felt it had been a fruitful first day that had resulted in a lot of interesting information that warranted further investigation, once Suparman had explained it a couple of times. The trouble was, all the face-to-face discussions with ExelComindo and the employment agency had been conducted in Indonesian, and Suparman had had to duplicate afterwards the entire thing in English to Special Commander Bryant, so when Suparman suggested he continued alone tomorrow and meet up with Special Commander Bryant in the evening so that Special Commander Bryant could do more important things instead, Special Commander Bryant thought it was a great idea provided Commander Unwin didn't find out. Suparman promised to get the print-out of all calls on the ExelComindo number since November two years ago to Special Commander Bryant first thing in the morning.

Special Commander Bryant was under strict orders never to call the ExelComindo number to see who answered, and had stressed the importance of this to Suparman without really understanding why. When Special Commander Bryant had emailed the list of all outgoing numbers dialled from the target phone to Superintendent Smith, he was asked where the record of incoming numbers was, and Suparman had found out that ExelComindo doesn't keep records of incoming numbers, even those automatically forwarded to another number, unless the phone happens to be 'roaming' at the time and incoming call charges apply. Provided the phone remains in greater Jakarta, in effect, there would be no record kept of any incoming calls. Suparman was very interested in the 'automatically forwarded' bit, and told Special Commander Bryant he was going back to ExelComindo offices to speak to the technical people.

"If I understand this correctly, what they seem to be saying is, a ProXL phone can receive a call and automatically forward it to a pre-set number. The phone's records will show an outgoing call made to the pre-set number, charged to the ProXL account, but not the incoming call that was diverted by it. I need to know whether the ultimate receiver of the call, at the pre-set number, will see the call coming in from the ProXL phone, or the actual originating phone. It could mean your victim received a call from somewhere else, diverted via this ExelComindo ProXL phone. I need to know if that's possible, and whether ExelComindo can trace the origin of any call that is diverted".

'We have an interesting lead and I'm going back to ExelComindo to speak to the technical people', Special Commander Bryant emailed to Superintendent Smith just after Suparman had gone back to ExelComindo to speak to the technical people. 'If I understand this correctly, what they seem to be saying is, a ProXL phone can receive a call and automatically forward it to a pre-set number, and beyond that we're completely in the dark. Got to go now' and Special Commander Bryant went to the pool to catch some rays, safe in the knowledge that Suparman would get to the bottom of it.

— o —

"The last time I tried to urgently contact Tarzan was when Bryant's phone had been off all day and the hotel said he'd checked out", said Superintendent Smith to Commander Unwin. "Tarzan's office told me he had gone shopping in Singapore for a couple of days with Special Commander Bryant. Bryant is obviously back now, but it is apparent that the phone issue is a lot more complex than originally thought, and I don't think this is an appropriate investigation for someone of Bryant's rank. I'm getting information from Bryant that seems incomplete or not fully understood. I'm also convinced that whether the phone is a live lead or a carefully set up red herring, it can be connected directly to Pimpinan. Gouder was called from this phone in Jakarta, but the question now seems to be whether it was a direct call from the phone, or someone called the phone from somewhere else and was redirected to Gouder by it. I've asked Bryant to ascertain whether it's physically possible someone called the Indonesian phone from London, knowing he would be redirected by the phone in Indonesia back to Gouder in London. If so, it would indicate Pimpinan has somebody in Jakarta holding the phone and programming it to redirect calls to numbers he provides, but I am not satisfied Bryant understands what I am asking him. It is apparent that Indonesian phone companies do not keep records of all incoming calls, unlike our own phone companies. I propose we urgently send a team of two detectives to make sure nothing slips through the cracks".

"Never mind Bryant's rank, this investigation is not appropriate for someone of his IQ. God help us if he screws this up; he's not a detective, he's a politician who's never worked an actual case in his life. He has trouble detecting his own arse".

Commander Unwin thought for a moment. "What a nightmare. What was I thinking, when I sent Bryant? But it won't go down well in Jakarta if we pull Bryant and send a couple of lower ranks to work with them; they would see that as a snub, it's not the way they like to do things. I have full confidence in the Indonesians' capabilities once they get to work – look how impressive their performance was in rounding up the Bali bombers after 2002. They had a lot of international assistance available, but they didn't need it, and the world took notice. This time, though, they don't have the full story, and are unaware of the significance of the work. For now, we'll keep it that way. Okay, let's keep Bryant there, but get two nominees prepared and ready to catch the next available flight, and we'll see what we get from Bryant in the morning and make a decision tomorrow. Meanwhile get Bryant to spin the possibility to the Indonesians as a gesture of appreciation for their outstanding work. Spin is one of the few things he seems able to do reasonably well. And above all, remind him not to call that number unless and until your officers get there, or he is specifically instructed otherwise. We will only get one crack of the whip on that one".

— o —

"The Yahoo account is a dead end. The only activity is incoming email bills from ExelComindo, and it's only ever been accessed from mobile devices. We might be able to get a lead on it if he accessed it from a land-line terminal, but he never has and he's just going to a different Starbucks each time with a Blackberry".

Suparman was looking as though he had just delivered good news, which confused Special Commander Bryant until he continued "But ... I won the grand prize with ExelComindo. Most of their customers have pre-paid accounts. They register their details and buy a card, which they top up with credit whenever they run out. Pre-paid cards usually cannot get roaming, or international calling or call divert. But this is a ProXL post-paid card, normally provided only to businesses and proven credit-worthy individuals, which can do all those things and more, provided the balance doesn't exceed the monthly credit limit. He can divert all calls to any number in the world, as long as the phone stays in Jakarta, and he can change the number it diverts to as often as he likes. The person on the other end only sees the ExelComindo number, which makes sense considering most people only ever divert their cell phone calls to their wives when they're on the golf course. If he had two ProXL cards, he could daisy-chain them and make it even more confusing".

Special Commander Bryant recognised an opportunity to make a sensible contribution. "So what we have to do is ask ExelComindo what number it's programmed to divert to right now".

"Unfortunately, no. It's stored on the SIM card. They don't know until it is actually used".

"So we should arrest Waite and check his SIM card right away!"

"What? No! Listen, when we spoke to him, the phone was active in Senayan. We were with Waite, three or four kilometres away. It cannot be his phone now, unless he knew we were coming to visit him. But what we *could* do", said Suparman slyly, "is get ExelComindo to send a bill now, hope the suspect doesn't notice it's eight days early, and sit in the ExelComindo office waiting for him to come in and pay". Suparman was stroking his gun now. "And, if you really want to impress your office, why don't we call the phone from ExelComindo's offices while you're on the line to your boss in London, read him the number it's forwarding to, and he can have people on the road to the subscriber while his phone's still ringing".

Chapter 8 - Morgan Freeman

It had been another eventful day. At around seven, Emma Gajewski arrived back at the Mostyn hotel after a short taxi ride from Paddington Green, and headed straight for the bar for a couple of Manhattans before she even thought about dinner, and tried to make sense of what had happened. A padded envelope had been delivered to Superintendent Smith first thing that morning by the mail room, labelled simply 'Supt. Steve Smith – CONFIDENTIAL' in felt pen. Usually the routine mail would be opened before delivery, but the confidential endorsement meant it had been x-rayed, checked for explosive traces and then delivered intact. Superintendent Smith had found a pack of playing cards inside, with no note or anything else accompanying it, and had immediately realised the possible significance of the parcel and sent it for prints, activating emergency protocol. Apart from his own fingerprints dropped during the package opening, Superintendent Smith had been informed there was a complete but smudged set of prints from another person on the card pack, arranged as though they had been provided for a Police ten-print record, which were quickly identified as being those found at the scene of the two killings attributed to Pimpinan. Superintendent Smith was wary of making the assumption that even if Pimpinan was a lone operator, the prints were from the man seen in the killing videos, and pointedly refused to refer to them as 'Pimpinan's prints'.

There had then followed a laborious but frantic series of tasks to try to quickly ascertain who had delivered the package to Paddington Green station. A person assumed to be a bicycle courier had dropped the package at the front desk the previous evening, no signature required and without any paperwork, and left within five seconds of arriving. CCTV showed a young woman wearing black and purple Lycra cycling shorts and top, tinted glasses and a cycling helmet drop the package with a smile, speaking briefly to the reception clerk, and leave without further incident. It was noted the young woman had handled the package with bare hands, as had the reception clerk, but she wore no visible markings identifying any particular courier service. She had walked down the front steps and disappeared in the direction of Edgware Road station, and Superintendent Smith had requested CCTV footage from the station and street cameras to find out if she had in fact entered the station or had mounted a bicycle anywhere nearby.

It was next to impossible to recover usable fingerprints from a coarse paper package like this one by normal dusting methods, but the lab had ordered a cyanoacrylate lifting in an attempt to trace the courier. The trouble was, the package would be riddled with fingerprints from many different people, and if no record was found of some of the full or partial prints recovered, it would be a million to one chance of finding her that way. The package would be placed in a humidity controlled chamber, where the moisture in the air would rehydrate any trace residues left by fingerprints, down to the paper fibres below the surface but which may have been contacted by the fingers. Once that had been done, a small heated dish containing a type of cyanoacrylate, very similar to commercially available Super Glue, would be placed in the chamber. Vapour from the heated dish would fill the chamber and attach itself to the now-moistened residue from the fingerprints, fixing it and hardening into dusty white imprints that were visible to the eye with the help of a simple magnifying glass. Any prints discovered in this way would be carefully lifted onto special plastic film, taking care to get deep into the pores of the paper to produce a flat-line copy of the fingerprint. It was a very time consuming, detailed process and Superintendent Smith had had to decide on a compromise between speed and thoroughness which favoured speed. He would nevertheless have to wait a further day for the results.

Meanwhile, the pack of playing cards was opened and examined with gloved hands. No fingerprints had been found on the glossy surface of any of the cards, but they had been shuffled and seemed in random order, and Superintendent Smith requested that before anything else, the exact order of the cards was noted for future use. The cards were examined under ultra violet light, and nothing unusual was noticed. The box was slit with a razor and laid flat, and in minute letters on the inside surface was written '22 December 1962' in indelible laundry ink, probably using a tiny mapping pen. When Superintendent Smith looked over the order of the playing cards, paying special attention to the three of diamonds, he discovered that not only was it present, but there were *two* three-of-diamonds cards and no jokers, making a fifty-three card deck. The first three of diamonds was the eleventh card in the deck, and there were ten cards between the two three-of-diamonds cards, which were, in order, the jack of clubs, ace of hearts, nine of spades, eight of spades, five of diamonds, ace of spades, seven of clubs, king of hearts, eight of hearts and nine of clubs. The day had ended with the leadership team of Operation Krakatoa holding a thirty minute debrief to agree that the importance of Pimpinan's first direct contact with them could not be overestimated, and that the relevance and significance of the immediate clues presented and any hidden connotations not yet discovered would need a great deal of investigation, and they all went home exhausted.

Emma Gajewski wondered whether all of this amounted to more than a hill of beans – okay, so Pimpinan has succeeded in getting a package placed into the heart of the Operation which clearly said 'this is from me', but did any of it mean anything? The date, the courier, the fifty three card deck, the ten cards between the two three-of-diamonds, the eleven cards before them and the thirty cards after them, the mass of partial fingerprints which would undoubtedly result from the paper analysis – all would require enormous resources to decode, analyse and follow up, and all might be completely meaningless; a diversion of effort. Or not. She was feeling that the fundamental question of why Pimpinan took the risk of getting into Paddington Green by proxy at all was being overlooked on account of the mass of detail provided by the package, and she understood that that was almost certainly the entire reason for it. This was not a cat-and-mouse game being played; if the significance of all the 'clues' turned out to be nothing or, as was more likely, remained uncertain forever, it was a very clever and successful effort to directly insert spurious evidence into the investigation, to divert attention from the real issues at hand. And one of the issues at hand was the fact that Pimpinan seemed to have access to information from within the Operation itself. The package had been addressed to 'Supt. Steve Smith', and no-one had appeared to pick up that Superintendent Smith's key involvement in the Operation was something supposedly known only to the Operation itself. Further, until today Emma had been unaware that Superintendent Smith's first name was 'Steve'. The fact that both of these things were known by Pimpinan was probably more pertinent than any of the clues in the package. Emma would have to sleep on this before raising it as a concern.

Emma finished her Manhattan and had ordered a second when a man beckoned to the stool beside her.

"Do you mind if I sit here?" asked the man, and Emma thought he looked vaguely familiar. She guessed he was mid-forties, handsome in a plain sort of way, well groomed and physically well built, and smelt strongly of cologne.

"Be my guest", she replied, and although she was far too tired to contemplate being hit on by a stranger in a bar, she found that generally Englishmen were a lot less bothersome than the men at home, and she was pretty good at reading the signs. This man did not have the unmistakeable vibes of a man in search of a quick fling. "But I warn you, I'm having a bad day".

"Well, I'm certainly familiar with that feeling, and I know the perfect remedy". He turned to the barman.

"Would you pour me a large Glenfiddich, please, landlord, in a nice big Old Fashioned tumbler, just a splash of water, no ice", and the barman, who was wearing a name tag that said 'Ahman', grinned with pleasure.

Somehow I never tire of those quaint English manners, thought Emma, feeling the Manhattans starting to make her day seem a whole lot better.

Gregory appeared to be the perfect gentleman. During the ninety minutes they sat and talked in the gentle buzz of the Mostyn bar, he never once stared at Emma's chest as he spoke, or steered the conversation to lewd or suggestive topics, or touched her arm in an overly-familiar way, or made her feel uncomfortable in the slightest. He was a man for whom conversation flowed easily, and he instinctively rose from his seat when Emma excused herself momentarily to visit the rest room, which he called the W.C. and which Emma discovered from Googling 'WC' in the rest room, stood for 'water closet'. Emma explained that she was in London on an exchange arrangement between Police forces, a sort of working holiday if you will, and Gregory did not push her for any more information than she felt comfortable supplying. Gregory owned a chain of fitness clubs, and was expanding his portfolio of premises by franchising gymnasium facilities to four and five star hotels in the capital. He showed her a photograph of his children, a boy and a girl aged seven and eight on a white beach under palm trees which he said was taken in Bali, although Emma noticed he never mentioned his wife. Gregory's telephone rang just as Emma was feeling she had better go to her room and eat something before the Manhattans started getting the better of her, and he excused himself to go and take the call in the lobby. He had left his reading glasses in their case on the bar, and Emma signed her bill so she would be ready to say goodnight and leave on his return. Gregory never returned.

— o —

Emma eventually took a quick look around the lobby, and then told Ahman that her friend had left his glasses on the bar, and if he returned for them after she had gone to her room, Ahman should call her and she would bring them down for him. She felt slightly disappointed that

Gregory had disappeared so suddenly, which seemed out of character with the gentlemanly person he seemed to be, and hoped there was no emergency that had made him leave immediately and forget his glasses. Emma realised the reason for her slight disappointment was that she had been secretly hoping she might see Gregory again, and since they hadn't yet exchanged phone numbers, his sudden disappearance meant that the chance of that happening had diminished somewhat, but she decided to open the glasses case before leaving the bar to make sure he hadn't left anything important or valuable inside. She found only the expensive-looking Cerruti glasses she had seen him put on briefly, and was about to shut the case when a small, blue and white rectangular snippet of stiff linen paper, about a centimetre and a half long and with a rounded corner at one end caught her eye. Turning it over, she found it was a corner snipped from a playing card, and some unfathomable thing inside Emma told her that was a Bad Thing just as time immediately slowed to a crawl in inverse proportion to the crescendo of menace that erupted in Emma Gajewski's head as she saw it was cut from the *three of diamonds,* and she just managed to stop Ahman from picking up or touching Gregory's unfinished glass of whisky before she needed Ahman's help to sit down, legs and hands trembling through no fault of the Manhattans, to pull out her business phone and call for the help that would quickly make the Mostyn bar out-of-bounds for new patrons and keep the existing drinkers there for the rest of the night.

— o —

"She's really shaken up", said the Detective Inspector in cowboy boots, "In her words, she's shaken the hand that wielded the hammer. Bummer; I can see how that would freak you out".

"What do we know about the man?" asked Superintendent Smith. "I mean, I know it's early days, but is there anything to support her assertion that this was the actual video Pimpinan? Although if she says it *was* him, then I think that is a given". Superintendent Smith was out of uniform now, not being accustomed to being called back to duty until the small hours, and looked tired.

"Shorter hair, lighter colour. Three or four days beard growth, but neat. Better dress sense. According to her, education coming through more clearly in the voice. But it's unmistakably the same man, or his twin brother. Slight trace of an underbite; easily faked by thrusting the lower jaw forwards about half a centimetre and training yourself not to forget, it's amazing the difference it makes to a first impression. May have been wearing cotton pads inside the cheeks. But we have facial recognition software that my money says will prove it beyond any doubt before morning". The Detective Inspector in cowboy boots seemed to suddenly remember who he was talking to, and uncrossed his legs. "I've got all the hotel footage and we've made preliminary reviews. He stepped straight out of the front door and got into a taxi; didn't talk on his phone at all. We didn't get the license number from the hotel cameras so we're doing the full bit on tracing the taxi; the driver is most likely still on-shift now. If we can talk to him while it's still fresh in his mind, that will help us a lot. On top of the facial identification, we've got visible smudged prints on the glass and if we're lucky, we'll get DNA untouched by the alcohol. Glasses and case too; prints all over. Statements from everyone in the bar; a few of them need following up but it's probable that they shouldn't have been there with whoever they were with, and feel a sense of impending consequences".

"My God, this is frightening. How could this happen? She's a key member of a top-security operation. Supposedly secret within the entire Service except on a strict need-to-know basis – and the target wanders in and spends an hour and a half chatting to her, in full view of the whole world. Not only that, as if that wasn't enough, but she's here from the damned *FBI* because we begged for their help. They loaned her expertise to us, and ... well, they won't make *that* mistake again in a hurry. We look like total fuck-wits. We could have lost her".

The Detective Inspector in cowboy boots stepped outside the small conference room momentarily, then re-entered and told Superintendent Smith that Special Agent In Charge Gajewski and the rest of the Operation team were ready to leave for the Level 0 Secure House. The Operation would leave the Mostyn hotel, but a team from Serious and Organised Crime would continue to sterilise the scene without really knowing what they were looking for, which meant they would take ownership of the very public events that had taken place at the Mostyn the night before, and Operation Krakatoa's involvement would merge with a secretive, unrelated investigation until it no longer existed. The Level 0 Secure House, codenamed 'La Lune', was a short car ride away in Charles Street, Mayfair, and was identified only by a brass plaque which read 'La Lune Madagascan Vanilla and Produce Import

Company'. La Lune was accessed via an underground passage from a Level 1 Secure House two doors down the street, from which protected people would enter and leave La Lune via a lift to the hidden basement passageway without otherwise entering the Level 1 Secure House. Between La Lune and the Level 1 Secure House was a private house divided into a basement and ground floor office, and four luxury flats. No-one was ever to be seen coming or going from La Lune, except the staff who worked there and the people bringing catering supplies and other deliveries that frequently arrived. Both La Lune and the Level 1 Secure House, which was unmarked, were seven-bedroom fully serviced houses with staff quarters, protected round the clock by armed officers (of Malagasy appearance in the case of La Lune) who dressed in slightly unkempt business clothes. The Level 1 Secure House was accorded the highest level of security and secrecy within the Metropolitan Police, and La Lune did not officially exist; it was maintained by MI5 for situations when the presence of diplomats and foreign agents in the United Kingdom was a matter so secret that knowledge of the fact would compromise National security, and gravely endanger the life of the protected person. For now, Operation Krakatoa had borrowed it.

At three a.m., Commander Unwin was ashen-faced and needing a shave when he addressed the core leadership team in the first floor lounge of La Lune.

"I won't keep you from your beds long", he said. "Operation Krakatoa has been compromised and is now under lockdown. We will meet tomorrow at ten thirty in the strategic control centre to decide where we go from here. In the meantime and with immediate effect, all of us in this room will live at La Lune. Tomorrow we all need to assemble enough clothing and personal items to allow us to remain here indefinitely. Pack a suitcase as though you were going on holiday, but don't bother with sun cream. An unmarked van will collect your cases and bring them here inside removals boxes. Emma and Larry, I know you already have all of your effects here.

"We all know the protocols for entering and leaving, and travelling around. We only come in or go out during normal office hours, and never in groups of more than two. We only travel in Service cars masquerading as mini-cabs. Marked Police cars and uniformed officers will never come here. We spend all our off-duty time in this house. Everything we need will be provided or delivered by arrangement with the house manager. All telephone lines are secure and go through a central switchboard and all calls, in and out, will be recorded. Outgoing calls will be number-withheld and you will not be given the house telephone number. You may keep and use personal cell phones, but not Service cell phones. Do not make any personal calls on your cell phones; use the secure land lines. Your cell phones are only to be used to receive calls. The repeater cell on the roof is a spoofing cluster - I don't understand the technicalities, but if you use 'find my iPhone' to locate yourself, it will show you somewhere in Shropshire. Be very careful not to disclose to anyone at all your true whereabouts or any clue as to the location of your residence.

"From now on and until we can establish otherwise, assume Pimpinan knows every aspect of our investigation. We regarded the playing cards delivery to Superintendent Smith as a show of bravado and we're up to our necks in investigating the data that came with that. This is more than bravado. Our man knew where Special Agent In Charge Gajewski and Special Agent Donaldson were staying. He may even have known that Gajewski sometimes relaxes in the bar before dining. He may have watched her for a few days to familiarise himself with her movements and waited for the best opportunity to approach her. Our priority now is to determine how much else he knows and how he is getting his information. And for the moment, we need to be safe".

"You wonder how much he knows?" asked Special Agent In Charge Gajewski. "Let me tell you a few things he knows. He knows that Superintendent Smith is part of Operation Krakatoa. Nobody outside Operation Krakatoa knows that. He knows Superintendent Smith's first name is 'Steve'. Even most of Operation Krakatoa didn't know that until he informed us of the fact. He knows what I look like and where I was living. I don't believe you will see evidence of him ever entering the Mostyn hotel prior to last night. I hardly ever drink in the bar or eat in the hotel; I almost always eat outside. He knew I was not going outside to eat as usual last night. I told Larry I was tired and I wanted a couple of drinks in the hotel before bed. I told him that in the strategic control centre in front of ten other people. This fucker knows what is discussed in the strategic control centre and probably has access to photographic information from inside the Operation. He knows that if I succeed in getting inside his head, I am a huge threat to his liberty, so he decided to go head to head with me at my own game; by charming me with his eloquence. He knows he could have killed me instead if he felt like it, and he's fully aware I know that too. If he knows what is discussed in the strategic control room, nothing makes me comfortable he doesn't know what's being discussed right here, right now".

"Oh, come now", started Commander Unwin, clearly rattled, 'that is utterly absurd. Let's keep some professional perspective here. Are you seriously suggesting that someone working inside what is probably the most important undercover operation in the country today, is in league with a repeat killer we're all trying desperately to catch?"

"What I'm suggesting", suggested Special Agent In Charge Gajewski, as her cell phone began to ring, "is, um... wait... *holy shit*! Is this Jakarta? This is *Jakarta*..." and everyone fell over themselves to gather round and see the number on her screen.

"Oh shit..." wailed Larry, at the same time as:

"Don't let it ring off – you have to answer!" insisted the Detective Inspector in cowboy boots, who had recently become part of the core leadership team by accident, and

"PUT IT ON SPEAKERPHONE!" yelled Superintendent Smith, beckoning everyone to shut the noise up.

The room went silent and she answered on speakerphone. "This is Emma".

"I need you to listen very carefully, and above all don't hang up", said Special Commander Bryant. "You may be in great danger. My name is Special Comm...".

Commander Unwin turned purple and exploded. "Bryant, you fucking imbecile", he screamed, "get off this line. What did you... wait a second, what number did you call? Is this..."

"Commander Unwin?" stammered Special Commander Bryant, clearly confused, "Is that you? What are you doing on this telephone line? I was trying to see who the suspect was lining up next. We're making excellent progress here".

Commander Unwin gathered himself quickly; he didn't want to give away any more information than he needed, and said "No, that's fine, Special Commander, we'll take it from this point. I'll be in touch later this morning; it's just after three a.m. here now".

After Bryant rang off, Commander Unwin looked pensive. Eventually, he said "Well, it looks like Special Agent In Charge Gajewski's cell phone number is something else Pimpinan knows".

Emma Gajewski did not smile. "Commander", she began, and then thought better of it. When she resumed, she spoke very slowly and almost inaudibly. "Everyone. Who in the room can tell me, or could tell me after a reasonable amount of time to look it up, or ever tell me, what my personal cell phone number is? Not my official number. My personal number".

Nobody spoke. "You see, Commander, this is not my official business number. It is my own, personal, cell phone. I use it only for family and friends. Even Larry doesn't know it". She was noticeably shaking now. "Pimpinan got it, and had it programmed into the phone in Jakarta".

"Are you absolutely sure you didn't give it to this Gregory person? You didn't text him, or write it down for him?" The Detective Inspector in cowboy boots was looking agitated now, as Emma shook her head slowly, staring at the floor. "Do you have Bluetooth switched on? Did you access any websites using the hotel WiFi?"

"I may have; yes I did. He used an expression for the rest-room – I Googled it. But he wasn't with me. I was in the Ladies' Room at the time".

"Did you text anyone while you were there, or use the phone for anything else?"

"Yes I did. I input my number to the Delta Airlines web page. I booked a ticket. For my mother. I had to input my mobile number; my email address and credit card too. I hadn't spoken to him by that time, but he may have been nearby. It's a personal number, dammit, a pay-as-you-go, no name, no contract, no bills; it's not meant to be secure".

Superintendent Smith had been talking on the land-line phone unnoticed since Special Commander Bryant had hung up after blundering into their consciousness, and now he was saying "What? What? Are you sure? There's no mistake?" and eventually put the phone down and began wide-eyed to get everyone's attention.

"Mixed news from the lab. Bloody weird news, actually. They're working through the night. Prints on the glasses and case – Pimpinan. Prints on the bar; on the stool – Pimpinan. Prints all over the bloody place – Pimpinan. Prints on the whiskey glass – one partial, two complete, several unusable, smudged. Not Pimpinan. Initially unidentified. Also, they are old. They had to refresh them. They ran every available record and got a match. It is Morgan Freeman, and yes, they are sure".

"What? Morgan Freeman, as in the actor?" asked Agent Donaldson incredulously, holding up his hand to stop Commander Unwin from asking 'Who?'

"No", said Superintendent Smith, "not Morgan Freeman, as in the actor. Morgan Freeman, the actor. Morgan Freeman – *the* Morgan Freeman".

Chapter 9 - La Lune

Special Commander Bryant was not happy to be back in London. His plan to make a senior management decision by overriding the standing instruction and calling the Jakarta mobile phone number had backfired spectacularly, and he had been half way to London, having been summoned back without delay by an abrupt phone call at four a.m. the following morning, when he remembered that at that very moment he was supposed to be meeting the British Ambassador for afternoon tea at the Ambassador's residence. Such was Special Commander Bryant's level of fluster that he had stood up Her Majesty's Ambassador to the Republic of Indonesia and just got on a plane and left, and he knew it was an oversight without precedent, and it was not his fault. What made it worse was the fact that Special Commander Bryant had had his office make the arrangements with the British Ambassador's people without telling anyone, and when the British Ambassador telephoned the Commissioner personally to complain, nobody except Special Commander Bryant's Personal Assistant knew anything about it, which had embarrassed the Commissioner deeply. Commander Unwin had reluctantly decreed that Special Commander Bryant be included in the core leadership team holed up at La Lune, or 'La Loony Bin' as Special Commander Bryant had immediately nicknamed it, and being the last to arrive he had got the worst room, the only one without a television and with a view of a wall and the back fire escape. Now, Special Commander Bryant had the day off to get over his jet lag, and once the others had all departed for the strategic control room he set out to determine if any of the staff of La Lune were named 'Claire' or 'Clair' or 'Clare', so he could make a spontaneous and witty remark along the lines of 'Oh, Claire de La Lune!' later that evening.

Inspector Suparman's plan to have ExelComindo issue a bill for the phone and wait for the suspect to come to the office to pay in cash had not worked, either. After waiting for four days without result, ExelComindo had, upon Inspector Suparman's suggestion, tried to charge the account to the credit card of Russell Waite in order to see what happened, only to find the charge rejected, as Russell Waite had terminated the credit card some three months previously. Russell Waite had moved his local banking arrangements from HSCB to CIMB Niaga at the Jakarta Stock Exchange building due to his HSCB credit card being the object of a cloning scam, and everything checked out. Inspector Suparman and Special Commander Bryant had surmised that the phone had now been abandoned and left to die, which led Special Commander Bryant to try calling it while it was still active in a last-chance effort to gain some further clue, only to find himself being loudly sworn at by Commander Unwin. Having exhausted all available options, including establishing that Russell Waite could provide no insight as to who had stolen his phone, Special Commander Bryant thought that being so rudely ordered back to London was perfectly timed, since he was able to call Grand Commissioner Tarzan as soon as he was awake and apologise for not saying goodbye personally, say he had decided to leave for London on a matter of utmost urgency and thank him for all the invaluable help. Special Commander Bryant had travelled to the airport in a hotel limousine to avoid the inevitable uncomfortable questions from Grand Commissioner Tarzan, and it was only during his preliminary debrief with Commander Unwin and Superintendent Smith that Special Commander Bryant learned he had not been dealing with the head of the entire Indonesian Police Force, as he had assumed, but that there are some five levels within POLRI superior to that of Grand Commissioner, and there are other Grand Commissioners all over the place. As he recalled the vague feelings of doubt he had had in Grand Commissioner Tarzan's shabby smoke-filled office, Special Commander Bryant reflected that while his assignment to Jakarta had not produced the case-cracking results and series of diplomatic coups he had hoped for, it could have been much worse.

— o —

Meanwhile, in the strategic control room, on the third day since the panic-inducing contact between Pimpinan and Special Agent In Charge Gajewski at the Mostyn hotel, feelings of vulnerability and paranoia had all but completely dissipated. Security arrangements had been put in place for the Operation which hadn't been deemed necessary before. For example, Gajewski's habit at the end of the day had been to simply step out of the front door and hail a taxi to the hotel. That did not explain how anyone could know she was assigned to Operation Krakatoa, but it would have been easy to watch and follow her. Now everyone travelled by mini-cabs that were owned and operated by the Metropolitan Police and did not carry fare-paying passengers. As they disassembled and reassembled the facts, it began to be apparent that apart from the identities of the core leadership team assigned to the Operation, most of what Pimpinan obviously knew about them could be explained without suspicion pointing to inside help. Superintendent Smith did not ever use his first name on duty and many of his colleagues were even unaware of it, but his full name had been used a couple of times in the past in quotes for the London Evening Standard, and surprisingly there was only one Smith at the rank of Superintendent based at Paddington Green. All you needed was Google and a bit of intuition.

But this was not the way the FBI did things, and Emma Gajewski's first inclination as she awaited evacuation from the Mostyn had been to get on a plane and get the hell out of there – she had been left vulnerable and had ended up in a very unsafe situation as a result. She was used to a ring of steel being around her while she worked, with secret identities and guns and bullet-proof cars and tracking devices and back-up agents tailing her every move. In London, she and Agent Donaldson hadn't even been able to get clearance to carry their side-arms. In London, you were expected to act like a normal member of the public and blend in, and it had nearly ended in catastrophe. Pimpinan had got next to her and effectively said 'You know that thing you're doing now? Don't do that, it doesn't work'. Similarly, Pimpinan had programmed her personal cell phone number into the Jakarta phone to reinforce the point, but she was confident after the initial scare that Pimpinan had no intention of targeting her for the white room – he only targets men, criminals, predators. She fit no part of his psychological profile, and she was comfortable betting her life on it. A technician had demonstrated how her phone profile and all screen actions could be duplicated and recorded by a pocket-sized device costing 'a couple of hundred quid' from fifty feet away - shocking but simple.

"The Americans have effectively ruled out asking any questions of Mr Freeman", said the Detective Inspector in cowboy boots. "Their position is that Mr Freeman is without doubt uninvolved in the case and is unaware of it, and would be unable to provide any information that might help us. What they did tell us is that Mr Freeman has visited London on several occasions in the last few years, dating back to February the fourth two thousand and ten, when he attended the London premiere of his film 'Invictus'. He occasionally stays in secure apartments used by the entertainment agencies for A-list celebrities, but sometimes he stays in top hotels. They wouldn't tell me where, but said of course he would never stay somewhere like the Mostyn. Anyhow, they don't want to risk the American tabloids getting wind of a story that Morgan Freeman is being interviewed in connection with a series of murders in London. They are scared that Mr Freeman's management's lawyers would crucify them for any ugly rumours and scandal that would result, since they would be without foundation. I was only asking for a ten minute phone call, but that's not going to happen. They also said that it's not uncommon for big name stars to have their cups and glasses and cutlery and what-not kept by souvenir hunters after they have used them, and there would be no possibility of him knowing or remembering".

"I happen to agree with them", said Special Agent In Charge Gajewski, "and I don't believe we would get a thing from it. Morgan Freeman is one of my favourite actors, and believe me, I would have noticed if he had sat next to me drinking whiskey. The suspect was specific about the glass he wanted – he asked for a large Old Fashioned tumbler. He switched the glass when I was out of the room, simple as that. It's a common glass used by good hotels and bars everywhere, and the Mostyn's own glasses are indistinguishable from it at first glance. He knew we would look for his prints, having left them all over everything else, and he added shock value by giving us prints from a person known the world over as an actor at the pinnacle of his career. Not an easy thing to do. Apart from once again showing us how clever he is, this was a distraction, nothing more. We shouldn't waste time on it, and we shouldn't lose focus because of things like the playing cards delivery. We need to involve resources outside the core Operation to investigate the peripheral issues. It would be great if we could get Superintendent Smith to head up a kind of secondary investigation, to keep us free".

"For now, let's leave it at that", Superintendent Smith interjected. "Let's recap. Let's recap and update ourselves on who we are looking for".

"Okay, well, this man is a vigilante", Gajewski counselled, "and more than ever I'm convinced he's acting alone, and has access at some level to Police intelligence. His motivation is not that of any ordinary serial killer. He seeks to deactivate certain kinds of organised crime. He publicises himself to potential targets, and there is evidence that in some cases, it works without need for further action. He makes available to his selected target, in graphic detail, images of what he threatens to do to that target if he continues to do what offends him. If the target stops, it satisfies him. Thus, he does not kill for the pleasure of it; he has no need of killing, but he has no qualms about killing if the circumstances dictate. Now, what kind of person did I just describe? I'll repeat it – 'he does not kill for the pleasure of it; he has no need of killing, but he has no qualms about killing if the circumstances dictate'".

"A soldier?" suggested the Detective Inspector in cowboy boots.

"Bingo! A soldier, or some kind of Special Forces or special operations-trained Police officer would seem to fit. Now, let's look at what he does. He snatches people. We don't know where from or how, but it is safe to assume he does it relatively undetected. Accomplices of the people snatched are unlikely to come to the Police to report the fact, but the general public either didn't see anything, or kept quiet about it if they did. So he is skilled at surveillance and aware of security measures. They say you can follow a person from any house or office in Greater London to any other house or office in Greater London by watching CCTV, regardless of whether they walk or drive or take the bus or take the Underground, if you can get the footage from all of the various sources. London is awash with cameras. He is skilled at working out who is observing him and where he can effect a snatch without triggering a response. He takes victims without making a fuss. This suggests to me he would not be just a common soldier – he is probably specially trained in defeating security arrangements, silent warfare, infiltration, martial arts, that kind of thing. Some kind of special operations fits the bill. This is simple deduction.

"Let's now look at vigilantism in general. A vigilante is someone who hits back at someone or something that severely pisses him off when the law fails to protect him, and nine hundred ninety-nine times out of a thousand it's petty and fairly temporary. The guy who gets fed up with dogs crapping in his garden and leaves out poisoned meat, or goes out and beats up a couple of the kids who bully his own child or who hang around the estate doing drugs. Remember the 'Guardian Angels' who used to ride the subway in their self-styled uniforms? Vigilantes, supposedly protecting the public from muggers and thieves and robbers on the train. You never hear about them now. The law takes a dim view of vigilantism and clamps down hard on it, which is why it is unwise to be an active vigilante. The one time out of a thousand when it's not petty, when it may not be so temporary, is the kind of 'Death Wish' movie scenario. The guy who goes out to attract muggers at night so he can kill or hurt them, that kind of thing. In real life it almost never happens. Most people are not prepared for confronting violent criminals on their own territory, and if they try, sooner or later they end up the dead ones. But a thousand times out of a thousand, the vigilante has been touched by whatever it is that he sets out to combat, and it's always personal. If we assume that our man is a vigilante, and he's the one in a million who has the training, the drive and the skill to carry it off, that means he has a history. He has been personally touched by the crimes he wants to destroy. It's personal between him and the crime, but when it comes to his treatment of his victim, it's all in a day's work. The victim is an object, a symbol, nothing more. He can detach himself from the humanity of the victim, just as a soldier does when following orders to kill.

"Finally, let's look at the man himself. I've met him and chatted with him. He is charming, well mannered, educated; in fact he oozes good breeding. He drinks twelve year old, single malt Scotch whiskey, with a little water and no ice. That is a traditional, purist British way of taking whiskey; Americans generally prefer ice or drink it straight up or, heaven forbid, mix it with sweet, flavoured soda mixers. He displayed no element of snobbishness or disdain concerning my own choice of drink, which featured American whiskey mixed with other flavours and ice. This may show lack of interest in pressing his own views on others; something surprisingly rare among repeat killers. He is clearly highly intelligent. The rage and anger inside him does not show through in any way. He is sure of himself. He does not seek to be the centre of attention, but he is not afraid of attention being thrust upon him. He wears a little too much cologne, which for someone as well bred as he seems might indicate a little too much self confidence".

Noticing the slightly sceptical looks on the other faces in the room, Special Agent In Charge Gajewski grinned and continued "As a psychologist, I am never off duty, and I find myself studying everyone I meet. He was one of the few people I've met for whom nothing would surprise me. I am almost certain he speaks multiple languages; he reacted to something the bar keeper said in Arabic as though he understood. It was a subtle, momentary change of facial expression to one of comprehension - I'm sure it was a 'tell', in poker parlance, and it was a slip. He showed me a picture of his children – I believe they really *were* his children, and I noticed his wife was not in the photograph. He pointedly did not mention a wife when he talked about his family. That may be significant.

"The children were pictured in Bali, which is in Indonesia. I'm kicking myself for not having my suspicions aroused by this coincidence. It may, too, be significant. I strongly suspect from all the evidence as a whole, he knows Indonesia well and probably speaks Indonesian. He was built like a soldier or a martial arts expert; not overly muscled like a body builder, but lean, fit and wiry, which he covered with a story about a fitness club business. This was bogus.

"So here we have my assessment of who we should be looking for: a military man; an officer, maybe currently serving but probably recently decommissioned. Special Forces trained, perhaps a sniper; has probably killed multiple times in the line of duty, expert in avoiding security systems, silent warfare, infiltration, martial arts and the like. My feeling is he has real-time access to intelligence on Police investigations, criminal activity, that sort of thing – which is not the sort of thing a Special Forces operative has. That is the puzzling thing. He is cunning, confident, resourceful, spent time in Indonesia, probably speaks Indonesian and possibly Arabic, married with kids, may have lost his wife, has been profoundly affected by organised crime involving the drugs and protection businesses. One possibility from this is that his wife may not be in his life any more because of the crimes he now targets, and as a result he targets those crimes because they took his wife".

"You mean, killed?" asked Detective Sergeant Robbins, who was unaware he was the only person in the room who didn't currently live at La Lune.

"It is something which we should bear in mind as a possibility and a pretty good motive. One of the keys to understanding this man's psychological make-up is how and why he selects his targets. Your teams have put a lot of effort into trying to trace his actions in taking the victims – looking for dates and times, places, eye witnesses, video footage of the snatch, how he transports the living victims to either the white room or the public place of death, where the white room is, where and how he disposes of the bodies. Results have been very disappointing. You've been looking for victims' known movements, whether they knew each other, what their criminal activities entailed and who they affected. What I've been doing in the meantime is looking for common denominators in all the victims we know about, from the psychological viewpoint of the killer; basically we have to find out what it is about each victim that drove him to wipe him from the face of the earth, what it is that inspires his hatred that the victims each possessed. I propose that since we have time on our hands in the evenings, we make a start together on dissecting the victims tonight".

"No pun intended?" grinned Detective Sergeant Robbins, and Superintendent Smith glowered at him. "But surely", Robbins continued, "every soldier or Policeman would have their fingerprints on record? Even special operations were new recruits once, SAS officers had to be greenhorns at one time. Do they pull all the records of their operatives when they pass the tests? I mean, if I committed a crime and left fingerprints, you'd identify me in a minute, you have access to identification of everyone on the entire Force".

The Detective Inspector in cowboy boots leaned back in his chair and crossed his legs, showing off half a yard of white and grey snakeskin beneath his Armani trousers. "If he's ex-SAS or SBS, it will be next to impossible to get information on people matching this profile", he said. "These people don't talk to us. At all. You would need a court order, and you won't get it. Anonymity is guaranteed for the rest of their lives, unless they choose to give it up. I suggest, with Superintendent Smiths agreement, I take another tack and take a chance on Indonesia itself. If such people are or were stationed there, it's worth a shot, and the Embassy would probably know about it. I have a friend who was in Thailand until last year, training the Police elite divisions there in security, VIP protection and counter-espionage, anti-people smuggling, that sort of thing. Part of the international friendship and trade arrangements; he is Army and he did it based from the Embassy".

"That is a very good suggestion", chimed in Commander Unwin, "and let's hope our recent faux pas hasn't queered our pitch too much with the British Ambassador. Let me talk to some people. Someone may need to go there and meet with the security people in person".

"I wouldn't give that top priority if I were you, unless you can easily spare the resources", counselled Gajewski, "because, don't forget, Pimpinan has been leading our direction all along, playing us like puppets, and the Indonesian connection may be just another distraction. The mobile phone lends a lot of credence to the theory of a heavy Indonesian connection, but it is possible all this was set up by someone who knows Jakarta well, but has had no military or diplomatic presence there. If that's the case, it could just as easily have been Barcelona, or Timbuktu. Let's not overestimate the importance of it, other than as something that has to be followed up and eliminated".

"Except, it is vital to this Pimpinan person that the phone company cannot provide a list of incoming calls, unless the phone is located outside Jakarta". Superintendent Smith was looking tired now, as though speaking was an effort. "It takes more than a casual acquaintance with a place to know such a thing in any given city, and it is not something that could be expected or anticipated with any degree of certainty, or found out from the internet. Furthermore, our investigations have included focussing on banking arrangements in Indonesia. It is one of the easiest places in the world to obtain a bank account in a name differing materially from the account holder's real name. People's names in Indonesia are not accorded the importance they are in the West. Misspellings are tolerated, and people even spell their own names in multiple ways. Many people have no family name at all. People with long names have their account names truncated by the banks, due to screen field limitations, and records or cross-references to the full names are patchy. Partly for those reasons, Indonesian banks rely more on identity card numbers than they do on names, to provide positive identification. For foreigners, who have no Indonesian identity cards and may have multiple passports or replace their passports periodically, this leaves a glaring gap in security. Even if a foreigner opens an account in his real name, it is entirely possible that no connection is possible to his other banking arrangements outside the country. Thus, you can find yourself tracing worldwide accounts in the name of Joe Bloggs, date of birth X, and anything in Indonesia may not be picked up. Joe Bloggs can be gadding about all over the world, charging flights to an Indonesian credit card, and your enquiries with MasterCard or Visa could miss the connection".

The Detective Inspector in cowboy boots, who had already started checking out the Jakarta nightlife on his iPhone and was fired up by what he saw, could now see a potential expenses-paid trip to the party capital of Asia on the cards, and didn't want the opportunity to slip through his fingers.

"In my view this makes it essential one of us gets ourselves over there and opens up the issues. We need to investigate the security forces' presence there, or rule it out. We also need to put more effort into finding out how money gets into the country, and where it goes from the correspondent bank or banks. If Pimpinan runs, say, a credit card with an Indonesian bank, he must be moving funds there from somewhere else, almost certainly England, or making money from a source within. Plus, whoever is programming numbers into his phone for him must require to be paid for it somehow".

Commander Unwin liked what he heard.

— o —

Special Commander Bryant was listening to the accounts of the past week as the core leadership team finished their dinner at La Lune, and had taken an instant dislike to the Detective Inspector in cowboy boots with his gung-ho, braggadocio attitude and his annoying habit of making astute observations and well-judged suggestions about half a second before Special Commander Bryant thought of them. Special Commander Bryant was wary of ambitious upstarts who gave opinions above their station and tried to ingratiate themselves into conversations with their superiors, and he recognised the need to interject sagacious and authoritative comments and nods of approval from time to time to keep his finger on the managerial pulse. Special Commander Bryant mentally elevated his 'smart comment opportunity awareness' level from yellow to orange.

"I tend to agree with Agent Gajewski", said the Detective Inspector in cowboy boots, "that speaking to Mr Freeman would not bring anything of value to the investigation. Pushing the issue would just rub the Americans up the wrong way, and we need to keep in their favour. Criticising their decision would not help, and circumventing them would be counter-productive. I understand their fears about creating unfounded adverse publicity for Mr Freeman".

"It is a common misconception", jumped in Special Commander Bryant, "that America does not respond well to criticism. On the contrary; for instance, America was criticised for being late for the two great World Wars, and subsequently has been first to show up ever since, at the merest hint of a war in the offing".

There was an awkward silence during which Special Agent In Charge Gajewski was, for once, at a loss for words, until Superintendent Smith said "Well, be that as it may, I think we're all agreed that we'll let the Morgan Freeman avenue drop. Now, I have an important update on the playing cards. We have tried to get something from the order of the cards, among all the other things, and first of all we focused on the ten cards between the two three-of-diamonds. We thought at first this was just coincidence, but if you disregard the suits of the ten cards and note them in order, by the first letter of the card value – that is to say, 'n' for nine, 't' for ten, 'j' for jack and so on – it spells a name. J-a-n-e-f-a-s-k-e-n. Jane Fasken. It is an uncommon surname in this country, but there are three people named Jane Fasken on the record in Greater London. One of them is a recently graduated student of English Literature, and she runs a small bicycle courier service with four or five other recently graduated students who are looking for full time employment. She operates by distributing flyers around the offices in the square mile mainly, and picking up packages when she gets a call, payment on collection".

"Holy shit!" exclaimed the Detective Inspector in cowboy boots, "This is a huge deal! Why didn't you... I mean, have you spoken to her?"

"Naturally, we have. She is indeed the courier who delivered the package, and she remembers it well. She was called to pick up the package from Starbucks at Liverpool Street Station, by a man named Smith who paid in cash and did not require a signature for receipt. That makes the service a bit cheaper, since she does not need to archive or provide evidence of the delivery, and is not unusual. She identified a still taken from the Mostyn video footage as the man who met her in Starbucks. Telephone records show the call was placed from a payphone on the station concourse, and she can recall the noise made it difficult to hear. She picked up the package within an hour of the call. We are trying to obtain video of the man on the station concourse, but the main security system deletes recordings automatically after twenty four hours. We are looking at many private systems at the shops and eateries around and above the concourse. We hope to see him with the package; if we get lucky we will see him pass it to Jane Fasken".

"So let me get this straight", cut in the Detective Inspector in cowboy boots, "we're pulling out all the stops to get film of the suspect sending a package to Superintendent Smith, by courier, which package comprises solely coded information that identifies the sender and tells us the name of the courier who delivered the package? It doesn't make sense; it's like me sending you an email via Yahoo saying only that I'm using Yahoo to send you an email".

"It makes perfect sense", countered Special Agent In Charge Gajewski, "if you remember that he's probably very aware of security and surveillance systems and highly adept at avoiding them. There are very few places more open to the public and under the gaze of security cameras than a train station. Liverpool Street Station is no exception, and he knows that. He picked the location for that reason. He was putting on a show; he wanted to be seen".

"That is my thought, too", said Special Commander Bryant, hoping that it would be Commander Unwin's thought also.

"I still don't get it. Why would he bother? He is just taking an unnecessary risk".

"How many hundreds or thousands of man-hours have we spent on this one event? How much lab time has been expended in analysing the package, how many people have we tied up searching records for fingerprints, trying to find a lead on the supply of the padded bag or job-lots of packs of playing cards, trying to trace the courier leaving the Police station through all of the various video sources, figuring out what the double three-of-diamonds means, what the order of the cards means, if it means anything at all? Then when we finally did understand this carefully planned clue, there was interviewing the courier, accessing her phone records, gaining access to all the video from around the station. How much time have we spent sitting around talking about it, just as we are doing now?" asked Special Agent In Charge Gajewski. "And that is before you think about the cosy little chat he and I had at the Mostyn, and the huge amount of work that led to. Look at us. We've been trying to speak to A-list Hollywood celebrities, for heaven's sakes. We've all fled our homes and hotels and are hiding in a safe house. It is pathetic. He made me tremble and shed tears, and I don't tremble or shed tears".

"So you think he took a big risk, just to try to scare us and swamp us with things to follow up on? Does he imagine that there is a limit to our resources; that we won't be able to catch him because we don't have enough time, or because we're scared?" The Detective Inspector in cowboy boots puffed out his chest and leaned back in his chair, trying without success to look like Dirty Harry. "Do we look scared?"

"Don't misunderstand me; I'm not saying we should have done anything differently, or ignored any aspect of the evidence we've been presented with. Everything, however small, needs to be analysed and investigated until it can be discounted. The fact that he ensured we would spend so much time deciphering his playing-cards stunt, and that we would then come up with a major breakthrough that will probably lead to absolutely nothing is his way of reinforcing the point that nothing can be overlooked, and that everything we find will likely be disappointing until he makes a mistake. There actually *is* a limit to your resources; however that's not the point. The point is, there was in reality very little risk in the courier playing cards thing, which is why it makes sense. Another point is that while we have been figuring out what it's all about, we may have overlooked other, far more significant and material factors that would have taken us closer to catching him, which is why it makes sense. From a psychological perspective, between the flaunting himself on the station concourse – sending us a courier delivery, no less

– and shaking my hand and buying me a drink in my hotel and leaving us with film of the two of us laughing and chatting and admiring his kids, he's portraying himself as tantalisingly close; he's just an inch away, he's instilling a feeling in us that we are on the verge of an arrest. That is an illusion. He is not an inch away, and we are no nearer to a breakthrough than we ever were. You see, there is nothing more frustrating, when you desperately want something, than knowing that person or thing is right next to you, in full view. It makes us far more despondent when we fail to get it, than if it had never been seen, nearby, looking like a possibility. It stems from childhood; if you take away a favourite toy from a child and hide it, the child will pretty soon forget about the toy. But if you take it away and put it on a shelf in view but out of reach, the child will go crazy until you give it back, or hide it, and will forget about all the other far more attractive toys. The proximity diverts our attention, impairs our judgement, affects our morale and eventually makes us feel all our efforts are increasingly futile. *That* is why it makes sense, and that is why if I were in his position, if I were brave enough, I would do exactly the same thing".

"Chess mate!" laughed Special Commander Bryant, slapping his thigh in delight. "If there's one thing I've learned in my position, it's never to cross swords with a psychiatrist".

"I am not a psychiatrist, I'm a *psychologist*", corrected Special Agent In Charge Gajewski, "but if I were thinking of becoming a psychiatrist, you would definitely be the inspiration for my doctoral thesis. But one thing puzzles me about Jane Fasken. Did Pimpinan look for a courier whose name could be spelled with playing cards, or did he pick Jane

Fasken as his courier and just happen to notice all the letters of her name correspond with playing cards? It wouldn't have been possible if the courier's name had been Melanie, for example, or Alice. It's something we need to think a bit more about".

"Plus, we shouldn't forget the other matter of the date", said Superintendent Smith. "We have been trying to establish a connection or a meaning related to it, so far without luck. Police records, newspaper archives, the internet: all are awash with information about events that happened on every date since time immemorial, and nothing correlates so far". Remembering Special Commander Bryant was unaware of the tiny date written on the inside of the playing card carton, he said "The card packet had a date written in minute letters on the inside surface. '22 December 1962'".

Special Commander Bryant blanched. "That is my date of birth", he said, wide-eyed.

* * *

Superintendent Smith was heading up a brain-storming session with the core team.

"I want to talk a bit about Paul Adrian Kingston. You may recall the weapon of choice used on him was the side-cutting snippers. He died a terrible death, we think from a heart attack, after some eleven hours of mutilation had rendered him unrecognisable. I want to pay special attention to him at this stage, as there are a number of unique and puzzling angles about his case which might help us get a lot closer to Pimpinan once we understand them. Like all the other video victims, his body has not been found. Unlike the others, Kingston was brought to our notice via an anonymous tip-off at the same time as Pimpinan took an interest in him, probably for the same reasons, and we'll discuss the implications of that remarkable coincidence in a moment.

"Now, this is a brief summary of what we have on Kingston's background. Two convictions, both minor, eight and ten years ago, for possession of high-grade cannabis resin. Both times it was a toss-up between simple possession and possession with intent to supply, but both times he was let off on the lesser charge. Serious and Organised Crime suspected he was indeed a supplier, and for that reason kept him on their *persons of interest* list in case his name came up anywhere. It did regularly; he was hovering on the sidelines of several drug-related stabbings and two major cocaine busts, but he was never fingered or named as a player, and they couldn't find anything to warrant bringing an investigation, at least not until the recent tip-off.

"He came from a relatively well-to-do family – father an accountant, mother a nurse. Lived in Fulham until about four years ago, since when he's been living in a village in Essex called Barmley. Don't worry if you've never heard of it; nor had I, and it's an unremarkable place. He lived alone in a large house on the edge of the village green, which in hindsight is pretty unusual for a life-long city boy. Locals say he kept himself to himself, and no-one really knew him. He wasn't unfriendly, but made it clear that he wasn't interested in getting to know people. Appeared to have money; he lived in a nice house, drove a Discovery and wore a Rolex, that sort of thing. His neighbours reported he commuted by train to London two or three days a week, dressed in smart business clothes, and they assumed he was some kind of important figure in the City. He held a first class season ticket from Colchester. On days he stayed at home, he wasn't seen at all, but the car would be there all day.

"Then SOC received information that an anonymous phone call had come in on the hotline, informing that Kingston was the ultimate source of crystal methamphetamine supplied to a firm which distributes it around Central London, with particularly focus on some of the gay bars and clubs. They were told he brings it into London by train several times a week and makes delivery in the afternoons in public locations including Covent Garden, Oxford Street and Piccadilly Circus, but was thought to have no further connection with the distribution and sale of the product. This was of great interest to them because at the time, an operation was under way to shut just such a crystal meth syndicate down and find the source of the supply, and this operation had all its ducks in a row ready for a sweep-up except for one thing – it had hit a brick wall when it came to finding the link between the heads of the distribution syndicate and the manufacturer or supplier. It was as though the stuff was just appearing in their possession, and they were beginning to think the syndicate had access to a huge stock of product which they were unloading in relatively small amounts, over time, so as not to draw too much attention to their activities. So SOC set up a surveillance team and only three days later, they had Kingston making a switch in Starbucks Piccadilly Circus with a known distribution leader from this very syndicate. Unfortunately they lost him right afterwards after he got into a cab and disappeared into the traffic. He didn't arrive home that night, or the day afterwards, and his car was still parked at Colchester railway station on the third day. By then they had a warrant to search his house, and to keep a long story short, they went in to an empty house and found the smoking gun. The upstairs of the house was a fully self-contained, one-man meth factory. It was a state-of-the-art set-up, with complicated vapour extraction and a deep-well waste neutralisation and disposal system, and it is likely he could produce upwards of four kilos of methamphetamine from pseudoephedrine every month. Pure stuff, nicknamed Millie in club-speak, goes for around fifty quid a gram to end users, so that gives you an idea of the scale of it. This was not a hobbyist or a basement user refining Night Nurse for his own consumption, or to make a few quid selling dodgy product. This was the real deal. Once cut, this would produce possibly twelve or fifteen kilos of retail product a month. There was nothing to suggest he cut it in the lab, or 'stepped on' it in dealer parlance, meaning he is likely to have sold the pure stuff to his contacts and they cut and distributed it.

"What SOC also found, which was not discovered for a further week, was a sealed package containing a DVD of the murder of Richard Leighton on Kingston's dining table. Leighton, as you recall, was another of our video victims; the hammer victim. Now then, this was interesting because SOC had already got a copy of this very same DVD, which had been received by Essex Constabulary in Colchester and had made its way to the Met, and eventually to Operation Krakatoa. And here we have another unique feature of Kingston: unlike the others, he had been sent a copy of the disc, on a full size DVD. The original recording on a mini-disk was the one sent to Essex. All the others were sent originals, mini-disks recorded direct from the camera. Not only that, but the packaging had clearly been opened and resealed, and we think it was intercepted somewhere en-route to Kingston, copied and sent on. SOC decided to work backwards from Kingston's dining table, to the postman who delivered it, to the local sorting office, to the transport from the origin's sorting office, and so on. See at what point we lose the track, and if anything on the way throws up anything. We got a red flag immediately, from the postmaster of the Barmley sorting office, one Ravinder Singh. Mr Singh has nothing to tell us, and cannot elucidate us on the package or it's movements, but his reaction when we revealed the subject of our enquiries was very peculiar. He flushed like a beetroot, looked very spooked, and had to sit down, complaining of feeling dizzy. He rapidly maintained his composure when it became apparent we were not there to accuse him of anything, and we lost the momentum, but it was clear to those present he had something he was hiding. We put it to him that he had opened the package and, having viewed the disk and seeing what was on it, showed (and I quote) "admirable civic responsibility" by sending it to the Police, albeit anonymously, and sending a copy on to Kingston. We assured him we were not interested in pursuing any action in respect of illicit opening of Her Majesty's mail or such like, but he will have none of it, and repeatedly questions why we think he would ever want to open people's mail. A background check found no history of mail theft or accusations of mail tampering or suspicions of the same associated with Barmley. The only odd thing is that Barmley has always had, and continues to have, a very high instance of complaints against utilities and credit card companies, who seem to keep losing payments and erroneously crediting payments coming from Barmley. Whatever connection there is, and whether or not Singh saw the video or redirected it, we don't think there is anything immediate our continued interest in Singh will find to benefit us, and we've let the matter drop for now.

"Now, the big questions - why did Pimpinan target Kingston; did he get his intelligence from the same source as us; did he know we were also just about to pounce on him, and if so, does he appear to have access to the Operation's database?"

Commander Unwin looked stunned. "Are you suggesting that this man might be a Police officer?" he gasped. "Close to one of the team? One of us, even?"

"I'm suggesting that from everything we've learned in the last twenty four hours, it appears he knows many of the things we know. He knows about the team and its personal details. He knows about who the Met is targeting and why. He knows where to find people we're after. He knows where to find us. I am not suggesting he is an office of the Met or has direct links to this operation, but he seems to have inside information. It's possible it is either being provided to him from someone with privileged access, or he has accomplices who are very skilled computer hackers, or he is monitoring us to gather the information he then acts upon, or any combination of those".

"Or", said the Detective Inspector in cowboy boots, "maybe it's the other way round. Maybe he's the one passing information to us. Maybe he made the anonymous call about Kingston, maybe he sent the Leighton video to us and only sent a copy to Kingston. Maybe he wanted to ensure we were spectators, alerting us to Kingston and ensuring we get there just too late. It's what he seems to do; get there just before us, all the time. Like Special Agent in Charge Gajewski says, keep us feeling impotent, if you'll pardon the expression".

Chapter 10 - The London Evening Standard

Commander Unwin didn't know which was worse – the fact that Operation Krakatoa had crashed into the British public's awareness with the highly critical, exclusive front page article in the London Evening Standard on the day after they had all gone home from La Lune, or the fact that the Commissioner had resolutely insisted that Special Commander Bryant be present to answer questions at the hastily-arranged press conference, having been named by the Standard as the officer in charge of the Operation who had promptly gone shopping in Singapore as soon as the first lead was found. The press conference was being called in an undisguised attempt at damage limitation, with a view to giving the impression that the Met's handling of the case was not at all like the bumbling, Keystone Cops version of events described in the Standard, and to counter inferences made that the incidence of violent crimes in the Capital had actually fallen as a direct result of the violent crimes the Met was now half-heartedly investigating. It would be the first time that the television press had access to any of the investigating team or, indeed, access to any of the crime information apart from the reports in the London Evening Standard, and Commander Unwin thought that bringing Special Commander Bryant to the event would be like bringing a lighted match to look for a gas leak.

What Commander Unwin desperately needed was a strategy, and once he had a strategy he needed to establish tactics, and he had around fifteen hours between the story breaking in the London Evening Standard and the start of the press conference. The Commissioner had been very clear that the objective of the press conference was to kill any erroneous information contained in the Standard's report, clarify the scope and nature of Operation Krakatoa in general terms, and above all, assure the public that their security was in safe, capable hands, while not disclosing any of the critical details of the investigation. Commander Unwin regarded this as a lose/lose situation, a bit like being asked to play high-stakes poker wearing boxing gloves, not least because Bryant would be there ready to go off unexpectedly like the loose cannon he was.

EXCLUSIVE – LONDON'S CRIMINALS UNDER SIEGE IN TURF WAR

Parts of the Capital's drug and organised crime figures are expected to drop for the first three months of the year as a result of a series of murders by a secretive, previously unknown gang, which ruthlessly preys on key underworld figures. The well-organised but so far unnamed gang is well known to the criminal fraternity, and is thought to be coordinated from outside the UK. Several underworld drug suppliers and heads of organised crime have been killed by the gang in recent months, and video recordings of the killings have been distributed to many others in an apparently successful effort to discourage their activities. Police fear the motive for the murders may be an attempt by the gang to move in on lucrative drug deals and organised crime, leading to a turf war on London's streets. However, in a clear sign of the impact the killings have had, many street drug traders in and around Hackney were noticeable by their absence yesterday, and customers were left trawling the area looking for supplies. One resident, who did not wish to be identified, said "The pushers have been running out quickly since about a month ago, and now they don't come. They don't seem to be getting the goods to sell. To be honest, it's a lot better now, we feel safer on the streets".

A spokesman for Scotland Yard denied the existence of the gang. However, sources confirmed that Operation Krakatoa, named after a mountain that exploded in the Sunda Strait in 1883, has been set up to investigate the killings, after two previously unconnected gangland-style murders were linked to the gang, uncovering many more abductions and murders which have never been made public. Since its inception, thought to be up to a year ago, Operation Krakatoa has made little progress in finding the gang responsible, and Police have taken the unusual step of appealing to known criminals that have been contacted by the gang to come forward with evidence for their own safety.

The commanding officer of Operation Krakatoa has been revealed as Special Commander Bryant, who is believed to specialise in strategic operational planning and whose first move was to bring in the help of the FBI, raising eyebrows in some quarters over the apparent lack of capable resources within the Metropolitan Police. Special Commander Bryant personally travelled to Asia as part of the investigation, and publicly accessible records of his expenses filed reveal that his first port of call was Singapore, where he spent two days shopping after his passport, uniform and a consignment of olive oil were stolen. Bryant also spent "more than a week" at one of the top luxury hotels in

Jakarta, reportedly trying to locate a mobile telephone without success. Special Commander Bryant was earlier unavailable for comment.

In a bizarre twist, it emerged that other senior officers of Operation Krakatoa have personally met one of the key ringleaders of the gang on at least one occasion, and may have been seeking the assistance of a well known Hollywood actor, named by a source as 'Johnny Depp or possibly Jack Nicholson', concerning key aspects of the enquiry.

An unnamed spokesperson from the Mayor's office said "If the enthusiasm of the Police to find those responsible for committing murder in London is diminished by any side effect reduction in crime where the Police themselves have failed, this will not be tolerated. Crime reduction attributable to committing of other crimes is not justice, nor attributable to Police performance".

Commander Unwin held a briefing meeting in his office with Special Commander Bryant, Superintendent Smith and Special Agent In Charge Gajewski, who was due to return to California in two days' time. The Detective Inspector in cowboy boots and three other lead detectives would be briefed later, and were to be present at the press conference but not participate in the presentation or the questions and answers session.

"The first task is to quell the notion that Special Commander Bryant is in charge of the Operation", said Commander Unwin, "and to this end I will begin by formally introducing us and describing our roles. This will establish from the outset that the information in the Evening Standard's report is not reliable.

"Now, note that none of the details reported are attributed to named sources. We will not question whether the Standard has actually interviewed any of these unnamed sources or ask to know who they are, since from bitter experience, if a paper chooses to name its sources at a later date, it can prove highly embarrassing to have publicly called their bluff. Libel laws are very complex, and generally speaking, the news media is free to quote anything told to them, even from undisclosed sources, provided it is done in good faith and it is clear the report is the allegation of a third party and not held up as the opinion of the media itself. What I am saying is, we are to be careful to treat the report as flawed because of the erroneous commenting of unnamed sources, and not as the result of any misrepresentation by the newspaper. Okay, we have about ten minutes before my next meeting. You have all been given a copy of the Commissioner's briefing notes. Let's have some suggestions on how to play this. Remember, we must not go into specifics about the investigation".

Special Commander Bryant knew from observation that a mark of an influential leader was to speak first and speak loudest, without regard to whether your contribution was particularly relevant. "First we must get to know the colour of their teeth", he said, and then for the benefit of the blank faces in the room, which was all of them, he continued "We don't know whether they will be questioning aggressively, or mocking us, or simply trying to establish facts. We need to cut our britches accordingly".

"I think it's fair to assume that there will be elements of all three", replied Commander Unwin, "and it would be helpful to a satisfactory outcome to limit the use of mixed and simply nonsensical idioms and metaphors. But I agree, we should not be defensive, but react according to the tone. There will certainly be awkward questions, not least because this has been an active investigation for some weeks now, not the year that The Standard speculates, and the public has until now been unaware of any of it. Above all, we must not get flustered, and must project an image of being a cohesive team in full control. We need to retain secrecy in many areas, due to the nature of the investigation, and this should be our position when faced with anything that may embarrass us".

"How are we going to address the implication that I went shopping in Singapore and spent my time living it up at taxpayers' expense and failed to get any results? That's not how it was at all. Tarzan put me up to it; he's the one that did all the shopping, he bought more jewellery than you could shake a tree at. And who the hell told them my passport was stolen, that's what I want to know".

Commander Unwin winced. "Thank you for that abject lesson in what we are facing, and exactly how not to deal with it", he said. "You travelled to Indonesia to secure the cooperation of the Indonesian Police in investigating certain lines of enquiry. You held a high level meeting with senior Indonesian Police officers, and others, in Singapore as a vital part of the process. As a result, valuable information is flowing. That is all you need to say, and I sincerely hope that is all you *will* say".

Superintendent Smith, who had been instructed to take the lead in the presentation and field most of the questions, said "One of the key aspects I expect questions on is the role of the FBI, and why we brought them in. I would like to get alignment on our position. In my opinion, and if I am interpreting the Commissioner's notes correctly, we can rightly deny that we brought in the FBI per se, but obtained the technical advice of an FBI expert on a very narrow field of specialisation. We should also stress this is not unusual".

"Exactly right, although don't be too emphatic about the 'not unusual' part. Emma obviously will not be present at the press conference since her usual employment is of a highly classified nature, and we don't want photographs of her all over the internet. Emma, do you have anything to add?"

"Only that your approach is probably the right one, under the circumstances. Keep the idea of this being a gang alive for the time being. Remember Pimpinan himself will see and hear everything you do and say, so try not to be drawn in to discussions about suspects or motives. Don't mention the word 'Pimpinan' at all. Keep as much as possible up your sleeves, and make it plain that is a conscious decision. Remember too that some people watching may have received videos or other contacts from Pimpinan – we want them to feel confident enough to bring this to our attention, without us actually saying so".

"Right, I'll see the rest of you in the Press Room at twenty minutes to ten. I, for one, will be saying a prayer before I leave".

— o —

Special Commander Bryant felt he had been born for occasions such as this, and couldn't wait to see the look on Mrs Bryant's face when he walked in the door later that evening. He made a mental note that if the day went particularly well, he would pick up a bottle of good champagne on the way home, so they could toast his new beginning as a public face of authority of the Metropolitan Police. He noticed with a glimmer of satisfaction the less optimistic look on Commander Unwin's face, as the reporters took their seats and the cameramen conducted their final checks and talked to their unseen control desks and the sound crew fiddled with microphones that looked like long side-handle batons. Superintendent Smith was looking relaxed, acknowledging faces in the room and smiling, and the Detective Inspector in cowboy boots and the three detectives whose names Special Commander Bryant had trouble remembering had taken their seats to the left of the front table, sitting in a row diagonal to the assembled crowd.

At ten o'clock on the dot, Commander Unwin welcomed everybody and asked that everyone listen to what the team had to say first, following which questions would be invited for as long as time allowed.

"My name is Commander Alan Unwin, and I am the commanding officer of Operation Krakatoa. On my left is Special Commander..," and Commander Unwin stumbled and turned pink as he realised he had no idea of Special Commander Bryant's first name, and Special Commander Bryant pointedly offered no help at all, so he continued "ah, Special Commander Bryant. Special Commander Bryant is responsible for tactical and operational planning, and coordinating cooperation between the Metropolitan Police and all other Police services as the need arises", which was news to Special Commander Bryant.

"On my right is Superintendent Steven Smith, who is in charge of operations, heading up a team of some thirty dedicated detective officers. Superintendent Smith will now brief you on the background and status of the Operation, but before he does that I want to just remind you all that this meeting is being held in response to an article in the London Evening Standard, published yesterday, and subsequently followed up by news media worldwide. Certain aspects of the case reported to date include factual inaccuracies, which we will clarify. We ask you to focus on the facts of the case as presented, and not on any apparent contradictions. Whilst we will endeavour to be as forthright as possible, please also remember that this is a top priority investigation and some of the information we have to hand is of the utmost sensitivity at this stage. We hope you understand that we cannot discuss the Operation other than in general terms".

Special Commander Bryant realised with glee that the Commissioner would surely pick up on the fact that Commander Unwin didn't know the name of his most senior colleague, and wondered whether it would be a feather in Special Commander Bryant's cap or a blot on his copybook if he animatedly pretended to introduce himself to Commander Unwin in front of the assembled journalists when it was his turn to speak. Special Commander Bryant decided to rise above using such low tactics for a cheap laugh for now, for the sake of a good impression, and decided to rely on polished professionalism and understated leadership to speak for him.

Superintendent Smith talked for forty minutes, during which he painted a picture in calculatedly vague terms of an efficient, effective investigation with multinational cooperation and steady progress, and managed to portray the idea of a single criminal enterprise affecting the crime statistics of a city the size of London as frankly absurd. Commander Unwin then told the assembly that the meeting would field questions, and the room erupted into a pandemonium of clamouring shouts and bawling demands for explanations, which Commander Unwin was alarmed to note were all directed at Special Commander Bryant.

Special Commander Bryant spotted an opportunity. Rising to his feet, he outstretched his arms toward the throng like a holy man blessing the crowd, and stood without moving with his eyes closed while the hubbub died down, until the room was silent.

"Please, ladies and gentlemen, let's remember where we are", he said, and everyone wondered what that had got to do with anything. "We have plenty of time for questions, and we are at your disposal for as long as it takes", and Commander Unwin let out an audible groan. "But I must ask you to address your questions one at a time, by raising your hands. Each person will be allowed at least one question. I will point to the person whose question will be dealt with next. Please remember to state who your question is meant for".

Everyone in the room raised a hand in unison, and Special Commander Bryant pointed into the mob.

"The lady in the red jacket".

"Special Commander Bryant, why were you removed as the commanding officer of the Operation, and why are there two officers at the rank of Commander heading up the investigation, and what is your specific role in the enquiry now that you ..."

"I'm sorry, that seems like more than your fair share of questions, so I'll stop you there. For the record, Commander Unwin has been the commanding officer since the Operation's inception, and I have always been assisting him in a kind of consulting role, due to my wide experience of the big picture. My expertise leans toward strategy and direction, and accordingly I have been involved in diplomatic assignments with other countries' Police forces. I can't be any more specific than that. Yes, there are two Commanders, but Commander Unwin is a basic Commander and I am the *Special* Commander. That's why I'm here, and that's not to say I'm the superior officer, at least not on Operation Krakatoa anyway".

Commander Unwin looked startled and opened his mouth to speak, but Bryant pointed again. "The man in the Rolling Stones tee shirt".

"Special Commander Bryant, again: is there any connection between the Operation and the theft of your passport, and could you explain why you were in Jakarta at all?"

"I was in Jakarta to establish top-level cooperation with the Indonesian Police, during which time there was an unrelated theft from the hotel's secure depository which I was not aware of at the time. One of the items reported stolen by the hotel was my passport, however my Indonesian colleagues had recovered this and all of the other guests' property by the time I found out about it. There are peripheral aspects of the case which require investigating in Indonesia, however that is not to imply that Indonesia is in any way the focus of the Operation. Next question – the gentleman in the dark suit".

"Special Commander Bryant, this operation is obviously accorded a lot higher priority than most organised crime in the Capital, and the public is concerned about the effects if some kind of criminal turf war breaks out. Superintendent Smith dismissed the claim that crime figures are falling as a result, but anecdotal evidence indicates such a claim has a basis in fact. The public is concerned about the secrecy to date, and the fact that the Police have not named casualties or even given numbers. My question is, do the Police take a more casual approach to the operation than would otherwise be the case, given that your work in reducing crime is effectively being done for you, and that as far as the public is concerned, the crimes are so far victimless?"

The room began to buzz with murmuring and nodding of heads.

"That is a very good question, if a rather leading one. On point one, I am not personally qualified to comment on recent crime statistic trends, so I will defer to the statisticians, whoever they may be. On point B, hypothetically assuming anecdotal evidence about a fall in statistics is proved accurate, the Police are no less passionate about bringing the perpetrators to justice than ever, regardless of who the crimes in question are directed at. The last thing we want Londoners to have to endure is a territory struggle between criminal factions. The second point deals with secrecy, and identities of casualties. The fact is that up to now, all we have is a list of possibly missing persons, and certain evidence that suggests they may have been involved in violent encounters connected to the Operation, excepting the two murder victims who have been named. What we do not have is a procession of dead bodies to account for. And as far as these crimes being victimless is concerned, I would point out that everybody is somebody's son, brother, father and husband, except of course if they happen to be of the woman gender".

A woman stood up and shouted out her question without being invited. "Special Commander Bryant, is it true that the FBI has identified the ringleaders of the gang and, contrary to what Superintendent Smith told us, actually held meetings with the ringleaders without the Operation's knowledge with a view to negotiating a satisfactory outcome?"

"Absolutely not. The FBI is not involved in the Operation, other than providing specialist advice directly to us in a very narrow field, as Superintendent Smith stated. Negotiating a satisfactory outcome is not on our agenda, and from what I know of the FBI, such is not the way they do things either".

"So are arrests imminent?"

"I'm sorry", said Bryant, "I cannot discuss that, since to do so would alert the suspect to our intentions. Suffice to say, when the time comes for an arrest to be made, you will be the first to know about it. The second, if you count the suspect himself".

The room was becoming agitated now, and Special Commander Bryant felt his authoritative presence being challenged as more questions began to be called out without his prompting.

"So you have identified a suspect?" "You said suspect, singular, what did you mean by that?" "Why can't you be more specific about the Indonesian connection?" "Is the FBI involved to teach you about termination with maximum prejudice?" and "Are Johnny Depp and the olive oil cartel related?" all rang out in unison.

"I'm sorry, I'm sorry, none of these questions can be answered by us at this stage", said Special Commander Bryant in a raised voice, doing a good job at hiding his fluster. "All of these things concern highly confidential issues of the utmost, um, confidentiality, vital to the Operation. When we can disclose more, we will let you know. Until then, please accept our assurances that we are making every effort to apprehend the suspect or suspects and are making significant progress by the hour. We hope to have good news very soon".

"Special Commander Bryant", said a lone voice, "I fully understand you need to hold your cards very close to your chest at the moment, but..."

"No", interrupted Special Commander Bryant, "No cards. The cards are another area of the utmost secrecy which we cannot divulge to you now".

"Huh? What cards? Tell us about the cards!" clamoured a dozen voices at once, and Commander Unwin started to stand up to call a halt to proceedings before things got completely out of control.

Special Commander Bryant blanched. "You just mentioned the cards ... what cards indeed! You brought up the subject of cards. There are no cards, unless you just mentioned them, and they are highly classified", and Commander Unwin politely but firmly wrapped the meeting up and they left the room within seconds.

— o —

Commander Unwin was still furious as Special Commander Bryant arrived, late and last, at the debrief meeting with a party-pack of coffee and a box of muffins he had stopped-by for in Starbucks. Special Commander Bryant knew that it was a mark of an effective leader to periodically treat the workforce to snacks and drinks out of one's own pocket when things had gone well, even if the workforce included swaggering upstarts such as the Detective Inspector in cowboy boots, who was even more annoyingly sure of himself since he had received his assignment pack and travel briefing for a trip to Jakarta.

The Commissioner, who had sought the private opinion of Special Agent In Charge Gajewski on how she thought the press conference had gone, had sent an email to Commander Unwin and copied it to the entire leadership team, congratulating them on a job well done and singling out Superintendent Smith for his concise summary and Special Commander Bryant for his 'masterly' piece of work at being vague and hard to pin down in a precise and clear-cut way. Commander Unwin, wrote the Commissioner, might in future think about contributing a little more to press conferences at which he was the senior officer, and

Special Commander Bryant's style of taking charge of unruly proceedings should be emulated wherever possible.

"The Commissioner feels that the press event was as successful as it could have been, under the circumstances", said Commander Unwin through gritted teeth, unaware of Special Agent In Charge Gajewski's influence on the Commissioner's opinion, "which surprises me, as I felt we were a hair's breadth away from having an unmitigated disaster on our hands. I would like to invite feedback from the non-panel team members present at the press meeting. How did you all think it went? Anyone? Any lessons learned, or general comments?"

The Detective Inspector in cowboy boots, who seemed to be affecting a trace of an American accent lately, raised his hand and said "Sir, I think your strategy of establishing command of the Operation and then delegating responsibility for leading the meeting to Superintendent Smith and Special Commander Bryant was a great plan. It came across as an unspoken, complex chain of command, with everyone knowing their place and with authority at every turn. The art of high level delegation is a delicate one, Sir, and it was right to distance yourself from the control of the meeting in favour of Special Commander Bryant, even though he is technically the senior officer, as he pointed out. It went down well with the press, who saw a well-woven tapestry of management in play".

"Are you trying to be smart, lad?" demanded Commander Unwin menacingly, who had glanced across at Special Commander Bryant and noticed he was jotting down 'well-woven tapestry of management' on his notepad, and who now had an extra layer of sheen on his dome and a newly-apparent vein throbbing under his left temple, "Whoever told you Bryant is the senior officer? Are you mocking me?"

"Oh no, Sir", faltered the Detective Inspector in cowboy boots, clearly flummoxed. "I just thought you handled things noticeably well, that's all".

"Because the Commissioner feels that I ought to think about contributing a little more to press conferences at which I am the senior officer. Do you think I should have thought about contributing a little more to the press conference, as the senior officer?"

"No, Sir, that's just what I was saying. You handled it exactly right".

"So", began Special Commander Bryant, who had identified this as one of those rare occasions when starting a personal confrontation was both a good idea and relatively risk-free, "what you are saying, is that the Commissioner's advice to Commander Unwin is wrong? That you, in fact, know better about commanding-officer-ship than the Commissioner? Because it strikes me that is a dangerous position to go out on a limb above the parapet from". Special Commander Bryant turned to Commander Unwin hoping for a look of support, but found only a stone-faced glare, as he continued "If you play with sleeping dogs, as they say, you are going to get burnt. That's what I would do".

Commander Unwin didn't know which one of the two he hated the most right now, and just wanted both of them out of his sight, and was saved from having to speak to either of them by Gajewski, who was increasingly feeling like she was tasked with holding the hands of other people's children at a party that was not hers either.

"Well, the main thing is the Commissioner is relatively happy, and on-line news channels suggest the press have taken a positive view, despite there remaining a lot of unanswered questions", she said. "I suggest we put this behind us and get on with the job. As you may know, San Ramon has agreed to extend me here for another two weeks, so it looks like you're stuck with me for the time being. They were impressed with the way you discounted negative assumptions about the FBI's involvement. They were watching you at three a.m. when they should have been in bed".

"There is one more thing", said Commander Unwin glumly, "Since Operation Krakatoa is now public, we are to commence issuing press updates daily. The press updates are to follow the guidelines issued prior to the press conference, that is, a minimum of detail and emphasis on the continuing highly sensitive nature of the investigation. Formal press updates are the only, *the only*, means of communication with the Press. No meetings, no emails, no phone calls, no chats in the pub. This is to be hammered out in unmistakeable terms to all ranks, Superintendent Smith. Further, the Commissioner has decreed..."

He paused for a full twenty seconds, during which time Special Commander Bryant wondered whether it would be polite to offer a glass of water, or enquire whether Commander Unwin was having a stroke.

"The Commissioner has decided that all press updates are to be edited and approved by, and sent from the desk of, Special Commander Bryant. I am therefore delegating that responsibility to Bryant with immediate effect, in keeping with that well-woven tapestry thing. God help us all".

Special Commander Bryant purchased two bottles of the best champagne he could afford on the way home, and arrived to find his house full of his friends and neighbours offering congratulatory remarks and drinking his gin, and for once Mrs Bryant had nothing but praise for her husband, although he might try to restrict his animated arm movements a bit and speak more clearly next time.

Chapter 11 - The Survivor

The day following the day of the press conference started off uneventfully with a daily progress review in the strategic control room, but the meeting was soon disturbed by a flurry of activity that had kept Superintendent Smith away and had him talking in huddled groups with detectives who were hurriedly coming and going and excitedly speaking a little too loudly for Superintendent Smith's liking. It was obvious to Detective Sergeant Robbins that something big was going on, and now Special Agent In Charge Gajewski had been called over to the discussions and was looking more agitated than he had ever seen her.

"Where is Calamity?" yelled Superintendent Smith, referring to the Detective Inspector in cowboy boots, who had been nicknamed 'Calamity Jane' by colleagues in an attempt to put down his faux-Texan demeanour, but who had annoyed everybody even more by embracing the nickname with relish.

"He's gone, Sir! He's on a plane to Jakarta!" called out a voice in the room.

Superintendent Smith re-joined the main group after a few minutes, and looked flushed.

"All right, listen up, we appear to have a major development. It seems we have a survivor of the white room, and he is available to us for questioning. This is what we know at this stage. Last night at around ten p.m., a man was dumped from a moving vehicle on Kingsland Road, Hackney. He was in pain and hysterical, and was taken to A&E at

Homerton. Police attended the hospital, where it was determined that the man had been administered an unknown noxious substance into his urethra, which was still lodged there and causing great pain. In layman's terms, he had had something inserted into his dick. He had to be restrained, and pain control was not immediately administered as he was thought to be under the influence of alcohol. Since the object needed to be removed and the man could offer no clues as to what the object was or why it had been inserted into him, he was sedated and transferred to the Chelsea and Westminster hospital, where they have him now. On the way, it was established that the man is a serving Policeman, one PC Peter Collinson. Collinson claimed to the Police officer in attendance that he had been kidnapped while on duty and had been shown video footage of torture and murder, carried out by the man who was holding him, in the same place he was being held. He seems to have had a lengthy conversation with the abductor. We understand that a small object has been successfully removed, and is being examined for identification. Collinson is said to be recovering quickly, and is already being held in a guarded room on Commander Unwin's orders. All the preliminary evidence suggests that this Collinson was in direct contact with Pimpinan, was taken to and from the white room seen in the videos, and also that he was let go by him. If so, this is the only known survivor, and we need to move fast and interview him. It sounds at first glance like another carefully thought out gift from Pimpinan. I will go there now; I had wanted Calamity but seeing as he is otherwise occupied, D.S. Robbins will come with me. Gajewski will interview Collinson later after we have finished, unless we determine that there is no need for a follow-up. Everyone be back here for an update briefing at three p.m. Remember, regardless of what may or may not be already in the public domain concerning the Operation, this turn of events is absolutely secret until further notice. That is all".

"One more thing", said Detective Constable Sameera Watson, "we've just heard Collinson was AWOL yesterday and the day before. Not exactly unheard-of, apparently, but this time Collinson's wife filed a missing persons report on him two days ago after he failed to return home after shift".

— o —

Special Agent In Charge Gajewski joined Superintendent Smith and D.S. Robbins after lunch. Smith and Robbins had followed Gajewski's suggestion of reverse-interviewing Collinson; a technique whereby, once the high-level chain of events has been established, the detailed interview is conducted in reverse timeline. In this case the timeline was divided into four 'buckets', starting with the departure from the place of incarceration and dumping on the street, followed by conversations with the abductor and occurrences during the abduction, followed by the snatch and transportation to the place of incarceration, followed by the normal activities of Collinson prior to the snatch. The interview would then be repeated in true chronological sequence, and the two accounts would be compared for inconsistencies and contradictions. This technique was claimed by Gajewski to be effective with hostile witnesses or witnesses who may have something to hide, since the illogical initial timeline made it difficult for someone to 'think on their feet' the first time round; to coordinate the account if it included lies, half-truths or if areas of the actual chain of events were being hidden, and although Smith and Robbins were not familiar with this method of questioning, comparison of Collinson's two accounts had revealed more holes than a worn-out colander.

Gajewski had decided that rather than be present with Collinson at the interview session, she would review the transcript for obvious signs of psychological stress and look for pointers to concentrate on later, if necessary. She had planned to have a brief meeting with Collinson to determine his state of mind and find out what, if anything, scared him more than anything else, and why. What Gajewski hadn't expected was to walk in to the room to find an irrevocably traumatised man who had clearly said goodbye to his career as it disappeared down the toilet, but had something much more important on his mind. She had expected a traumatised man who was part of the team and looked to the team to protect him and bring him back into the fold, not someone who regarded that team as a threat.

Gajewski's briefing by Smith and Robbins had given her the following starting-point for the discussion with Collinson:

- Attending a reported break-in at a charity shop with his partner, one P.S. Patel. Became separated from Patel when Collinson went to look around a yard at the back of the shop.

- Collinson was attacked from behind with a canvas hood which was placed over his head and locked in place, and soaked with a pungent liquid. Lost consciousness, and came to bound and gagged in a van.

- Driven for two to five hours, then dragged conscious from the van into a house. Blindfold and gag removed, and left bound on the floor of a white tiled room by a man later identified by Collinson as Pimpinan from photographs taken from the Mostyn.

- Videos were shown on a portable television screen for one to two hours of the slow murder of unknown individuals in the same white room. The chair featured in the videos was present in the room, and Collinson assumed he would be murdered in the same way.

- Pimpinan returned with a stool, which he sat on, and a discussion took place for approximately one hour. Collinson was assured he would be released, but would be subjected to similar treatment as the victims in the videos if he did not agree to fulfil all of Pimpinan's demands.

- Pimpinan's demeanour was firm and unflinching, but Collinson reported it as strange that he repeatedly apologised for Collinson's discomfort and the pain he said he would suffer, also for the fact Collinson had been made to soil himself.

- Blindfold and gag replaced, and left alone for 'some hours'. Collinson then dragged back to the van. Driven for two to five hours, then Pimpinan stopped and climbed into the back and removed the blindfold but not the gag.

- Pimpinan put on a pair of surgical gloves, then undid Collinson's trousers and extracted his penis. Pimpinan said he was going to leave Collinson with a reminder of their conversation. He inserted a small plastic tube into the penis, pushed a thinner plastic rod into the tube, and extracted the entire assembly. Collinson reported feeling a foreign object lodged that immediately began to impart a burning sensation which escalated continuously beyond being unbearable.

- Pimpinan fastened the trousers, apologised again and returned to the driving seat, discarding gloves. Collinson did not note any identifying features of the van, but noticed it seemed new and had no windows in the rear. After some minutes, Pimpinan reached behind and removed the gag and held Collinson by the collar; Collinson began screaming. A side door slid open, probably electrically, and the van swerved at the same time as Pimpinan pushed, and Collinson was ejected onto the street.

- Collinson reported it was several minutes before anyone arrived, despite screams for help. He had been dropped quite close to the point he was snatched from. People were wary of helping, since his arms and legs were still bound by tape.

- Collinson and Patel had not been formally assigned to a charity shop break-in by their controllers. Collinson has back-tracked on this point, and now maintains that it was a genuine assignment which was discovered during routine patrols.

- The charity shop in question has not reported a recent break-in, nor been attended by Collinson and/or Patel at any time.

- Patel has been interviewed separately and is unable to verify Collinson's account. It transpires Collinson frequently takes leave of Patel and has, in the past, insisted on an ongoing, informal arrangement of Patel covering for his absences, which Patel is not comfortable with. Patel affirms he has in the past been offered money for his cooperation, which he claims to have refused.

- Patel last saw Collinson when Collinson left him close to the charity shop at six p.m., not eight p.m. which Collinson reports as the time of visiting the charity shop. Patel is unable to account for Collinson's movements after that time, and cannot verify whether or not Collinson entered the charity shop.

Gajewski was following the same line of reverse-interviewing, since Collinson did not seem adept at dealing with it. Collinson had been brusque at first, defensive on the one hand, yet also seemingly resigned to whatever trouble he had got himself into, and it was clear that he considered his personal survival was at stake. Gradually, Gajewski succeeded in coaxing him into being a little more forthcoming, by focussing on his feelings and opinions related to what had happened, and what appeared to motivate the abductor. Gajewski decided to be very subtly abrasive and non-empathic, since it was clear Collinson was not looking for a friend, and she decided to terminate the interview as soon as she had established psychological status of both Collinson and Pimpinan without emphasis on covering the entire timeline.

"What went through your mind when he put on gloves and undid your trousers?" she asked.

"I was terrified, really terrified. I couldn't scream, my mouth was taped up. I thought at first he was going to castrate me".

"Did he seem to be preparing for some kind of sexual assault? When it became apparent he wasn't going to mutilate you?"

"I had no idea, but it didn't seem like it. It struck me the gloves wouldn't have been part of it. He seemed to be preparing to hurt me. I was expecting pain, since he had apologised before ... we were talking before, and he said..."

"We'll get to that later. But when he assaulted you with the tube, did he appear to be doing something he enjoyed, or that gave him a thrill?"

"No, he seemed more like it was an effort; something he'd prefer not to do. He seemed a bit repulsed by it".

"I can imagine. After that, what went through your mind after he had withdrawn the tube and fastened you up?"

"It started to burn right away, and got worse every second. I thought he had put in some acid, or an ant; some kind of insect that was starting to eat its way out of me. I've never been so frightened in my life, or in so much pain. It hurt so damn much I couldn't think, and got worse every second. He said he would let me go, but now I thought he was going to leave me to die. I'm still scared they will have to amputate it or operate on it, or I'll be disabled sexually".

"Would you like to know what it was? It was a seed of some kind, almost certainly from a hot chilli pepper. Probably a Scotch Bonnet. Just a tiny little seed. The capsaicin is what gives it the heat, and it works by locking onto pain receptors in mucus membranes, giving the feeling of heat where no heat really exists. It's actually an illusion, part of the plant's survival and reproductive mechanism, but humans have grown to like it in their food in small doses. It will continue to burn for a while, particularly when you pass water, but will eventually dissipate with no long-lasting effects. You're lucky that the hospital didn't decide to cut you open and remove it, which they probably would have done if they had thought it was some kind of burrowing insect".

Collinson was wide-eyed and was looking as though he had just heard a sure-fire truth that couldn't possibly be true.

"How does that make you feel, now that you know it was something comparatively trivial?"

"Like a fool, if it's true", said Collinson. After a long pause, he continued "I wish I'd known at the time, I could have fought the pain. I thought at the very least I was losing my manhood; it felt like I was being dissolved in acid or something. I can't believe it; it was sheer agony, and now you're telling me it was like eating a hot curry? I'd seen what this guy was capable of, and believe me, you don't want to see what I saw. And I had been there, in the same place". Collinson shivered. "What if he comes here? He's going to come for me for sure, because there's no way Management will play ball with him. You lot won't protect me. I'm probably going to be fired and arrested before I get out of this bed, if he doesn't get to me first".

"Let's talk about the place. The white room. Why did you think he took you there at the time, and why do you now think he took you there?"

"I didn't know, I thought he was a psycho who wanted to butcher me. Looking back - he is a psycho for sure, but he wanted me to be a messenger. Luckily for me. He wanted to make demands, and wanted to be sure I'd take him seriously. Well, I take him pretty fucking seriously, let me tell you".

"The demands. Only two. You are to convince the Metropolitan Police to take out a full page advertisement in a national daily newspaper on behalf of all Police services in the country, admitting their failure to control drug crime and protection rackets, and promising to make immediate restitution. Not to issue a press release to that effect, but to take out an actual advertisement. Is that correct"?

"Correct".

"He didn't specify any particular newspaper? Or suggest any"?

"He said it didn't matter which one, as long as it was a national. He said the BBC wouldn't care where they read it, when they jumped on it".

"That's the word he used, restitution? It seems a strange word to use. Well, that's going to be a pretty tough demand to meet, I have to say. It's not going to happen. The second demand, you are to own up to being a part of the problem by admitting that you regularly took bribes to allow street drug trading to take place and to tip off criminal contacts with information about Police anti-crime operations in the locality. Is that it?"

"Yes, only I never did any of those things".

"'A rotten-to-the-core, dirty cop'. That's the exact expression he told you to use?"

"Yes. But like I said, I have contacts, but they are potential informers, not the other way round. Yes, I met them, but not like it sounds. Patel will tell you. But I've already made a confession, just like I was told, like the dirty cop I apparently am. You lot don't frighten me, but this guy does. Taking me was a piece of cake to him".

"There's one thing I don't understand. You said that he didn't tell you to resign ... why do you think that was?"

"I said he actually told me not to resign. He said the Police could announce my sacking as the first step to restitution". Collinson paused. "My wife will leave me after this, no doubt about it".

"Maybe not, now it seems you will probably still have a functioning dick. Or maybe she will, for the same reason. Let's go back to your contacts. Your 'potential informers', as it were. Did any of them speak to you about being at risk from some kind of vigilante gang that is trying to get them off the streets?"

"They read the papers, but it's not news to them. They knew about it before. There were rumours about one of the high-up suppliers who disappeared, but he turned up again. Some people are nervous, but some think it's all a rumour being put about by us. Some say London's a big place, and the chances of them getting attention are next to nothing. Others talk big about it; say 'bring it on'".

"You seem to know a lot of them, and what they think. Did it occur to you that the man who put a tiny seed in your tiny dick may be part of that? Part of a vigilante gang trying to get your friends off the streets?"

"Well, really, do you think so?" asked Collinson, sarcastically.

"Did it occur to you that this man would want you to convey the details of your little ordeal to your 'potential informers'? To tell them, 'Hey, this is real, watch your step'? To tell them, 'Taking me was a piece of cake to him'?"

"That's not going to happen now. I'm off the force, for sure".

"Did it occur to you that 'The Management' might just want that to happen too? Or that this man would know that 'The Management' might want that to happen too, and that's why he told you not to resign?"

"What are you saying? The Management wants me to get banged up on a five year stretch, more like".

"I'm saying that things aren't quite as clear-cut as you might think. I'm saying that if you admit your guilt, which we all know and which, despite his best efforts, Patel has been unable to hide, everyone will know where they stand and will be able to decide a path forward. I'm not trying to help you; I personally think you're rotten. But there is a bigger picture here".

Special Agent In Charge Gajewski stood up to leave, and said "Expect a lot more visitors today. The Management. Meantime, try to get some rest. And I suggest you refrain from pulling that little thing of yours around for a few days, until the pain has completely gone. Give it some rest and recovery time".

Gajewski turned and walked to the door, and as she leaned for the handle, in a single flowing motion swiped her skirt up at the rear, giving Collinson a two-second vision of her perfect bare ass which set Collinson's rest and recovery back by several days.

— o —

"To my mind, this changes everything".

Special Agent In Charge Gajewski was addressing Commander Unwin at the extraordinary planning meeting Commander Unwin had called with Gajewski, Special Commander Bryant and Superintendent Smith to agree a path forward, and to decide on recommendations to make to the Commissioner. Detective Sergeant Robbins was also present to fill in any gaps, since he had interviewed Collinson and Patel and had also carried out back-up investigations with Collinson's wife and the charity shop, but Commander Unwin intended to dismiss Robbins before any strategy ideas were discussed.

"This has opened up a whole new window into Pimpinan's psyche. He has never followed this line of behaviour with us before. This is no longer about showing us how in-control and determined and clever he is. The only reason he would have taken Collinson and scared the shit out of him and let him go – with precise instructions for the Met – is because he wants to actually push the Met to commit publicly to being a lot more proactive at taking certain types of dangerous criminals off the streets in future. He sees you as not doing all you can to stop the type of crime he's fixated about. He's exposed a dirty cop, and given you a chance to do something about it. He wants to humiliate you into action. He assumed it's certain the public would find out about Collinson being dumped on the street and taken to hospital, and also that the public will likely find out he's a corrupt officer who was dragged into your operation by 'the gang', one way or another".

Special Commander Bryant was rarely one to let his emotions get the better of him, but something about Gajewski's tone rubbed him up the wrong way.

"I notice you always revert to speaking in the second person when things go wrong", he said. "When everything is hunky dory, it's 'we are this, we will do that, and we're all part of a team'. But now, when faced with difficult decisions and uncomfortable situations, it's 'he wants to humiliate you' and 'your operation'".

"Special Commander, we most certainly are all part of a team. But my role is to be an advisor, and at the conclusion of all this, you will still be here and I will have moved on to other things. You are the Metropolitan Police, and I am not. Sometimes it is necessary to remind ourselves of that. I meant no offence but I stand by my choice of grammar".

"So was it us, the team, that Pimpinan fooled into having a drink with him at a hotel bar, or you, as an advisor? I'd be interested to know your choice of grammar in that case".

"Bryant", interrupted Commander Unwin, a little more forcefully than he had intended, "This isn't helpful. Please refrain from diverting the meeting to non-issues".

"The Special Commander has a point, drawing on his fine command of the English language", said Gajewski with more than a hint of irony. "I will in future speak in the first person plural when discussing any aspect of the Operation. I do apologise, Special Commander, I did not intend to upset you, and will defer to your wishes.

"Getting back to my point, though; Pimpinan must know that the Metropolitan Police is highly unlikely to accede to his demand for a public admission of failure and promise to make amends. It is more likely he assumes that by exposing a corrupt officer and it becoming publicly known that the exposure was carried out by him, or the 'gang' as it is still assumed, the effect will be the same. We will be humiliated into making a grovelling admission and a promise to do better. But here is the key point, whatever we decide to do about this and however it turns out: if he sincerely wants us to make more effort, as suggested by his pushing us into having to try harder to take certain types of criminals off the streets, to take the reins and get results: that may mean he wants to stop, or at least to wind down his activities. And getting Pimpinan to stop is our number one priority, even higher in priority than the close second, which is arresting him and bringing him to justice. And with that in mind, we should be very careful in how we respond to this".

Commander Unwin decided to lay his cards on the table, to prevent a lengthy round of suggestions and 'what-if' scenarios being discussed that would not result in a feasible course of action.

"The Metropolitan Police will not take out any advertisement or issue any press release along the lines of the demands", he said, "and I am not prepared to recommend such a thing to the Commissioner. For one thing, the sentiments expressed in the demand are simply untrue – we are not failing. We are under extreme pressure to allocate limited resources effectively, which sometimes leads to results not being ideal, but that is not the same thing at all. For another thing, the Commissioner does not have the authority to proceed with such a thing, even if he agreed, which he would not. There is no individual in the country with the power and the inclination to authorise such a move – it would be political dynamite, which would need to be owned by the Home Secretary and the entire government up to the Prime Minister himself. It is simply not going to happen".

"I understand that position and I fully accept it, but does that mean we have to simply ignore the events of the last couple of days and hope they go away?" asked Superintendent Smith. "We should obviously not consider giving in to demands of the most wanted of criminals, but it seems to me that this will not be the end of it if we are seen to do nothing at all. I have never experienced a situation remotely like this, but it seems to me that unless we catch this man right away, which at present seems unlikely, other people may be put at risk. But how to handle the situation is beyond me".

"The public notice issue is set in stone, and that is the end of the matter", replied Commander Unwin. "But the issue of how to handle Collinson is not so crystal-clear. Firstly, nothing appears to have been picked up by the Press; not even that a bound and injured man was found in the street and taken to hospital, let alone him being a serving Policeman, or that he was injured by the 'gang' Operation Krakatoa is seeking, or that he has admitted being corrupt, or indeed any of it. Surprisingly.

"Secondly, Collinson has not formally admitted guilt and maintains his innocence, claiming his statement of guilt was made under duress and that he was following orders to protect his own safety. This is a bizarre situation, since Collinson also appears to want us to take appropriate disciplinary proceedings and terminate his service on the basis of his statement of guilt, but at the same time agree unofficially that he is not guilty of the charges. Clearly an impossible course of events. His ideal outcome would be a change of identity and relocation with the Met, which he knows is also impossible. His perceived 'probable outcome' is dismissal, following which he would be likely to disappear and fend for himself. This is also highly problematic, since he would almost certainly reappear with a lot of awkward questions about his treatment at our hands as soon as Operation Krakatoa is successfully concluded".

Gajewski noticed this was the first time anybody had spoken with an assumption of a successful conclusion being reached by Operation Krakatoa, and found it refreshing.

"So let's look at the facts, and discuss options with a view to making a recommendation to the Commissioner, who is taking a very keen interest in what we have to say", continued Commander Unwin. "Fact – Collinson is suspected of being guilty of widespread corruption, and it would likely not be difficult to prove that his so-called 'statement of guilt made under duress' is actually an accurate statement of fact. Fact – in the meantime, Collinson may be in further danger from Pimpinan if nothing is seen by Pimpinan as being done by us in response to Collinson's admission, whether real or under duress, although I consider this unlikely. But we do owe Collinson a certain duty of care. So now we come to the options as I see them. Please feel free to comment or add to them.

"Number one – the status quo. Do nothing, and allow Collinson to continue to serve as a Police officer. This option is unacceptable on all levels, and to my mind is not worth even discussing. We do not knowingly employ corrupt officers, full stop. Collinson himself will not cooperate with this option.

"Number two – investigate Collinson's involvement in corruption and instigate disciplinary proceedings. These would probably result in Collinson's dismissal, and may lead to criminal charges being brought. This option would open a viper's nest of problems for us. It would be very public, and would have the effect of embarrassing us into the kind of situation Special Agent In Charge Gajewski described. Further, it could lead to Collinson later protesting his innocence publicly, and accusations of the Met hanging Collinson out to dry to save its own skin, in another bungling of Operation Krakatoa. The ramifications of this cannot even be imagined, and it is a very undesirable option.

"Option three – persuade Collinson to admit his guilt without duress and resign. This could be relatively risk free for us, except for the fact that Collinson has made it clear he is not willing to cooperate. He considers he would be under grave threat of retaliation, since he would have failed to comply with Pimpinan's demands on all counts. He does not want to be the one to determine his own fate. He has indicated an intention to accuse other officers of corruption and demand substantial payments if we try to force his hand. This option has the potential to become the worst option of all".

"So there we have it. We are between a rock and a hard place, as they say. Suggestions, or comments"?

Special Commander Bryant was experiencing a strange, growing sense of déjà vu, like the feeling of dreaming a dream which one was certain one had dreamed before, many years ago, or maybe last night, but despite the certainty, one could not be certain.

"We should not risk the Press getting hold of this", began Special Commander Bryant slowly, noticing it seemed as though someone else's words were tumbling out of his own mouth. "There should be no sacking of Collinson. There should be no initiation of criminal or civil proceedings against Collinson. There should be no disciplinary hearing, and no announcement. No attempt should be made to scotch any rumours among the troops about Collinson's recent absence, or activities that led to it. Rumours should be neither confirmed nor denied, nor even commented upon, and would remain simply rumours".

Nobody spoke, and Special Commander Bryant wondered what the voice tumbling out of his mouth was going to say next.

"Well", Special Commander Bryant continued, "we have a bit of a Pandora's nest here. I think a high degree of diplomacy is required to prevent yet another round of tabloid publicity criticising the Police generally and further tarnishing the public perception of the Met's professional capabilities in particular. Perhaps a complete restructuring of the offending party's status as a Police officer is required involving the cooperation of two Services at the highest level".

Everybody was staring open-mouthed at Special Commander Bryant now, and still nobody spoke. Commander Unwin hoped upon hope this was going to be something worth waiting for, and didn't want to be the one to break the spell.

"What if I were to write in my inimitable style to Constable Collinson, in strictest confidence, informing him of these three salient points: number one, he has been found guilty by a top level internal review panel of gross misconduct and dereliction of duty, and accordingly is formally issued with a written warning stating that if his conduct deviates from the exemplary at any time during the effective period of the written warning, he may be dismissed from duty forthwith without the requirement for further disciplinary proceedings; number two, as a condition of this written warning Constable Collinson is to be seconded with immediate effect to, say, Thames Valley Police stationed at Reading or somewhere, with no loss of service, and number three, the effective period of this written warning is three years from the date of issue, following which in the absence of any further disciplinary misdemeanours it will automatically be removed from his file and deleted from Police personnel records.

"Collinson's immediate superiors would be advised that Collinson has been granted a transfer to Thames Valley for personal reasons. So you see, Commander Unwin, we may have found a solution to our problem, and the problem may have gone away with absolutely no ringing of alarm bells or need of press conferences. Collinson would move to Thames Valley at Reading to avoid the prospect of his certain dismissal from the Met, oblivious to the fact that the Met could not possibly dismiss Collinson because to do so would unleash a firestorm of negative media publicity damaging all of our careers and probably resulting in further dismissals or sanctions higher up the ladder. Collinson would commute to his new place of work in Berkshire every day until he gets his career back on track, or as is more likely, he will become disillusioned due to the overwhelming amount of commuting, find another avenue of employment and would leave the Force of his own accord".

The silence was deafening now, and Special Commander Bryant wondered whether anyone was actually listening.

"I'm listening", said Commander Unwin. "Do you know; with a bit of tidying up it may just work. Please, do go on".

"Of course, such a damage limitation exercise is fraught with risk". Special Commander Bryant was on a roll.

"So, how do you propose we mitigate that risk?" asked Commander Unwin.

Special Commander Bryant leaned forward conspiratorially. "We need someone capable and high-level to be on hand day and night taking control of the situation from within. What would happen if Collinson made some kind of cock-up and his disciplinary record was pulled? We cannot risk the spectre of a serving Policeman being dismissed in consequence of a minor disciplinary offence, due to previous charges involving corruption and collusion with organised criminals. It would smack of a cover-up the first time around, and the publicity simply doesn't bear thinking about".

"I'm still listening", said Commander Unwin eventually.

"That is why I am suggesting that you, Commander Unwin, to be seconded to Thames Valley on a special assignment until the three years is up or Collinson departs the force, whichever is the sooner. Don't worry, you won't need to..."

"We don't need to go as far as that", interrupted Commander Unwin, "but I get the gist of your thinking, and I like it. I will discuss your idea with the Commissioner, and we may be able to develop it into a plan. Perhaps we could even throw in a relocation package, to make it financially hard to refuse. I will of course give full credit for the idea to you, Bryant, and the Commissioner will doubtless want to hear it from the horse's mouth, so to speak".

"Well, I do owe Thames Valley a long-standing favour. It would be up to the Commissioner to decide how much Thames Valley needs to know about the corruption allegations, which let's not forget do not officially exist yet, since we haven't investigated them. And, of course, no record of the disciplinary sanctions would ever appear in Collinson's file, because you refuse to be on hand day and night taking control of the situation from within".

Detective Sergeant Robbins, who hadn't said a word since the meeting began, was now also experiencing a strong feeling of déjà vu for some reason, and Commander Unwin suddenly remembered that he had completely forgotten to dismiss Detective Sergeant Robbins from the meeting before they started to talk about strategy ideas.

— o —

Superintendent Smith had an update.

"We have effectively ruled out the DNA suspect. We have spent an inordinate amount of effort in trying to link him with Pimpinan or determine categorically that he is not connected with him, and we have had a lucky break. We managed to obtain video evidence from the Good Luck hotel on Whittal Street in the N10 area, which clearly shows the entrance to the public lavatory the other side of the road. This hotel is a private guest house. The public lavatory is the location at which the suspect was reported to have committed an act of indecency, for which he was later arrested. The day following that event, Pimpinan can be seen entering the public lavatory at four minutes past ten in the morning, and emerging four and a half minutes later".

"I'm way ahead of you", jumped in Special Commander Bryant, always on the lookout to prove his credentials as a leader of men and people of the woman gender. "The hair in Gouder's shoulder wound came from the DNA suspect. Pimpinan and the suspect both frequent the same public lavatory. So there is a connection between them after all. Either Pimpinan is a victim of the suspect soliciting homosexual participation in the toilet, or more likely he is actually the suspect's gay lover. I'll bet it's the latter; that would explain why the DNA suspect's hair might be on Pimpinan, and how he transferred it unknowingly to Gouder. All we have to do is bring him back in and grill him for the name and address of his boyfriend".

Superintendent Smith laughed, and looked at Special Commander Bryant quizzically to see whether he might be yanking Superintendent Smith's chain before responding. "Really? That's what you think?"

Special Agent In Charge Gajewski, against her better judgement, tried to make life easier for Bryant.

"I think what Superintendent Smith is telling us, is that we have video footage of Pimpinan preparing to lay yet another red herring. Superintendent Smith did say we have ruled him out".

"Correct. At the exact time that we have footage of Pimpinan entering the lavatory, the suspect was in custody, in the process of being charged for the offence committed the day before. The two events at the lavatory are not directly related. Incidentally, the indecency offence has not yet been prosecuted; it is not a high profile case".

"I don't get it", said Special Commander Bryant. "Are you telling me that the two prime suspects in the same case have been found to share the same toiletry facilitation, and that this is nothing more than a coincidence? Because, call me old fashioned, but I don't believe in coincidences".

"It's not a coincidence", said Gajewski gently. "Pimpinan wanted to plant random, unconnected human DNA at the scene of the crime to throw us off the scent; to lodge false leads. Where better to obtain random hair and microscopic skin samples from unconnected members of the public, than on the floor of a public washroom? He was there to collect sweepings from the floor, which he took away and used at the murder scenes. He inserted a hair from the sweepings into the shoulder wound of victim 1, Gouder, and lodged dust from the floor under the fingernails of victim 2. Dust in buildings is comprised mainly of shed skin and hair debris. The underside of any escalator is absolutely full of the stuff. The hair and some of the skin dust he collected came from the DNA suspect, who had previously been engaging in, shall we say, energetic activities at the same location. That, I believe, is the extent of the connection. I have heard of this exact modus operandi before; the Unabomber was found to pack bombs together with sweepings from public toilet floors. In this case, it is only due to the DNA suspect's previous arrests for similar offences that we had the DNA from his hair on record. Don't forget, we also had a lot of unidentified DNA under victim 2's fingernails".

Special Commander Bryant was catching up. "All I'm saying", he said, "is that we should be careful to fully discount the idea of a gay lover before we accept the more obvious red herring scenario. This Pimpinan person seems more than capable of setting up a gay lover / red herring double bluff".

"Point noted", Superintendent Smith sighed.

"This chap certainly does get around, though", continued Special Commander Bryant. "He's left victims in East London and Central London. His white room could be anywhere. He's shown up at the

Mostyn, near Marble Arch in central West London, and at Liverpool Street Station, in central East London, the Square Mile. He grabbed Collinson in Hackney. Now he's appeared in N10, North London. If you look at all the pins in a map of London, it looks like someone fired a shotgun at it. How does he travel? Is he intimately familiar with the whole of London? At this rate I wouldn't be at all surprised if one of us bumps into him in the street somewhere, or having a picnic in Hyde Park".

For once, Special Commander Bryant had elucidated exactly what was on Special Agent In Charge Gajewski's mind.

Chapter 12 - Calamity Jane Bites the Dust

The Detective Inspector who wished he had brought something to wear on his feet other than cowboy boots had had a somewhat less eventful journey to Jakarta than Special Commander Bryant, and a much less enjoyable one. For a start, he had flown with British Airways via Hong Kong, and had not got to see Changi airport in Singapore, which he had heard so much about. But a worse part was that he had been ticketed in a seat in Economy, with mediocre food and no champagne or business class slippers, and had arrived at Soekarno-Hatta frazzled and stiff after a seventeen hour journey, with swollen feet that made him wish he owned a pair of sandals. POLRI had been less than enthusiastic about collecting a mere Detective Inspector from the airport, and instead had pointed out to the Met's central travel office that if their officer arrived at a meeting without a valid business visa, he may be liable to immigration violation sanctions. The travel office had arranged for a single entry business visa for Calamity at the Indonesian embassy in London, and made arrangements for the Crowne Plaza hotel to collect him from the airport with the hotel minibus.

Calamity Jane dumped his bag on the floor and collapsed onto the bed, boots and all, and promptly found he was too tired to sleep. It was five o'clock in the afternoon, local time, and although he did not feel jet-lagged, it felt like midnight while his watch was still showing ten o'clock in the morning. After a time spent resting while his mind raced, he went to the pool to look around, but felt conspicuous as he was the only guest wearing long trousers and boots. He found a shop in the lobby that sold Balinese attire and bought a pair of garish, knee-length shorts and Dr. Scholl foot-massaging sandals, but then decided he was too lazy to change in his room and go back to the pool, and went to sit in the lobby-lounge and have a coffee. The Crowne Plaza was nicer than he had expected, with a spacious airy bedroom and gleaming marble everywhere in the public areas, and was probably the best hotel he had ever stayed at, but he knew it was a lot less opulent than the place Special Commander Bryant had been to, and wished he could have opportunities to sample the high life and travel in Police convoys and be served free champagne by pretty girls. After a while, Calamity decided his plan was to have a couple of early-evening cocktails in the bar, have dinner and then get to bed and be ready in the morning for his first appointment with the Security Advisor at the British embassy. Calamity's meeting was scheduled at eleven o'clock, which would allow ample time to have a good breakfast, prepare himself and take a Silver Bird to the embassy. After the meeting, he would send reports to London by email or by telephone if necessary, from a room that would be provided for his use at the embassy, and he would be free for the rest of the day.

Calamity ensconced himself in a plush leather high-backed bar stool, and ordered a Bali Sunset, which he had never heard of before but was on promotional offer on a buy-one-get-one-free basis. He had only recently found out Bali was in Indonesia, having assumed it was in the Caribbean or somewhere, and noticed that references to Bali were everywhere despite it being some six hundred miles away. Calamity wondered whether he could arrange for a couple of days vacation time after his assignment was over and fly there to see what all the fuss was about before going home, and resolved to check the cost of flights and hotels.

There were many Western guests in the bar, most of whom seemed to know each other, and fairly soon a couple of English guys next to him began to include him in their conversation. Calamity was happy to talk to them, since he had been keen to discover the famous nightlife of Jakarta and great places to eat, and it was difficult in a strange town without knowing anyone. Rob and Robert were colleagues at an oilfield service company; Robert had lived in Jakarta for four years and Rob was a regular visitor from his base in Kuala Lumpur, and was staying at the Crowne Plaza.

"The worst thing about Jakarta is the traffic", said Robert, "and it is totally unpredictable. Friday nights are always bad, and when it's raining, but the rest of the time it varies between pretty awful and totally gridlocked for no apparent reason. You can never be sure of arriving at an appointment on time, or catching your flight, although having said that, the traffic is a great excuse if you wake up late with a hangover".

"I remember the first time I came here", Rob added. "I was staying at the Four Seasons, going back to the hotel around five o'clock. It took me three hours for a two mile journey. I could have walked, but didn't want to run the risk of getting hit by a million motorcycles on the pavement. I nearly had a stress-induced stroke when I sat at a red light just down the street from the hotel for fifteen damn minutes while happy hour ticked away, listening to an Indonesian version of Chirpy Chirpy Cheep Cheep the driver insisted on playing. It's the only time in my life I would have been willing to pass the time reading a Dan Brown book if I had one. Next day I got the hotel BMW 7-series to pick me up – it comes with a well stocked cocktail cabinet and Wi-Fi, so I didn't care too much about the traffic after that".

"The girls seem to be very friendly here, and some of them are stunningly good-looking". Calamity was looking around and fishing for information now. "I'm not married, so I'd be interested to know the chances of getting some pleasant female company while I'm here; things to avoid saying or doing. I have no experience of local culture, obviously".

Rob and Robert grinned at each other knowingly, and rubbed their hands together and shifted in their seats as though they were about to impart some top secret information.

"Okay", began Rob, "a quick idiot's guide to the local culture, and surviving with your goolies intact. First thing to remember is most people here are Muslim. Around the central business district where the international offices and embassies and all the good hotels are, people are generally used to Westerners. They are mostly quite liberal; dress in Western clothes, listen to pop music and eat steaks when they're bought for them. They are mainly polite and friendly, and like to associate with us, provided we don't offend their Muslim sensibilities. A lot of people we work with are good sorts; smart and street-wise. Further out into the sticks, people are more conservative and are less likely to speak English. They are more wary of Westerners.

"Jakarta is a safe city; violent crime is rare, but con-artists and tricksters are rife. Being a white man is like having 'I'm Rich' tattooed on your forehead – everyone will assume you are. So you need to be alert. Also, being British, everyone will think you're a fan of Manchester United".

"Yeah, well, that's all very interesting", broke in Robert, clearly feeling the point was taking too long to be arrived at, "but the question was about getting along with the local girls. In my view, Indonesian girls are the most beautiful in the world, and friendly with it. Expat wives here often feel threatened by it. But they're very hard to read; hard to see where you stand with them. The girls in the office are more likely to be married, and married Indonesian women don't generally play around, at least not with us. You have to be careful not to get the wrong message from their friendly disposition. The single ones are the most difficult ones. A white boyfriend or husband can be seen as a trophy, or a ticket to an expat lifestyle, and if they are interested in you it won't be for a bit of fun. It will be for keeps".

"So what I am hearing is, an Indonesian girlfriend is only interested in getting a ring on her finger? Isn't that a bit of a sweeping generalisation?" asked Calamity, sounding a little more disappointed than he intended.

"Well, yes and no", Robert went on. "If you want female company to hang out with, for coffees and talking and all that, plenty of girls will be keen to mix with you, and that's as far as it goes. If you're looking for the kind of 'friends with benefits' scenario, having a good time with sex thrown in but no strings attached, say 'bye bye' at the end of it, that's a bit more difficult. The best place to meet someone like that is at the up-market hotel bars. Like BATS, at the Shangri-La; it is probably the best place in town. We're going for dinner there tonight, actually. At BATS you find a whole mix of women: professional women who are out for a few drinks after the office, who may or may not be keen to socialise with Western men; hookers who want to sleep with you one time for money; girls looking for men who want what they call a 'Jakarta wife', who don't care if you're married or not but want to live with you as a wife while you're in town in return for being wined and dined and taken shopping, and then the girls who simply want to pair up with you and see how it goes. The trouble is, they all dress like supermodels and look like a million dollars, and they're very hard to tell apart to the untrained eye. Alternatively, you've got the whole thing repeated in the seedier bars, like in Blok M, but where every unaccompanied girl is almost certainly a hooker. Indonesian girls tend to be petite; have smaller breasts than our girls, but if you're more interested in quality than quantity, they're the ones to go for".

"I'm not really into seedy bars and hookers", said Calamity, "especially not when I'm on my own in a strange place". Calamity hadn't had a conversation along such chauvinistic lines for a long time, and it made him feel a little uncomfortable. "So what is BATS? Is it like a hotel bar or something?"

"It's a restaurant and nightclub, the best in town, at the best hotel in town, the Shangri-La. BATS actually stands for Bar At The Shangri-La. Fantastic food, heaving with expats and rich Indonesian kids, great live band from America, pretty hostesses who remember your name and your exact order and tab without writing it down, barmen who set fire to bottles and juggle them like Tom Cruise wished he could in 'Cocktail' and wall-to-wall beautiful girls. They make you feel like a big-shot, which is why people love it. But bloody expensive".

"Why don't you come along with us tonight, and see what you think?" suggested Rob. "It's not far, and if the traffic is okay, we'll be there in twenty minutes".

"I don't know", hesitated Calamity, "I'm a bit worried by the 'bloody expensive' bit. I'm not an oil tycoon like you guys, you know; the Metropolitan Police won't pick up a huge tab for me. Besides, I have an important day tomorrow".

"We're not going to be late", said Robert. "Just dinner and a bit of music. See what pans out. I tell you what, though, I'm in the chair tonight. Have dinner with us and I'll put you down as a company man on expenses. Meal and a bottle of wine on me; you're on your own for other drinks. You can split any time if you get lucky. At any rate, see what it's all about, and then you'll know where to go if you want to come back next time".

— o —

Calamity signed his bill and left his shorts and sandals in the hotel plastic bag with the concierge, then walked outside the lobby with Rob and Robert, expecting them to beckon to a Silver Bird, but Robert spoke in Indonesian to a uniformed man behind a desk that said 'Car Call' on it, and Rob lit a cigarette. Presently a Toyota Fortuner pulled up, and Rob stubbed his cigarette into a sand tray and they all got in the back of the big sport utility vehicle.

"Yanto, how's it hanging?" said Robert to the driver, as he climbed in. "You had your dinner yet?"

"Yes, Mr Robert", smiled the driver. "Pak. Sunardi is standing by with Mr Rob's car; you are not bringing the other car tonight?"

"No, Yanto, Sunardi can go home now. I'll call him", said Rob, picking his cell phone out of his pocket.

"To Shangri-La, Yanto, and don't spare the horses!" said Robert to the grinning driver, "And pump up the volume a bit. We want to get in the mood", and the big car purred effortlessly onto the highway with its sound system filling the world with the thumping beat of D-Note's 'Shed My Skin', and Calamity already felt like a big shot.

— o —

They pulled up at the dazzling lobby of the Shangri-La, and two uniformed doormen swooped over and opened the car doors as though they were greeting old friends, while a row of pretty, smiling girls in immaculate white uniforms stood by on the lobby doors, ready to open whichever one of them Calamity and his friends decided to go through. Calamity had never seen such a magnificent hotel, and his amazement that they would employ a whole troupe of people solely to open the doors was only surpassed when he noticed the immense crystal chandeliers, dozens of smiling staff in attendance and carved stone artwork everywhere.

"Welcome back, Mr Robert!" said half a dozen people, and as they descended the marble staircase towards the sound of music, Calamity realised that Yanto and the Fortuner had glided off without being told where to go or what time to come back.

"He'll hang out with the other drivers in the drivers' room, watching TV and drinking coffee and playing chess", explained Robert. "You just ask the car call desk out the front, when you're done, and they call him by name. Every office and hotel and mall has a car call here in Jakarta".

Robert led them past a queue of people waiting to pay to get in at an oversized door that said 'BATS', and a large security man recognised him and escorted them down a flight of up-lit stairs into a complex of rough brick walls and exposed joists and haphazard electrical cabling and pipe work. At the centre was a square, ridiculously well-stocked bar with bar stools along all four sides, and in front were an empty dance floor and a stage full of instruments and speakers. Along the far side was a segregated restaurant area that allowed a full view of the stage, and the room seemed to be populated with as many hosts and hostesses in yellow shirts and black trousers making everyone welcome as there were guests.

"It's done out in a theme of a kind of New York club set up in a semi-derelict warehouse", explained Rob. "No expense has been spared in giving the impression that every expense has been spared, and it's all deliberate. The exposed steel joists and the half finished brickwork and the haphazard cabling – it's all fake. The wires hanging down and the pipes everywhere are not real. You can come here a hundred times and notice something new every time. I love this place. You see that grubby roof?" He pointed up to a grimy translucent ceiling several stories up, held up by gigantic, bronze art-deco muscle-men figures, through which the dusk seemed to be dimly glowing. "It's not real. Remember, it's dark outside, and anyway there are thirty five stories of hotel right above it".

They ordered lobster tails and creamed spinach and the biggest pizza Calamity had ever seen, served on a steel sheet with a bricklayer's trowel for dishing out the slices, and the wine flowed, and the place was becoming busier. The background singer thanked the clientele for their support, to a round of half-hearted applause, and Calamity noticed out loud that every time he caught an Indonesian female customer's eye, she would smile sweetly, whereas the Western female customers would pointedly never catch his eye at all.

"They start to ramp it up a bit now", said Robert. "The main band will be on soon. They play four forty-minute sets, and each one is a bit more up-beat than the last. In between the sets, the DJ takes over. You won't be able to hear yourself speak before long".

Calamity asked for a round of drinks to go on his bill, having decided that it was the least he could do to repay such splendid hospitality, but he knew it would set him back as much as a whole night out at home. Before the drinks came they stood up and moved to an empty table by the dance floor on which was a card reading *Reserved for Mr Robert*, and as if reading his mind, Rob explained that the hostess would never lose track of him or lose his bill.

"The secret to this place is always to tip everybody", said Robert. "The rest-room guy will sense you coming, and open the door for you. He'll turn on the tap for you when you wash your hands, and hand you clean towels when you are finished. You never need to touch a thing. Give him a dollar or two and he'll remember you for life and greet you by name next time. The security guys and the hostesses too; they'll all remember your name next time. It impresses your friends no end".

— o —

Calamity was a lot more relaxed about the size of his forthcoming bill after his seventh after-dinner drink, especially since Rob had told him his receipt would simply say 'BATS – Dinner' on it, and as the band opened their second set with Van Halen's 'Jump' and the crowd went berserk, Rob and Robert dived onto the dance floor with four of the girls who had been mightily impressed with their carefree spending, and Calamity decided to stay put with the other three and cultivate his big-shot appearance. Their yellow-shirted hostess named Dewi appeared, and Calamity threw caution to the wind and ordered 'a bottle of your finest champagne and four glasses', and the girls huddled closer to him and two of them put their arms on his shoulders, and Calamity thought if he didn't get laid after that, there was no hope for him. When Dewi appeared moments later with a bottle of Dom Perignon and Calamity had downed the first glass in one go, one of the girls announced she was 'not that keen on champagne' and could she please have a Cosmopolitan, and the other two girls said 'ooh yes, let's all have Cosmo's', and Dewi disappeared again to fetch three Cosmopolitans and a Staten Island Punch, which Calamity felt sounded a little more macho than a Cosmopolitan since it was made of around five different spirits with a dash of fruit juice.

By the time the band started their fourth and final set, BATS was so full you could hardly move, and Calamity had completely lost track of Rob and Robert, whom he hadn't seen since the time they had ordered another bottle of Dom Perignon and Rob had been dragged onto the stage so everyone could sing 'happy birthday' to him. The girls around Calamity seemed to have multiplied now, and the shouted conversation had taken a lewd turn and kept going back to discussions of threesomes and foursomes and how many girls would fit into a Shangri-La bath, which were pretty big by all accounts. Calamity was having trouble following what was going on, and the girls would suddenly laugh out loud at him whenever he struggled to articulate whatever it was he was trying to say through his increasingly fuzzy consciousness. And then it was late and there were the two big security guards with his arms round each of their shoulders, who flawlessly maintained an air of respect and dignity despite the fact that they were assisting him drunkenly up the stairs with around a dozen girls following, and the sofa in the lobby while the girls solemnly arranged things and the security guards checked he was all right, and then they were all helping him to the lift to go to one of their rooms, and Calamity felt sure it would all turn out okay in the end.

The security guards helped Calamity to sit down on one of the armchairs, and as soon as they were gone, the four remaining girls attacked the mini-bar with such ferocity that within minutes a call was necessary to room service to bring ample supplies of spirit miniatures, wine, beer, snacks and orange juice. They started to pull off Calamity's clothes, and when the general consensus seemed to be that they would all take a bath together, Calamity didn't resist and hoped above hope he wouldn't fall asleep and miss his lifelong fantasy come true. The trouble was, Calamity was not very mobile by that time, and was doubtful he could make it to the bathroom without falling and splitting his head open. One of the girls appeared from the bathroom wearing a hotel bathrobe, and sat down on Calamity's lap as he slumped on the bed now, as helpless as a rag doll, then pulled open the robe and thrust her bare breasts in front of his face while they all shrieked with laughter and took photographs with their mobile phones, and pretty soon there seemed to be a competition to see who could be uploaded onto Facebook doing the most outrageous thing to Calamity. Calamity was vaguely aware someone was inserting a tongue into his ear, and he was on a huge bed with four of the most stunning, laughing, frolicking naked girls he had ever imagined and things were not stirring within him that should have been, under the circumstances, and suddenly it all ended and he had to stop that bloody noise in the dark that pierced his soul. The noise stopped and started again, and Calamity groggily realised it was the bedside telephone.

— o —

"Mr Jane, this is the front desk, Sir. Will you be staying with us tonight?" asked the voice.

Calamity was confused; it seemed a stupid question, as he had an itinerary showing a confirmed booking for seven nights, which he could cut short if necessary. Oh man, he thought, I feel like death. What the hell happened? Alcohol is what happened, he remembered, lots and lots of alcohol, and a very late night on top of jet lag. Thinking caused his brain to hurt, so he tried to do it quietly.

"Erm... er, yes. Of course. What time is it?"

"It is five minutes past six, Sir. Thank you for staying with us. Would you like Housekeeping to come and service your room?"

"What? No. No, no, no ... I'm not ready. Why are you calling me at six o'clock?"

"I'm sorry, Sir. We needed to confirm your room".

Calamity put the phone down and decided he couldn't possibly get out of bed just yet. He could snooze for an hour and have plenty of time to get ready, and he tried to resign himself to the fact he would feel terrible all day and would have to put on a show for the Security Advisor at the embassy. It was pitch dark in the room apart from the glow of a digital clock, which said '6.08'. But Calamity couldn't get back to sleep due to the niggling questions in his head, such as 'how did I get back here in the early hours of the morning?', 'where did the girls go?' and 'have I still got my wallet?'.

That last question made Calamity sit upright with a start, and he fumbled for a light switch, knocking over a glass, and managed to find the table lamp.

The room looked like a bomb had gone off. There were empty and half full wine bottles everywhere, cigarette butts on the carpet, broken glass on the dressing table, and plates of dried food and Pringles tubs and crumbs and shrivelled, half eaten fruit on every surface. But the main puzzle was he didn't remember the girls coming back to his hotel, and besides, the room was peculiarly unfamiliar. It was larger than he remembered, and fitted with luxurious dark wood furniture that he hadn't noticed before. Calamity dragged himself out of bed and to the bathroom, which was not where it was supposed to have been, and which was strewn with wet towels and empty shower gel bottles and a discarded bra and was half submerged in water, and it dawned on him as he stared unblinking at the drunkard in the mirror that he was AT THE SHANGRI-LA and not at the Crowne Plaza at all, with no clean clothes or shaver or briefcase and he had to get himself back to the Crowne Plaza NOW.

He tugged at the curtains, which wouldn't open, and noticed it was almost light outside. He found the main light-switch and then located his wallet in his crumpled trousers, and his brief joy turned to horror as he realised that his American Express card was missing. Calamity pulled his clothes on in a panic and decided the only thing to do was to go downstairs and ask for the manager, and as he was preparing to rush out of the room, he noticed a small pile of cards and an envelope which had been pushed under the door.

One card said 'we were unable to make up your room, as your 'do not disturb' light was on. Please call Housekeeping if you would like your room serviced', another read 'we were unable to turn down your bed, as your 'do not disturb' light was on. Please call Housekeeping if you would like our turndown service'. Inside the envelope, Calamity found his American Express card with a note and a printed bill almost eighteen inches long. He almost cried with relief as he read the note: 'You left your credit card behind the bar in BATS as security last night. Please accept our apologies for requesting this, as we were not aware you are a residing guest of Shangri-La. Enclosed please find your bill, which we have charged to your room account. Please let us know if this is not what you require. Thank you, and have a pleasant stay'.

Holy crap, thought Calamity, as he unfolded the bill and stared uncomprehendingly at the cover sheet, which said 'BATS – Dinner - one hundred and eighteen million three hundred and seven thousand two hundred and nineteen Rupiah' and the attached itemised list of drinks and prices. The calculator on Calamity's cell phone told him that this came to around seven thousand seven hundred pounds, or nearly six weeks' salary, which Calamity could not possibly afford, but right now he had to shake off the feeling of still being intoxicated, and concentrate on getting himself moving and ready for his appointment. He would come back to BATS tonight if he hadn't died by then, and question whether there were really around twenty Cosmopolitans, thirty beers, five shots of tequila and five Staten Island Punches plus a host of things he had never even heard of, not to mention THREE bottles of 'Champagne Dom Per 2000', attributable to his account.

A quick call downstairs established that breakfast was included in his room rate, which was quoted to him in U.S. Dollars (eight hundred and twenty seven fifty plus service and tax, which caused Calamity's blood pressure and heart rate to hit new apices), and Calamity went down to eat the breakfast he had stupidly paid for and drink gallons of coffee before checking out and rushing back to the Crowne Plaza. When Calamity took his seat and asked for coffee and toast, the waitress had appeared slightly puzzled, and as he looked around, a couple of things about the scene seemed not quite right. For one thing, the breakfast room featured a vast, sumptuous buffet spread out with live cooking stations, with curries, soups, roasted meats, Peking duck, sushi and sashimi, oysters and lobsters, whole poached salmon, a steak-and-burger barbecue, cakes, pastries, a liquid chocolate fountain, Thai food, Chinese food, Indonesian food, in fact every kind of food except bacon and eggs and the other usual breakfast staples. Under normal circumstances, thought Calamity, he would happily stay here the rest of his life, but now the second thing dawned on him, which was that it was no lighter outside than it had been when he checked fifteen minutes ago, and actually seemed to be getting darker. Calamity beckoned to the waitress.

"Is this the right place for breakfast?"

"Yes it is, Sir. Breakfast is from six a.m. to ten a.m. on weekdays, and until ten thirty a.m. on Saturdays and Sundays".

"What time is it now?"

"It is six thirty five, Sir".

"In the morning, right?"

"Oh no, Sir, at night. Did you come from America? We quite often get new American guests who think it is morning in the night-time. It's half a day time difference when they come here, you see ...".

"It's night-time now?" asked Calamity, panic rising inside him for probably the fourth time that morning, which was actually that evening. "What day is it?"

"It's Thursday, Sir. Would you like more toast, or will you have your dinner now?"

Calamity sat for ten minutes, frantically trying to figure a way out of the mess he'd got himself into, and drew an absolute blank. He'd woken up in the wrong hotel, twelve hours after he had intended to wake up, looking and feeling like shit and with a bill the size of the defence budget which American Express would accept without question and then terminate his card when he was unable to pay it off in one go, having slept through his critical appointment with the Security Advisor. People in London and Jakarta would have been looking for him, and the embassy may even have sent someone to his hotel to see if he was all right. How the hell could he explain this away and salvage the situation; maybe even save his career? And now he had gone and stumbled his way into another ridiculously large bill for dinner. Calamity realised how hungry he was, and how all the urgency had gone away for a few hours, and decided he would be able to think better if he ate some of the glorious food he had unwittingly committed himself to paying for. This was not how Chuck Norris would have done things in 'Walker, Texas Ranger'.

— o —

Since it was still early evening, Calamity decided to go down to BATS and have it out with the manager there and then, in the hope of convincing him a large part of his bill was for drinks fraudulently added to his account by unrelated patrons. After that, he planned to confront the front desk about how he could have been tricked into taking a room against his will, and see if he could get out of staying a second night by accident. Early-evening BATS seemed to be in a different universe to that it had been in the previous night, with bright lighting and subdued background music and sparse pockets of customers enjoying after-work cocktails and chatting to the hostesses. Over in the restaurant area, every seat was taken with diners tucking into enormous steaks and racks of ribs. Calamity took a seat at the square bar, and Dewi appeared, smiling and friendly.

"Good evening, Mr Jane, how are you feeling tonight? We were a bit worried about you, you seemed very tired".

"I need to speak to the manager", said Calamity brusquely, and then added "Sorry. Yes, I was very tired, but I'm fine now. But I do need to speak to the manager".

"Certainly, I'll fetch him for you. I hope nothing's wrong – did you lose something?"

"I lost the best part of ten grand", Calamity replied. "People were charging drinks to my bill without my knowledge, and I need to sort it out".

"Oh no Sir, I was in charge of your account, and I never let that happen. I'll be happy to go through the bill with you".

Calamity pulled out the bill and said "Well, the first thing is the champagne. It is thirteen and a half million Rupiah a bottle – can that be right? That's around nine hundred quid – and I've been charged for three. You didn't think to warn me how much they cost? My friend Robert ordered one of them, and it should have gone on his bill".

"Mister Robert ordered one bottle, on his bill, Sir. You ordered three yourself, Sir. Sorry, Sir, but you asked me to bring the best champagne on three occasions. Our best champagne is Dom Perignon 2000. We have much better champagne in Rosso restaurant, Sir, but I thought you wanted the best we have in BATS. Sorry if that was wrong, Mr Jane".

"I did? I ordered three bottles of Dom Perignon? Okay, how about the thirty or so beers? I didn't drink any beer at all, and nor did my friends".

"Those were for guests on adjacent tables. You asked me to provide drinks for everyone nearby, if you recall, Sir".

"I did that?" Calamity was starting to get vague recollections of feeling like a huge shot in front of the girls.

"Yes, Sir. Several times, Sir". She studied the bill for a while, and said "This is all correct; I can remember every entry on the bill. Would you still like to speak to the manager, or is there something else I can help you with first?"

Calamity numbly gave it up as a lost cause with a groan, as his anxiety level hit yet another new peak. "No, thank you Dewi", he mumbled through involuntarily gritted teeth, "I guess I'll somehow have to sort it out".

Calamity was suddenly aware of a glass of what looked like fruit juice in front of him, and a fit-looking barman wearing a name badge that said 'Daaz' grinning at him.

"What's this?" he asked.

"Staten Island Punch, Mr Jane. You like them very much, yes?"

"No! No – please take it away. I didn't order this".

"It's on the house, Mr Jane, for our good customer. You like them very much. You told me I make them the best. My secret, I put a little extra Bacardi".

Calamity reluctantly tasted it, and it tasted good, in a highly inflammable sort of way.

"If you would like another, it's happy hour till eight o'clock. We give you a ticket with each drink you buy, which you can change for the same drink later tonight. But not for whole bottles".

Forget it, thought Calamity, I'm in enough trouble, as he almost didn't notice an Italian accent behind him which said "Mr Jane?"

Calamity turned, and saw a suave, dark haired man in a good suit bowing deferentially to him.

"I am Marco, Mr Jane, and I am the manager of BATS. I understand there was a mix-up with your order last night. I apologise you. We did not serve you the best champagne, as you are requesting. If you would care to accept this bottle of champagne to keep, courtesy of Shangri-La, I will make sure we offer you the choice from our cellar next time. We have Krug 1988 at Rosso, for instance, a very nice wine which is priced at around forty two million Rupiah", and with that he presented Calamity with a bottle of Dom Perignon 2000 and left.

Calamity was thanking his lucky stars that Dewi had not fetched the Krug last night, and was uncomfortably realising he was gradually starting to be surrounded with drinks again, although so far it had not cost him anything, when he felt a hand on his shoulder, and a tall leggy girl in a black dress who looked like she could be a model, and who Calamity vaguely recognised, sat down next to him.

"Here you are", she said lazily. "Again. I was worried about you. You were completely out of it last night, you know. They told me you are staying again, so I called your room. I guessed I would find you here".

She had the kind of face that made Calamity want to stare at it for hours, with stunning almond eyes and honey complexion.

"I'm not staying", said Calamity. "I missed my appointments today and I need to get back to my hotel. My other hotel". This girl had Calamity at a disadvantage, since he had no idea of her name, and it occurred to him this was the first time in his life he was talking to a woman he was fairly sure he had recently seen naked, but couldn't swear to it.

"You're not staying, even though you will pay for a room tonight?" she quizzed. "Why?"

"I have no clothes or other stuff here, and I only took the room again tonight because I was late waking up. I couldn't get out of it by the time I realised. Were you with me when I checked in? How come you could book me into a hotel against my wishes, and the hotel agreed to it?"

"You were in no state to go anywhere, baby, and the hotel was worried. It's the holy month of Ramadan, you know, and people cannot be drunk in public. It would offend everybody and get you into terrible trouble. Alcohol is only allowed at international hotels at this time, and if you were seen outside in a bad state, the hotel would be blamed. Anyway, you wanted to stay; you insisted, and signed the form. We helped you so you would not get into trouble".

"What time was all this?"

"About two o'clock this morning. When we got to the room, you wanted to party. My friends like to party, and we stayed until five. But after you fell asleep, no-one could wake you and it wasn't a party any more. We all slept in your bed for half an hour, but when you went pee-pee on top of the bed we went home".

This could not possibly get any worse, Calamity thought. He had to get home to the Plaza and sleep it off, and maybe it would all turn out to be a bad dream.

"I'm in trouble; so much trouble. I had an important meeting today, and I slept through it. I should have reported to London afterwards. It's still lunch time there now, and they know I've gone missing. I'm sure the embassy has told them I'm not responding at my hotel. They're probably checking with the Police and hospitals. I cannot think of a single excuse or lie that could get me out of it".

"So just tell them you were in an accident. A car accident, in a taxi. You're not badly hurt, but they wanted to keep you in overnight, for observation. I have a friend who is in charge of administration at Pondok Senang hospital; she can make you a receipt, with your name and medicines and everything. Say you had mild concussion or something. Even if your embassy checks it out, it will all be confirmed. They are foreigners; they know nothing".

"You could swing something like that? Get a fake receipt from a proper hospital when I was never even there?"

"Sure, they do it all the time. Half the claims the insurance companies get from expats are fake, because their girlfriends know someone who works at some hospital or other. It never fails. The best thing is, you could blame your company for allowing you to get taxis in a dangerous place like Jakarta, and make them reimburse the bill".

So she doesn't know I'm a Policeman, thought Calamity, which is a very good thing. And this could get me out of whole lot of trouble. It could even offset some of my expenses.

"So why don't you stay here tonight, since you've already agreed to pay and it's such a nice hotel, isn't it, and I'll call my friend and ask her to bring a bill here, tonight". She laid her hand on Calamity's forearm. "I can keep you company while we wait. How much would you like the bill for? Twenty million? Thirty?"

"This all seems so ... dishonest. It's not the money, but it could save my career. How much would I have to pay?"

"You do not have to pay for a favour from a friend in Indonesia. But you should buy her dinner. Here. She would love that". She nodded at the Dom Perignon. "And give her a glass of champagne. But don't try to party with her – she's a little ... conservative. Nice girl".

— o —

Rosette doesn't sound like an Indonesian name, thought Calamity, but some people here do have Western names. Calamity was sitting in the restaurant area of BATS with Rosette, grilling her on what they had all been doing in Calamity's room until five o'clock in the morning.

Rosette and her friends didn't seem at all like the typical Indonesian girls Rob and Robert had described, and seemed completely uninhibited by nudity and sex. Conservatism is all for show, said Rosette; for appearances. In truth, she said, most Indonesian girls dig other girls as much as guys, but usually don't admit to either, or act on it. The time in Calamity's room would have been all about good clean fun with plenty of sex thrown in, until Calamity's rapid onset of unconsciousness put paid to that. Calamity couldn't believe how stupid he was.

"You're a bit of a star on Facebook", said Rosette. "I'll write down my friend's name for you. Already, other expats here are trying to find out who you are".

"I wish I had a bit more of a happy memory about it", said Calamity glumly. "It's not every day something like that happens. Not to me, anyway".

"Poor baby. You never did judge which one of us had the best breasts", said Rosette. "We had a bet on it, remember? The winner gets coffee and cake. You can make judgement now", and she held up her cell phone, which showed a photograph of Calamity standing unsteadily in front of a mirror, wearing just boxer shorts and grinning like a loon with eyes like piss-holes in the snow, surrounded by four posing girls wearing nothing but panties of various colours and sizes. Rosette was holding her cell phone up to the mirror in the photograph. She was amused to notice the immediate effect the photograph had on Calamity as he had to discreetly adjust his posture slightly, and had just made the hairs on the back of his neck stand up, chuckling almost inaudibly, by stroking his calf with her stockinged shin under the table, when another girl joined them and sat down.

— o —

The receipt was perfect in almost every way. It was the real thing, and showed ambulance charges, specialist consultations, emergency room and observation room time, an MRI scan, various doctors' time and some medications that Rosette's friend explained were mild sedatives. It was ninety-five million Rupiah's worth of convincing proof of being taken out of circulation without warning, and being unable to make contact with colleagues. The problem was, there seemed to be a misunderstanding about the timing and duration of the hospital stay to which it related. The receipt was for two nights, not one, which would mean Calamity could not attend his planned meeting with POLRI tomorrow, which was Friday, since he would still be 'in hospital' and the earliest he could be 'discharged from hospital' would be Saturday morning. The receipt was post-dated to Saturday, two days from now. So having arrived on Wednesday afternoon, the earliest day Calamity could actually have a meeting and start doing some work would be the following Monday.

"You can't rush recovery after an accident of this type", said Rosette, "You need to follow the doctor's advice. I suggest you use this to your advantage. Take the day off tomorrow to recover from your jet lag and get the booze completely out of your system. Don't contact anyone until Saturday, or you might end up getting visitors looking for you in the hospital. I'll try to arrange you a late check-out tomorrow at five p.m., after your office is closed; stay here and relax until then, go to the gym and the pool, go to your other hotel when you feel like it. Spend the weekend in the sun".

"What will you do?" asked Calamity, noticing she hadn't included herself in the plan.

"I have to work tomorrow. I could meet up with you afterwards, if you like".

"And tonight? Any plans?"

"I have a date with my girls, and in case you hadn't noticed, I'm already dressed to break hearts".

"Can't you stay and break my heart instead?"

"Are you kidding? Have you seen yourself? You look like you just spent a month in the jungle, and smell like it, too. You could use a shower, you know. I shouldn't be seen with you in public, wild man". Seeing Calamity's disappointed and slightly hurt expression, she went on: "Clean yourself up. Send your clothes to the laundry, ask for three hour service. Stay in your room in your robe and watch television, or sleep. I will be back here in BATS at midnight. If you are here when I arrive, and if you look and smell good, maybe I will stay with you".

— o —

Rosette arrived in BATS with two of the girlfriends from the previous night at five minutes to one, by which time Calamity had used the seven happy hour tickets given to him and Rosette and her friend earlier, having previously finished the champagne in his room, which he was amazed to find was now spotlessly clean and tidy, and he was pretty tipsy once again. Rosette walked directly to him and simply said 'Come', and with her two friends took him to the lift and up to his room, and Rosette wordlessly ran the bath while the others took out vodka and tequila and weed from their bags and began to undress, no shrieks of laughter or uploading to Facebook this time, and Rosette lay face-down on the bed and commanded Calamity to kneel on the floor beside her and undress her himself, making him slow down while the others looked on, purring out loud as he groaned with lust, and then they all calmly and unhurriedly bathed each other in the huge tub while Calamity imagined he was in love with them all, and by four o'clock in the morning they were all glowing inside and satisfied, and shit-faced again.

— o —

Special Commander Bryant had been able to pull strings with Tarzan, and even Commander Unwin had had to agree that the relationship-building shopping trip to Singapore had paid dividends. The Detective Inspector in cowboy boots, big fraud that he was, had arrived in Jakarta two days ago and checked into his hotel and hadn't been heard of since, having failed to show up at the embassy for his meeting with the Security Advisor yesterday, and Commander Unwin had decided that the urgency was too great to sit around and hope he reappeared in due course. The trouble was, it was Friday morning in London and there was an email from the Security Advisor waiting for Commander Unwin when he arrived, which said that an embassy representative had gone to the Crowne Plaza to check on Inspector Jane's well-being at one o'clock lunchtime Jakarta time, and had found him drinking beer by the pool and slurring something about hospitals and an accident. Firstly it seemed clear that Calamity's unexplained absence was a case of him going off the rails, which the Security Advisor had said was not exactly unheard of in Jakarta, and secondly, to get the visa requirements for a replacement officer processed would take until Monday or Tuesday next week, which would get him to Jakarta by Wednesday or Thursday at the earliest, meaning at least a whole week would have been wasted. Special Commander Bryant had taken it upon himself to personally contact his friend Tarzan to see if there was any way round the problem, and Tarzan had assured him he would be able and willing to by-pass normal protocol and allow a replacement officer to enter Indonesia on a visa-on-arrival and do business with POLRI and British Embassy officials without the need for a formal business visa, provided Special Commander Bryant came along as well, since Special Commander Bryant already had previous credentials with POLRI, so a special dispensation could be made without the need for further shopping in Singapore.

It was most fortuitous and fortunate for Special Commander Bryant that his clout with POLRI had been demonstrated to Commander Unwin, and tickets had been accordingly obtained for Special Commander Bryant and Detective Sergeant Robbins to leave for Jakarta very early the following morning, prior to an email arriving from Tarzan which confirmed Calamity Jane's departure from the rails. Calamity Jane had appeared unannounced at Tarzan's office, five hours late at three o'clock on the Friday afternoon, which was eight o'clock in the morning in London, unsteady on his feet, slurring his words and smelling strongly of beer. This had deeply offended the entire Police station workforce, who were fasting for Ramadan and doing their best to be pure in thought, word and deed and resisting temptation and strong emotions of all descriptions in pursuit of their religious duties, and the appearance of a drunk foreigner mumbling about discharging himself early from hospital being a mistake had caused them to feel anger and contempt, and therefore to fail in their virtuous efforts for that day. Not least of the damning factors was that Friday is the holy day in the Muslim week, and the entire staff had been to the mosque for prayers and soul-cleansing just before Calamity showed up. Tarzan said that Inspector Jane was now persona non grata and would not be communicated with by POLRI under any circumstances, and he would probably be rounded up and put on a plane with his visa revoked before the day was out.

Meanwhile, a semi-comprehensible email had arrived from Calamity Jane himself, notifying his office that he had been in a car accident on Thursday morning and had been admitted to Pondok Senang hospital for observation, but had discharged himself early, and was not feeling well and was about to re-admit himself forthwith. Further, he was checking out of the Crowne Plaza and would be moving to another hotel, to be closer to his medical advisors, and he hoped the difference in hotel room-rates would be acceptable 'under the circstumstnaces'.

Commander Unwin recognised an out-of-control binge when he saw one, and was glad that Special Commander Bryant had managed to preempt a solution. Jane had obviously been spooked by the visit from the embassy representative, and had gone into damage limitation mode that had made the situation for him much worse, and was now clinging to reality by his finger tips.

Calamity had a strategy, which was to wait out the huge problem he had created until the weekend was over, after which he planned to come back into daily activity as though nothing had happened, and hope everything would turn out alright in the end. Never explain or apologise, someone had once told him. Sometimes burying one's head in the sand was the winning formula, and now he felt a tingle of delicious powerlessness and the masochistic danger of risking everything he had ever worked for, in the hope of a few more moments of time like last night with Rosette and Wiwid and Gita, and however much his American Express bill would soon ruin his medium-term living standard, the drinks told him it would be utterly worth it. Far from looking bleak, Calamity's future counter-intuitively seemed very bright indeed. Rosette and Wiwid and Gita thought he was a big shot with the embassy, which in a way he was, and now he had moved to a classy and expensive place called the Shangri-La on a carefully calculated whim that he knew in his heart was a huge mistake but right now didn't care, which would impress them, and he had texted Rosette to tell her the news. Calamity was starting to be tempted to stay in Jakarta and run his American Express card into oblivion and set himself up as some sort of expatriate security consultant. He might get two, possibly three weeks of utopia before American Express smelled a rat and pulled the plug. By Sunday night, Calamity's life would never be the same again, and not in a good way.

Calamity Jane had not had any response to his texts or missed calls to Rosette, and had spent the whole of Friday night in BATS avoiding conversations with bar girls in the hope that she would appear. By ten p.m., Calamity had resolved to play it cool and not think about Rosette any more, as a result of which he was unable to think of anyone or anything other than Rosette for the entire night. Calamity was alarmed to conclude this was evidence that he was in the process of falling in love, and like most men who fall in love with beautiful, wild, free-spirited women that have every man at their feet, he knew this would end in tears of hopelessness. Unwelcome clichés involving moths and flames began to haunt him, and Calamity eventually staggered to bed that night without seeing or hearing from Rosette at all.

On Saturday morning he was woken, bleary-eyed and hung over once again, by someone tapping on his door, and saw through the peep-hole it was Rosette, looking around as though she didn't want to be observed in the corridor outside his room. When he opened the door expectantly, his heart and a quick swig of mint mouthwash in his mouth, she busted him full-force in the face with her clenched fist before barging her way into his room, knocking him to the floor.

"You're a fucking *Policeman*?" she hissed. "You're a fucking Policeman and you're getting thrown out of the country? What kind of bullshit is that? My friend got fired from her job. They went checking up on you after you showed them the receipt, and she got fired. The receipt was dated on a day in the future, remember? You showed POLRI a receipt from a day that hadn't come yet! What the hell were you thinking? Fuck you, you loser", and with that she spat at his face and stomped out, pausing at the door to add "And they know you're here, or they will when I tell them. Lessons learned: it's not a good idea to fuck with me, or to be drunk in a Police office during Ramadan. I hope they kick your balls into porridge, as a favour to me. Goodbye, jerk".

Calamity lay on the floor nursing his bleeding eye, waiting for the turn of events to sink in, and in his grotesquely distorted version of normality, realised that his cringing at the feet of this mini-skirted goddess as she towered over him, making no effort to prevent him looking up her skirt and savagely ripping into and abusing him had been a weirdly erotic experience that would stay with him in his private moments forever, which was ironic as it would make the actuality of permanently losing Rosette's affections and life as he knew it more painful by an order of magnitude. Calamity transitioned into the most dangerous and self-destructive phase of his descent into nonbeing, that of fretful self-pity and total loss of self-esteem, and decided against planning his day since nothing seemed worth doing, and instead opened the mini-bar without standing up and looked for the most expensive alternative to reality.

— o —

On Sunday afternoon he was woken, bleary-eyed and hung over once again, by someone tapping on his door, and decided against looking through the peep-hole, since if it wasn't Rosette he probably wouldn't be able to muster the energy to open it. He had spent all Saturday in his darkened room sending increasingly pathetic, pleading mobile phone texts to Rosette, until he finally received the last communication he would ever get from her, a text message which said 'Fuck off and die'. A brief excursion into BATS had proved devoid of thrilling fun, and ended with him failing to consummate a business transaction in his room with a girl who had not even a tenth of the intellect or class of Rosette, which cost him sixty pounds' worth of Rupiah anyway, and he had ended the night drowning his sorrows with HBO and the willing help of Room Service.

"Can I come in?"

It took a good ten seconds for Calamity to place Special Commander Bryant into the jigsaw of what his world had become. Special Commander Bryant came in and declined Calamity's offer of a seat.

"What are you doing here?" was all Calamity could think of.

"Well, it's pretty obvious what *you* are doing here. The Crowne Plaza told me where to find you. Good grief, man, look at the state of you. What on earth has happened to make you be like this? It stinks in here. Let some light in, for heaven's sake. It's three o'clock in the afternoon", and Special Commander Bryant began to tug at the curtains, until Calamity pressed the button to make them open electrically. Calamity caught sight of himself in the mirror, and was shocked. He had three days of beard growth and dirty, unkempt hair, dried blood on his cheek and a purple, swollen right eye. He looked like a homeless beggar.

"I was in an accident..." he began, until Special Commander Bryant shook his head.

"No, you were not. I know all about the fraudulent hospital bill. I know about you being caught drinking beer at the time you were supposed to be at POLRI, and later turning up at POLRI in a state of ... well, in some kind of state. They don't have a doctor's opinion that you were drunk, but claim that in their non-medical opinion you exhibited all the signs of drunkenness. It was all I could do to stop them throwing you in jail, or at least out of the country, and causing a diplomatic incident. This has gone all the way up to the Commissioner. So I ask again, what happened? Was it over a woman? It's quite common in Jakarta, you know, especially with older, married men. They go bananas when they're suddenly the focus of attention from lots of pretty girls. Lose everything in a lot of cases – the job, the marriage, the house, the kids. You're not married, are you? I'm hoping Mrs Bryant doesn't hear the stories, as she's not the most trusting of people. I was quite a catch in my day, you know".

Calamity was numb.

"I really don't know", he whispered. "I don't know where it all went wrong. I was all prepared, had dinner with some new friends, got talking to some nice girls, and next thing I know I'm in debt up to my eyeballs and waking up in bed with three girls at a time and I can't stop myself. They spiked my drink, that's what must have happened". Calamity's utopia was rapidly morphing into an embarrassingly silly but severely damaging vagary.

"Every day, for five days? Get real, man".

Calamity thought for a while, and said "Special Commander, I know we have things to sort out, but can we do this later? I really need to sleep. I really am ill, you know". Calamity was turning green.

Special Commander Bryant took an envelope from his jacket pocket and opened it, and took a sheet of paper from it.

"I've said all I came to say. I don't really need answers, since they would make no difference. I'm just trying to sound a bit concerned and paternal, for the sake of the conversation, whereas in fact I think you only have yourself to blame and you probably deserve all you've got coming to you. Anyhow, I have to formally read you this communiqué, and then we're done.

"Callum Royston Jane, you are ...' - wait a minute, is that your real name? Callum Jane? No wonder they call you Calamity Jane; was your mother a fan of John Wayne or something? Ha! Fancy that! Were you born in Royston, or conceived there perhaps? But I digress.

"Callum Royston Jane, you are hereby suspended from all duties and responsibilities under your commission with the Metropolitan Police Service. You are to refrain from representing yourself as a serving Police officer until further notice, and any attempt to do so will be an offence under the applicable statutes. Charges of gross misconduct have been laid against you, which will be set out under separate cover, and you will be required to attend a disciplinary hearing at a time and place to be advised in due course, at which you will be entitled to legal representation, to account for your actions. Sanctions up to and including dismissal from the Service, without the right of appeal, may be applied by the disciplinary panel.

"Well, that's it, in a nutshell. Officially, it's a process, but in my opinion you can consider yourself fired. I've never fired anybody before today. I thought it would be a lot more exciting, pointing at people and saying 'you're fired!' like Donald Trump. It's up to you, of course, but in your position I would think seriously about resigning before it comes to an official sacking. The Commissioner has had nothing but heartache from our venture into Indonesia, despite my best efforts to build fences and mend bridges, and he's not happy with you, let me tell you. Use your ticket to get yourself on the first plane home. The Met will only be responsible for valid expense claims up to this afternoon, and by valid expense claims I don't mean the cost of setting yourself up in this hotel. Who do you imagine you are, some sort of rock star? Let me tell you something – when these girls you wake up with discover you are a salaried Policeman and not Jon Van Jovi or someone, they will drop you like a hot tomato. This is not real life. I wish you the best of luck in the future".

The last piece of self-destruction Calamity Jane achieved in Jakarta was to upgrade his ticket to Club Class with the help of American Express, so they could refuse to serve him drinks all the way to London in a better seat, and he and his Shangri-La receipt for more than four months' salary went home to think about career changes and salvaging his credit rating.

Chapter 13 - The Altogether Unexpected End Of North Korea

Special Commander Bryant had not been best pleased to find out that the Metropolitan Police's policy on business travel decreed that when two or more differently ranked officers with differing travel class entitlements travel, they all travel together according to the entitlement of the senior officer, however the excellent news that had arrived the day before he left on his return trip to Jakarta gave him something important to think about for most of the journey. Special Commander Bryant's rank entitled him to fly business class on journeys of over five hours airborne duration, while Detective Sergeant Robbins' rank would normally fly economy on all flights, but they had been accordingly seated together in British Airways Club Class. Detective Sergeant Robbins had never flown business class before, and Special Commander Bryant hadn't forgotten that he held a grudge against Robbins, but for now he had better things to think about, so they travelled in relative silence.

Special Commander Bryant's excellent news was that he had got a publishing deal of sorts, although it was a little more complicated than that, and now he needed a good pseudonym so that it would already be well known when *The Many Few* finally hit the bookshelves, probably a year or two from now. Special Commander Bryant had tried his hand at science fiction, since he knew quite a lot about the space/time continuum and generally agreed with Einstein when it came to matters of general and special relativity, and had submitted a short story to a literary agent whom he had selected at random from researching potential publishing houses' followers on Twitter. The literary agent had written back after some three months, saying that (1) Special Commander Bryant's story was the best science fiction idea she had ever come across, feeling it was 'an hilarious and powerful satirical commentary on the aggression and war-like tendencies of the human race', which was only hampered by the fact that (2) it was the worst composition of a story she had ever come across, describing it as being at once unputdownable *and* unreadable, which presented something of a dilemma. The literary agent had at first been keen to steal the idea and rewrite it herself, but any attempt to change the storyline to hide the fact that it was based on Special Commander Bryant's idea would have destroyed the very heart of the story that was so attractive. The literary agent had sought the opinion of one of her clients, an up-and-coming giant of the humorous science fiction world who fancied himself as another Douglas Adams, who had proposed that he re-write the story as a full length novel under his own name, giving credit to Special Commander Bryant as co-author and thirty percent of all author's royalties, and this was the opening that Special Commander Bryant needed. Special Commander Bryant had impressed himself by writing something described as 'an hilarious and powerful satirical commentary', especially since he had only meant to write an entertaining story with no commentary intended at all.

Special Commander Bryant's short story idea had been like this:

* On an Earth-like planet orbiting a Sun-like star in the Milky Way galaxy, twenty three light years from the Earth, lived a human-

like life form almost a million years more technologically advanced than Earth people.

* The planet (called Keeg, in the nearest approximation to Earthsounds) was suffering an ongoing energy crisis, and the inhabitants had researched nearby planets for sources of the rare minerals needed to catalyse reactions in their anti-matter generators. The Earth's oceans were found to contain unlimited amounts of such minerals, and plans were put into place to travel to Earth and set up factories to extract the minerals and produce anti-hydrogen in situ, in quantities that could be transported back to Keeg. Fifteen hundred Earth kilograms of liquefied anti-hydrogen would be sufficient to power the entire planet for five hundred Earth years, and would take around five Earth years to produce. The return journey of twenty three light years, a vast distance but practically on the doorstep in space terms, would take around six hundred and sixteen thousand Earth years to travel using the most advanced chemical rockets available on Earth, but could be achieved by the Keegians in only three and a half Earth days using technology that Special Commander Bryant brilliantly explained, which was credible to any sci-fi buff with only a moderate level of suspension of disbelief.

* The problem was, Earth was inhabited by tribes of primitive humanoids who were violently protective of their own little pockets of the planet, thinking little of killing each other over nothing more than abstract political or religious ideas, and who were inherently hostile to anyone not looking and sounding

exactly like themselves, or who supported the wrong football team. These primitive humanoids appeared to believe they were the ultimate life form on the only planet in the universe that supported life at all, and were thus content to be constantly focussed on warring amongst themselves. The humanoids would need to be neutralised and then brought into service.

- Five Earth minutes before the launch of an invasion against Earth, just before the point of no return, the Keegians detected and witnessed a nuclear weapon test performed in North Korea, which changed everything, and the launch was postponed to re-evaluate. Earth was known to have nuclear power of the most primitive and inefficient fission type, but until then it had been assumed that Earth did not have the technology to weaponise nuclear power for destructive purposes, since so much effort was being expended on developing less effective weapons. The Keegians' swarms of robotic fighting units, each about the size of a domestic cat, were constructed of metallic polymer hybrid materials with enhanced strong-force atomic bonds that were impervious to the kinetic energies encountered from conventional weapons, meaning explosions and bullets and fire simply didn't affect the materials at all, but intense gamma radiation was the Achilles heel, and even the stupid inhabitants of Earth might try to nuke the fighting units to see if that would help. A new plan was needed.

- Six Earth months later the invasion resumed, and this time it was centred on North Korea instead of the previously assumed command point of the Earth (Canada). The plan was to maximise the element of surprise and employ shock-and-awe tactics to quickly overwhelm the leadership of the Earth, and then to not bother with building them any pyramids to keep them guessing before departure this time around, since the humanoids seemed to have improved their historical record-keeping since the last visit by the Keegian's ancestors. Keegian logic determined, wrongly as it turned out, that no sane tribe of primitive humanoids would wage war against other tribes with conventional weapons when it had nuclear weapons available to it, and therefore North Korea must be unique in its nuclear capability, and three hundred thousand fighting units duly arrived in Pyongyang and immediately went to work to deactivate the nuclear weapons facilities and then enslave the humanoid population of the most advanced pocket of civilisation on Earth, namely North Korea, to work in Keegian liquid anti-hydrogen factories. Each fighting unit was programmed with fluency in North Korean dialect and no other language, since it was fairly certain that all lesser pockets of civilisation throughout the rest of the planet would be fluent in the primary language.

- Once America, Russia and China had stopped laughing at the North Korean leadership's claims and started to take the alien invasion seriously, they took turns to nuke the hell out of North Korea, reducing it and all the Keegian fighting units in it to a smouldering wreck that would remain uninhabitable for tens of thousands of years. America would later admit to erring on the side of heavy-handedness, as it had identified an opportunity to kill two birds with one stone, and it was better to be safe than sorry. The Keegian command ship went home minus its robotic fighting units with its metaphorical tail between its legs, and Keeg never again launched an attack on Earth, or any other planet in the sector, and the resulting scarcity of anti-hydrogen caused the cost of living on Keeg to escalate to levels previously unknown on any planet, ironically resulting in suppression of the masses and dictatorship and local protectionism that pretty soon made the quality of life on Keeg resemble that previously enjoyed in North Korea, only with better television.

Special Commander Bryant was so excited about the developments connected with his story, which he had tentatively titled 'The Altogether Unexpected End of North Korea' in the absence of any better ideas for a title, but which title the literary agent had said was the best thing about the whole story, that he had to make a mental note not to forget about meeting the British Ambassador this time around. Firing Calamity Jane as soon as he arrived in Jakarta was therefore a welcome distraction from important literary issues, and brought Special Commander Bryant back down to Earth (from Keeg?) so he could concentrate on the job in hand.

The British Ambassador had been warm and friendly and polite and had avoided mentioning the previous failed attempt at a meeting, although Special Commander Bryant noticed that there were no invitations to afternoon tea this time, and after introductions and chats and a getting-to-know-you lunch with the senior staff, Detective Sergeant Robbins had gone off with the Security Advisor to pursue the security personnel angle while Special Commander Bryant had a meeting with the embassy's trade and industry guru, who would be able to facilitate a meeting with an ex-Hong Kong Police forensic accountant who might be able to unlock doors to help understand what happens to transferred funds when they arrive in Indonesia. Special Commander Bryant was secretly wishing he did not have to deal with complicated finance issues on his own, since a lot of these types of discussions seemed like double-Dutch to him, so it came as a welcome relief to Special Commander Bryant when the trade and industry guru suggested it would be politically expedient to include POLRI in any investigative work involving Indonesian banks, and Special Commander Bryant was able to point out the excellent relationships he already had with Grand Commissioner Tarzan and, on a lower level, Inspector Suparman, which the trade and industry guru thought was 'tip-top-tastic'.

— o —

Events moved very quickly for Special Commander Bryant and Detective Sergeant Robbins over the next forty eight hours.

The Security Advisor was himself involved in training the Indonesian elite forces in VIP protection and counter-terrorism operations, teaching urban surveillance and neutralisation of targets undetected, and was himself a good match to Special Agent In Charge Gajewski's profile of Pimpinan except for the fact that he was constantly under the spotlight of the embassy and his Army bosses. The Security Advisor pointed out that a number of British ex-Special Operations personnel had made their adopted homes in Indonesia, often providing informal security consulting services under cover of unrelated businesses that provided dodgy training to firms engaged by mining and oil and gas companies in remote areas such as Aceh, Maluku and Papua, where Western firms operate under conditions that could be hostile, and where life could be dangerous. Identifying and tracking down these wandering mercenary loners would be nigh-on impossible, since their activities were at best semi-legal and were usually covered by ghost companies set up (on paper) to source and export clothing, textiles, furniture and such like. The Security Advisor was unable to identify a photograph of Pimpinan, but stressed it was very unlikely he would be able to recognise anyone presently or previously in Indonesia for those purposes.

The ex-Hong Kong Police forensic accountant had made Special Commander Bryant's head spin with talk of correspondent banks, forex controls and interbank debenture waiver notes, and he was pretty sure he had heard the ex-Hong Kong Police forensic accountant mention 'currency hamster baskets', but the one thing Special Commander Bryant did learn was that the most effective way of sending regular, small payments from another country to an individual in Jakarta, without attracting much attention, was by using one of the money transfer firms such as Western Union and bypassing the high street banks completely. The recipient would typically walk in with a serial number and his identity card, fill in a form, and walk out with cash. Special Commander Bryant and Detective Sergeant Robbins went together to meet Tarzan, and after a lot of catching up of old friends culminating in a three hour lunch at the Sultan Hotel on Special Commander Bryant's expense account, the three of them set about forming a POLRI task force to collate and analyse all the incoming transfer information they could get hold of. By ten o'clock the following morning, Tarzan's office was full of boxes of A3 music-ruled printout paper which a dozen or so mainly female officers were scanning and crossing things out on and marking in highlighter pen, and Special Commander Bryant thought that this was living proof that life without computer screens was conceivable after all.

"What we are looking for", explained Tarzan, "is receipt of funds originating from the UK to the central office, of eight million Rupiah or less. That's about five hundred pounds, which is the maximum you mentioned. When we have listed these, we look for receipts to the same beneficiary one, two, three months before that, to come up with a list of regular payments. If we can identify the beneficiary and the office they collect it from, and we find the sender is the same each time, we can discuss which you want to follow up on".

"It seems very painstaking work, not to mention the mountains of paper", observed Detective Sergeant Robbins. "Wouldn't it be easier to just plug it into a database and run it all through that?"

"Believe me, this is the quickest way. The firms are happy to provide us this information on paper, but would not be happy to give us access to their computers, and we would need the court to make them do it. Besides, every computer system is different, and my officers would need training on each one. We're not very keen on databases in Indonesia, which is why we haven't got one. We don't trust them to tell the truth". Special Commander Bryant shot Robbins a look that said 'don't go there – they have their own way of doing things', and

Detective Sergeant Robbins recognised the futility of pressing the point with someone who probably had only a rudimentary idea of what a database was.

"This is real needle-in-a-haystack stuff", noted Detective Sergeant Robbins after the two o'clock coffee break. "We're just guessing he might use one of these services, since no bank accounts are involved, making it less traceable. But he could be doing regular bank transfers anyhow. Or crediting funds to an Indonesian credit card number in the UK, or simply mailing an envelope of cash every month. Or he might have paid a full year upfront, or maybe he's not paying anything at all".

"Well, the main reason this method is the most likely, is the recipient doesn't need to have his own bank account. Many people here do not have one, especially those who normally get paid salaries in cash, like maids and drivers and home security guards. Anyway, we'll have to do the next step if we want to look at bank transfers", replied Tarzan, "and most transfers arrive at Bank Central Asia as an intermediary and then go to the target bank. Our first step will be to get access to BCA. But until now we have a hundred and twenty seven matches to your criteria, and we have just one major service to finish, MoneyGram".

"A hundred and twenty seven matches? Do you mean we've found one hundred and twenty seven possible leads?"

"Yes, it's right there, on the board". Tarzan pointed to the giant whiteboard which was by now covered with scribbled abbreviations and names and boxes and arrows and looked like something Albert Einstein might have drawn to illustrate the relationship between gravity and something equally important. "Not including MoneyGram".

Special Commander Bryant was temporarily at a loss for words, and when he found some words again he said "Well, do you think we could summarise this on a sheet of paper, in the form of a list with columns, you know, originator name, recipient name, originating office, dates and whatnot?", and a female officer carefully lined up a sheet of paper in the typewriter and got a bottle of Tipp-ex ready just in case.

— o —

Special Commander Bryant was beginning to see Detective Sergeant Robbins in a new light, since it was useful to have somebody keen and enthusiastic about solving clues around, and Detective Sergeant Robbins seemed to know what he was doing and didn't appear to mind Special Commander Bryant taking the credit. And he didn't seem to be a bad sort either; the two of them had had dinner together, and Detective Sergeant Robbins had been genuinely fascinated in The Altogether Unexpected End of North Korea and was able to offer some invaluable feedback, from the point of view of a layman, into Special Commander Bryant's explanation of how the Keegians might travel twenty three light years in three and a half Earth days.

"It's what I call string theory", explained Special Commander Bryant. "It's often said that the shortest distance between two points is a straight line. This is correct, on paper, but in practical terms it is untrue. If you stretch a piece of string between two points on a piece of paper, the string does indeed follow a straight line, and the quickest way between the points is along the piece of string. However, if you stretched it between, say, London and Jakarta, it would be an arc, since it would have to follow the curved surface of the Earth. A shorter line would be through the Earth's mantle, but this would be impossible. String does not like to be stretched through solid rock.

"When you get into space, it's even more complex. Everything is moving, relative to everything else. Hence the theory of general relativity, and a piece of string between two relatively moving points would get hopelessly tangled with pieces of string between all the other points. If you could stretch a piece of string between Keeg and Earth, it would be twenty three light years long. That's over a hundred and thirty five trillion miles, and the only way we could travel to Keeg, with our limited technology, would be to fly alongside the hypothetical piece of string in a rocket, which would take us six hundred and sixteen thousand years. Not practical, especially if you were flying in Economy. But the Keegians have discovered a way of curving the string around the space/time continuum, so that the two ends become very close and almost touch, so instead of travelling from one end to the other, they sort of short-circuit the string and it becomes more like a ball of string. That way, every point in the universe is pretty close to every other point, and at the same time almost infinitely far from it. That's the secret".

"So you could travel at a leisurely pace to the other end of the string, and get there before a photon of light which had made the same journey in a straight line", marvelled Detective Sergeant Robbins. "The photon of light would arrive almost twenty three years after you did. That could go a long way to explaining how the tortoise beat the hare. The tortoise knew his string theory, and the hare was relying on old-fashioned straight line speed", and Special Commander Bryant knew he was a very good theoretical physics teacher.

— o —

Detective Sergeant Robbins had an idea, which he decided to withhold from Special Commander Bryant for now, since he would undoubtedly take the credit for it immediately.

"How much effort would it take to compare the list of regular monthly cash transfers and come up with those sender's names that match names of KITAS semi-permanent residence permit holders over the last, say, five years?" he asked Tarzan. "The names of senders in the UK, not the recipients in Jakarta. I'm thinking that the man we are looking for is now located in the UK, but I'm betting he almost certainly used to live in Jakarta, and therefore he probably was a KITAS holder".

"I'll get my best man on it", said Tarzan, and after lunch a small truck with a dozen narrow steel filing cabinets, each holding twenty thin drawers and each drawer containing fifty stock cards in flip-up cardholders, arrived from the Department of Immigration and Tarzan's best man, who turned out to be three women, set to work.

"Don't they have computer records of KITAS holders either? There are twelve thousand names here. Each one written in pencil, with dates and serial numbers, on a separate stock card. On a truck".

"They sort of do", replied Tarzan, "but their data entry skills are not very good, and the computer records don't always match the cards. This is the most reliable method up to two years ago, when they stopped being so diligent with the cards. If we get nothing here, we'll look at a few more, maybe another truck-load, and if we still get nothing we'll look at the computer records starting from two years back and work to the present".

"Well, at least let me help", said Detective Sergeant Robbins, and sat down with his list and a pen and fairly soon figured out that the cards were held alphabetically (in the loosest sense of the word) according to first names, not surnames.

— o —

Detective Sergeant Robbins and Kombespol Tarzan were explaining what they were doing to Special Commander Bryant, and that they had got a positive hit-list of thirteen names of ex-KITAS holders who were now living in England and were sending regular payments from the UK to Indonesia, and Special Commander Bryant couldn't see the point of it.

"Who cares if our man had KITAS or not? Maybe he did, or maybe he didn't. So why are you wasting time looking for KITAS holders?"

"Lots of people send regular, small payments to Indonesia", said Robbins, "but ex-KITAS holders comprise only thirteen of them. The ex-KITAS holders are people who have lived and worked in Indonesia, who have now left Indonesia, and for whatever reason still send money to someone they left behind. Many of the non-holders have probably never been to Indonesia at all, or just passed through. Someone sending money to an accomplice in Indonesia who programs a mobile phone for him obviously knows that person very well, and the sender is therefore likely to have lived and worked for an extensive period in Indonesia, and is therefore likely to be an ex-KITAS holder. That's why I had the idea of searching for the regular senders on the ex-KITAS list. Well, up to now we have thirteen regular senders who used to live in Jakarta full time, and thirteen recipients in Jakarta. Now we will visit the recipients and ask them about their relationships with the senders; who they get the money from and why. I have a gut feeling about this one, Sir; I think we're going to get lucky, get a major breakthrough very soon".

Special Commander Bryant doubted it.

— o —

Commander Unwin hadn't been so excited since the day in 1997 when he had shaken Her Majesty the Queen's hand, and if this went well he was sure that his name would crop up in the forefront of Her Majesty's consciousness again very soon. And, astonishingly, it was all down to Special Commander Bryant.

Bryant had had the brilliant idea of matching up regular senders of small cash payments from the UK to Indonesia with a list of ex-KITAS Indonesian semi-permanent residence permit holders now living back in the UK, and he and a Detective Sergeant who was in Jakarta assisting him had worked sixteen hours a day for five days collating the information. It had taken so much hard work because all of the available KITAS records were held on paper cards, comprising pencil entries riddled with spelling and sorting errors, and Bryant had finally got the breakthrough he had been hoping for.

Gregory John Grigg was Pimpinan, there was no doubt. Special Commander Bryant and his assistant had interviewed six out of a total of fourteen recipients in Jakarta of cash transfers from ex-KITAS holders in the UK without success, and then the seventh of them, a recipient via MoneyGram, had immediately identified a photograph of Pimpinan as Grigg. The recipient's name was Bambang Uharti, and he was the privately hired driver of Grigg for three years, until about two years previously. Bambang described Grigg as an important private businessman who dealt with airlines and hotels, the Police and security organisations. During Bambang's employment, Grigg had undertaken to pay for the last two years of Bambang's son's schooling, and Bambang was adamant Grigg was a very fine man. Since Grigg had left Indonesia, he had continued to send money to cover Bambang's personal cell phone costs, which he called his 'handphone'. Grigg had also provided him with another handphone; a special handphone with a post-paid account at ExelComindo, and instructed Bambang to pay the bill in cash at the Exelcomindo office every month, and not to use it for any purpose other than to leave it always charged and switched on, and from time to time set it to redirect all calls to a number which Grigg would provide by text message. The monthly cash transfers covered all costs of both of these handphones, plus about fifty pounds-worth of local currency a month for Bambang's pocket money.

Bambang had no idea what the purpose of the second handphone was, other than it was an important part of Grigg's continuing business with some of his Indonesian contacts. He was utterly convincing in his innocence, and was obviously very rattled at suddenly becoming the focus of a lot of Police attention, including from a very important-looking foreign officer. Special Commander Bryant had remembered the manually operated 'lie detector' which his poor taxi driver had been the victim of, and obtained Tarzan's solemn guarantee that no such methods would be used on Bambang to look for further information which clearly didn't exist.

Back in London, Commander Unwin's immediate focus had been to find out everything he could about Gregory John Grigg, and the results were staggering. Gregory John Grigg had been born and previously known as Roger Alan Pedersen, changing his name to Gregory John Grigg by deed poll after leaving the military. Special Agent In Charge Gajewski's analysis of the background and psychological state of the man they were looking for proved to be spot-on on almost every count.

After school, Pedersen had passed through Sandhurst and eventually joined the Special Air Services. At that point the trail vanished, as it always does when digging into histories involving the SAS, but following a flurry of top level communications between the Commissioner's Office and the Ministry of Defence up to and including the office of the Deputy Chief of the Defence Staff, reluctant information appeared that confirmed Pedersen had been a top-rated sniper and urban anti-terror operative, detailed to the highest operational security classification. During his career he had been reassigned to special training duties in Indonesia, as well as Saudi Arabia and Iraq, further to which all other information, including what those training duties entailed, were matters of impenetrable secrecy.

Pedersen's career ended abruptly after his wife and her parents were all killed in a house fire in Durham in 2009, for which two men were convicted of arson and constructive manslaughter, having been found not guilty of premeditated murder, and sentenced to a mere nine years and seven months in jail. Pedersen's father-in-law was a newly retired Policeman who had been one of the senior officers of a team credited with smashing the UK branch of a pan-European drugs organisation with links to Columbian and Bangladeshi cartel exporters, and the convicted arsonists were small-time local thugs employed by the remnants of the gang to exact revenge. Pedersen's father-in-law was the first candidate they had turned their attention to, and they were behind bars less than twelve hours later, singing like canaries about who had hired them and what they had been told to do. They escaped the murder charge due to doubts in the minds of the jury that they had been instructed to kill the occupants of the house, or had deliberately set out to do so.

After the loss of his wife and parents-in-law, Pedersen was a broken man who was never able to effectively fulfil his military duties again, not least because he now had sole responsibility for his two very young children. Pedersen was subsequently discharged from the military on compassionate grounds, with full honours and an unblemished service record. At the time of their mother's death, his children had been spending the week at their paternal grandparents' house in Dorset, and within a year Pedersen's parents had become the children's legal guardians.

Information about what happened to Pedersen after he left the military was sparse and patchy. He immediately closed his bank account, but no information existed about newly opened accounts elsewhere. No information could be found about an address or employment once he had begun to fend for himself for somewhere to live and work. He changed his name to Gregory John Grigg five months later, giving his parent's address for court records, and his parents knew nothing about the change of name. Grigg had surrendered his passport in the name of Pedersen and at the same time used the court deed poll to obtain a new passport in the name of Grigg, but apart from that, no bank, address, tax, television license, medical registration or any other records commenced in the name of Gregory John Grigg at that time or any time thereafter. His parents stated that he had never lived with them because of his work on the outskirts of London as a security consultant; he didn't seem to be overtly wealthy, but was apparently comfortably off and provided adequate funds for the children's welfare, doted on the children and visited them several times a week for the first year, drove a ten year old BMW 5-series, and always made excuses to enable himself to not provide address or phone contact information. After around one year, the visits became noticeably less frequent and gradually stopped altogether. Occasional phone calls came for the children from their father for another six months, and then he simply disappeared. The children, now aged nine and eleven, hadn't seen or heard from their father for years, apart from the receipt of birthday cards and Christmas cards every year, often bearing foreign postmarks and always containing a brief message and a fifty pound note, and they no longer missed him at all.

— o —

Superintendent Smith was updating the team. "He sent the money from Chelmsford. Paid it by credit card every time. Provided a passport for i.d., provided a false address on the form. They kept a copy of the passport; it is Indonesian and it is genuine. However, Grigg never became an Indonesian citizen; never became entitled to hold an Indonesian passport".

"So how did he get one? And I presume the credit card was in the same name, matching the passport - what was the issuing bank, and the account address, and why didn't we pick it up on our searches?"

"The fact it is a genuine Indonesian passport doesn't mean it was obtained through the proper channels. Let me explain. For many years, during the Soeharto era, Indonesian citizens needed an official reason to hold a passport at all, and even then they needed exit visas to leave the country and had to pay advance taxes to get the visas. It was a government control intended to curb the influence of wealthy Indonesians of Chinese descent. It went hand in hand with strict currency controls. With the fall of Soeharto in 1998, all these controls evaporated, and the passport service was swamped with applications for passports from ordinary citizens. Like any other bureaucracy in Indonesia, bribery oiled the wheels and kept things in motion. If you were entitled to a passport and wanted it in less than a month, you paid an unofficial fee to speed things up. You could get it the same afternoon. If you couldn't find your birth certificate, or wanted to omit one of your names, you paid an unofficial fee and the birth certificate was overlooked. Things are much tighter now, but it is still possible to bypass pretty much any requirement for controls and paperwork if you know the right people and have some spare cash to throw around.

"Passports are computerised, but as recently as two years ago, the application process was not. The officer in charge had full discretion to approve or reject an application. It is doubtful you will ever find records of the approval or decision process of a doubtful passport, even if they exist. Put simply, Grigg's passport is a genuine passport but fraudulently obtained. Indonesian law requires a foreigner who gains Indonesian citizenship to give up his or her citizenship of all other countries - it does not allow dual citizenship, except for minors that have one Indonesian and one foreign parent.

"Grigg did not give up his UK citizenship in this way. However, he used his Indonesian passport to obtain a five year UK visitor visa, and came and went through UK borders on many occasions using a foreign passport, while retaining his UK passport for in-country i.d. This kept his movements completely off the British passport control database. That is how he obtained a second, foreign passport. He obviously is well connected in Indonesia".

— o —

"The bastard used his real name", said Special Agent In Charge Gajewski. "He sent the money using his real name; he even used his real name when he talked to me at the Mostyn! How cocksure is that?"

"Looks like he finally made the fatal mistake we've been waiting for", said Superintendent Smith. "Any use of either passport anywhere will now trigger a code red alert, likewise the credit card. It's just a matter of time".

"No, it's too obvious, too simple. He's been playing us like puppets all along. All the clues we've been following until now have been consciously provided to us by him. The Jakarta connection. The obvious fact that someone there was being paid by him. I can't believe he would overlook the fact that we would get the identity of the sender about two minutes after finding the phone guy in Jakarta, or that we'd find his background just as quickly. Changing your name legally doesn't erase your past life in any way. But in his case, a large chunk of his past life, his military past life, is shrouded in secrecy".

"So you think he's giving this to us, along with everything else? Why the hell would he? How close to the real man is he comfortable with us getting? Are you suggesting he has a whole other life complete with identity?"

"I don't know. We're getting this old feeling again, 'really close to a breakthrough', and look what's happened before - nothing changes. Maybe he has made a mistake, but if so, I doubt that this is it. But either way, he's getting help. There's still a big gap. There's a thread somewhere we haven't found yet, and when we find it and pull it, everything else will fall away. We should have focussed more on where and how he gets his information, that's the key to everything. He's got the skills to hunt and neutralise urban targets without being detected; it's what he was trained to do. But I don't believe he has the inside information necessary to select or identify the targets in the first place. Like any covert operative, he has to be told who and where his enemy is. He doesn't just go out and look for bad people to neutralise".

"You know we have fingerprints on file", said Smith, "for Pedersen / Grigg, and they don't match Pimpinan. It doesn't make sense. However adept you are at running rings round an investigation, you cannot change your own fingerprints".

Gajewski was aware of this, and it had lain quietly nagging at her in the back of her mind, and she knew that this fact was connected to her personally.

"We might have had to conclude", said Gajewski, "that Pimpinan therefore couldn't be Grigg, except for the fact that I personally saw him lay prints at the Mostyn. Perhaps that was the whole point of the Mostyn thing. Not the tracking down a Krakatoa agent thing, or the showing off with Morgan Freeman thing, but the actual *witnessed* fingerprint thing. But why? Why wouldn't he prefer us to discount Grigg on the basis of a print mismatch? He's somehow pulled off every criminal's dream, and promptly corrected the erroneous conclusion before we even found it".

— o —

Special Commander Bryant, who had been welcomed home personally by the Commissioner and congratulated for his stroke of investigative genius regarding the KITAS records, had an idea. "Has anyone checked whether this chap has an identical twin brother?"

"Of course", said Smith. "He has no siblings at all".

'Shame', thought Special Commander Bryant, 'that would have been interesting; might have helped *The Many Few* plot-line no end'.

Chapter 14 - Ravi the Suspect

Three weeks after Special Commander Bryant returned to London, Special Agent In Charge Gajewski had been called back to San Ramon by the FBI, having more than satisfied every expectation of her, and absolutely no further progress at tracking Pimpinan had been made despite the best efforts of Operation Krakatoa and a fifteen-strong task force team of special investigators, including a senior counter-terrorism expert from the City of London Police, intelligence analysts, covert operatives and cyber security experts. Even a former CIA pattern analyst-turned-private security contractor, who played a prominent role in the finding and elimination of senior Al Qaeda figures, had been drafted in at huge cost and it had yielded nothing.

"What you guys need is a starting point", said the former CIA pattern analyst-turned-private security contractor, who wanted to be called 'Bud' and liked to use expletives a lot, and called everybody 'asshole' to their faces, "because so far you've given me zilch to work with. You see, with all the technologies and expertise you have available, no-one is out of your reach, it's that simple. If some asshole uses his passport or credit card, you got him. If he turns on his mobile phone, or opens the lid of his iPad, or drives his car past a camera, or walks past a camera, or calls his Mom, or sends an email, or uses an ATM, or likes some shit on Facebook, you got him. But you need to know who this particular guy is, and you assholes don't know jack about who he is. You know his name, that's it. You know his identity. But guess what; it doesn't help, because he's shut down and killed his identity and you have no clue as to the identity he's currently walking around with. Your only hope, your *only* hope, except of course if he gets hammered one night and accidentally uses his old credit card, is getting lucky if his face gets picked up by facial recognition software on one of your cameras that has it available. If he goes through an airport, or a subway hub station, something like that. I'm betting you're getting a lot of false positives right now, and nothing else. He knows exactly what you're looking for, and he probably knows how to beat FR software. It doesn't work that well to be honest. All the rest - does he even have a mobile phone? Does he have an iPad? What name does he have cards in, or passports, or email? Does he have a car? What name is it registered under? How the fuck can I help you assholes if you can't tell me who we're looking for?"

Commander Unwin, who hadn't been called an asshole in front of subordinates since he was a boy scout and didn't like the reminder, made a mental decision to phase out Bud's participation in the task force team at his earliest opportunity. He also didn't like the fact that the most vociferous, assertive front-line participation to the Operation was again drifting towards that of the Americans, and despite Commander Unwin's satisfaction that Special Agent In Charge Gajewski's contributions had been utterly indispensable and of inestimable value, the fact that Gajewski had been an American on loan to the Operation had caused a certain amount of top-level discomfort.

"Bud, have you ever come across a case where pattern analysis has been distorted because the suspect turned out to be two identical twin brothers from entirely different backgrounds?" Special Commander

Bryant asked, and noticing a mortified-looking Commander Unwin was about to shut his question down, hurriedly continued "Only I'm currently working on a top-secret case which involves identical twin brothers who were separated at birth and discovered each other in later life, who collaborate to provide each other alibis and misdirect the efforts to …"

"Bryant, enough", thundered Commander Unwin, "I'm sorry, Bud, this is not an official line of enquiry and I'm sorry you had to …"

"That is a fucking excellent question, Sir; what's your name again? Bryant? A fucking excellent question, Mr Bryant, and yes I have. At least one of you assholes has your pants on the right way round today. One time, we had no idea this one guy had a twin brother, and we were effectively chasing two people. Confused the hell out of us. We even had confirmed, rock-solid sightings of our guy in two different locations at the same time, and it took us a week to realise that fact. Got them both in the end though, we pulled one from a bank's CCTV and got a hold of his mobile, got the other mobile from it, ran a GPS and pulled him an hour later. Did you know a mobile phone has more computing power than the entire network of Apollo mission control computer systems? Size of a fucking cruise ship and three times as expensive; now this little thing sits in your pocket, costs half a day's pay and fucks you up every chance it gets. Tells us where you are, where you're headed, what you're Googling, shows us your face while you're texting and the view to your right while you're talking on the phone, lets us listen to everything you say all day long, some of them even tell us your heart rate; tell us when you're stressed or sleeping or jerking off. First rule of going off the grid: throw your phone in the fucking river and walk away".

"Thank you for saying so, Bud", beamed Special Commander Bryant, clearly delighted at the prospect of being mentioned to the Powers That Be as the only asshole with his pants on the right way round, "because, call me old fashioned, but I always say that once you eliminate the impossible, whatever remains, no matter how improbable, must be the truth. So if twin brothers are not impossible, as you yourself mentioned just now, they must be the truth".

"Priceless! You're a regular Miss Marple!" said Bud, his arms outstretched wide and three gold molars gleaming inside his ear-to-ear grin. Special Commander Bryant was unsure whether Bud was being sarcastic or proposing a hug, and hesitated awkwardly, but was saved from having to gamble on the possibility of a faux pas by Superintendent Smith.

"We know for sure that a twin brother is impossible", said Smith. "He has no siblings. We know there is no possibility of a separated-at-birth scenario, as he was raised by his birth parents, who are still alive and together and have never been too poor to afford children, or had to split the family up because of social services or a war. He has never attempted to contact them in the last twelve months and they have no more idea of how to contact him, or where he is, or what his name is now than we do".

"So what does Miss Marple-here suggest we do now?"

Special Commander Bryant knew what he'd do if it were up to him. "We need to solve the riddle of why Pimpinan is Grigg, but the two have different fingerprints. If there is no identical twin brother, there must be another explanation. So lets get the postman in for questioning; there are a lot of loose ends there".

— o —

"Would you like some tea or coffee before we begin?"

"No, no thank you. I don't drink tea or coffee actually".

"Some water then? Or a soft drink?"

"No, I'm fine. Thank you".

"Alright then. Let's begin. Hopefully this won't take too long, then we'll have a car drop you home. Okay, let's start at the beginning. What was the reason you hated Paul Kingston?"

"What?"

"I asked, what was the reason you hated Paul Kingston. It's an easy question to understand".

"I … I don't hate him; I hardly even know him. Why … why would you ask me that question?"

"I'm sorry, maybe hate is a little strong. I'll rephrase that. Why did you hold a grudge against Paul Kingston for more than a year?"

"Grudge? A grudge? I don't hold any grudge against Paul Kingston; I've only seen him maybe five times in my life. I probably said good morning to him twice; that's all. I don't hate him or dislike him in any way".

"So you're saying you liked him?"

"I'm not saying that, no. I don't know him well enough to like him".

"So if you didn't like him, you must have disliked him".

"No, I don't dislike him. I suppose I like everybody by default, unless and until they give me reason to dislike them".

"So you liked him by default".

"Yes".

"You liked Paul Kingston by default? You would have us believe you liked a man who caused you all that disgust and aggravation by putting dog shit in the post box?"

"Dog … what is this dog shits? Kingston put dog shits in the post box?"

"Why do you sound surprised? Did you or did you not call the Police on two separate occasions in April last year to complain about excrement being posted in the post box situated outside Barmley post office?"

"Well, yes, but …"

"And did you or did you not tell the attending officer that you would have to clean up the letters as best you could, and seal them in plastic bags and rewrite the addresses and attach a note saying that the enclosed letters were health hazards due to the post box being vandalised and blah blah blah?"

"Yes, but what has that …"

"That sounds very inconvenient, not to mention horribly gross and disgusting. Which is probably why you told the attending officer that you would like to '*string up the little bastard that did this*'".

"It wasn't *Kingston*; he lives in a nice house and keeps himself to himself. It was probably kids. The Police never found out who did it. They just said they would keep an eye out, and immediately forgot all about it. Is that what you want to talk to me about? I'm sorry, I ..."

"For someone who only spoke to a suspect twice in his life, you seem to have ruled him out very quickly. How did he react when you confronted him? About the dog shit? Did he deny it with that supercilious look on his face - the one that says 'yeah, I did it all right'? Did you know he was lying all along?"

"This is crazy. Look, I told you, I have never discussed anything with him".

"Why not? Was it because he was a racist? You snubbed him because he was a racist, right? The worst kind of racist - the kind of racist that puts dog shit in post boxes".

"What? This is ... I'm sorry, I'm confused now. I thought you wanted to talk about my post office. I thought you wanted to know about how mail comes in, and is sorted and delivered. That's what you said. Has something happened to Paul Kingston? Why are you using the past tense when you speak about Paul Kingston? Why are you asking me about him at all?"

"You tell me".

"Tell you what? Tell you about Paul Kingston? I don't know anything about Paul Kingston. Five minutes ago I didn't know that apparently he is a racist, or that he put dog shits in the post box".

"Who told you he put dog shit in the post box? Now we're getting somewhere. I bet you must have held a bit of a grudge against someone you suspected of putting dog shit in the post box, since he knew it was you that had to clear the mess up".

"You told me that; you said he's the kind of racist that puts dog shit in post boxes".

"I didn't tell you that. Did I tell him that?"

"You didn't tell him that".

"No, he didn't tell me that; you told me that".

"Well, what can I say? All I know is that Paul Kingston was maybe a racist, although we have no evidence of that other than your say-so, and you think he put dog shit in the post box, and now he's dead. It doesn't look good for you".

"Dead? *Dead*? I want to stop this now; I changed my mind, I want a lawyer present. You said this would be a quick chat to see whether you overlooked anything. You said it was just to check a few facts. You're *lying*; you ask me all these aggressive questions about someone I don't know and then tell me he's *dead*? No more questions, I want to go home. I want to see a lawyer".

"It's a bit late for that now. You're not going anywhere, pal. You can't just drop a bombshell on us like that after two minutes of questioning and expect to walk out the door. This isn't Dixon of Dock Green, you know. Is this Dixon of Dock Green?"

"This isn't Dixon of Dock Green, Ron".

"That's what I thought".

"What are you talking about? What Dixon of Dock Green? What bombshell? You said Kingston is dead, not me…".

"So you're telling us he's alive? Paul Kingston is alive?"

"I'm not telling you he's alive, I don't bloody know if he's alive. Why wouldn't he be alive? You told me he's dead. Why would he be dead?"

"Because you killed him; that would be my guess. You killed that racist. I don't blame you, personally; I would probably do the same thing in your shoes. But killing people just because they put dog shit in the post box happens to be illegal. You can't just go around killing everyone you don't approve of".

"This is madness. I want a lawyer, right now".

"Was Richard Leighton a racist too?"

"I don't know who Richard Leighton is".

"And I suppose you never spoke to him either?"

"Not to my knowledge. I run a post office, so I deal with a lot of people; I come across a lot of names without seeing their faces, and I don't recall any Richard Leighton. You can't expect me to remember all their names, or put all their names to faces".

"Well, let me refresh your memory. Richard Leighton is the guy you and your friend killed with a hammer. Smashed his joints one by one. Poor bastard took an entire day to die. You videoed the whole thing, then you took the video to Paul Kingston and told him you would do the same thing to him".

[No response - 10 seconds]

"My guess is that your friend did all the grunt work. My guess is, all you did was operate the video and get the video to Kingston. Am I warm?"

[No response - 10 seconds]

"That makes you just as culpable in his death as your friend with the hammer. But if you cooperate with us now, it would go better for you. No deals, nothing like that; this isn't Kojak you know, but it would definitely count in your favour".

[No response - 5 seconds]

"You're very quiet, Mr Singh. Don't you want to tell us about murdering Leighton? Would you prefer to talk about murdering Kingston? What we'd really like to know, first of all, is where the bodies are. It's very hard to make dead bodies just disappear; they have an inconvenient habit of advertising their presence for miles around with this overpowering, distinctive stench. That's why a lot of people throw them in rivers and lakes. But in water, dead bodies fill with gas and blow up; even heavily weighted bodies often rise up and float away. Scares the shit out of people nearby. But I'm guessing you know all that already. Where are the bodies, Mr Singh?"

[No response - 5 seconds]

"Well, I guess I better cancel that car to take you home. This is going to take a while, and I haven't had my lunch yet".

"I'm not stupid. I know this is bloody … bloody bullshit. It's all bloody bullshit. You know I had nothing to do with any of this".

"But at the very least, you know who did, Mr Singh, that is the point, and I'm also pretty certain you were an accomplice. I'm not stupid either. Your reaction when I mentioned killing Richard Leighton with the hammer was not one of someone hearing upsetting and unpleasant news for the first time. It was one of someone being found out. It was a 'game over' moment. Would you like to see the moment on CCTV playback? I'd be happy to show you".

[Pause - 5 seconds]

"Okay. I saw the video. Of the hammer. The first minute or so, that's all - I couldn't bear to watch it. I've had bad dreams ever since. It came in to my sorting office and I opened it. It was a video disk. It was addressed to Paul Kingston. I didn't know what to do; if I sent it to the Police, Kingston would not get the warning on it, and would be in huge danger. But I thought it must get to the Police. I didn't want to get involved, I was scared. This was worse than anything I ever imagined. It was a dilemma. So I copied it, and sent it to Kingston. I sent the video disk to the Police. That's all".

"That's all? That's all? That story has more holes and loose ends than a Kings Cross whore's second best stockings. But let me ask you a question, if I may. About your post office. What happens to a letter that is posted in the Barmley post box outside your post office, if it is addressed to someone in the Barmley delivery area? How is it processed?"

"Well, it goes straight into Incoming, for delivery …"

"How do you sort all the posted mail? The mail for other towns and cities?"

"We send it to the main sorting office, they have machines. We separate it into air mail, surface mail for other countries, and domestic mail for north, midlands, south east and south west. They do all the detailed sorting at the main sorting office".

"And mail coming in for Barmley?"

"That's the Incoming. It arrives from the sorting office and we distribute it".

"So a letter mailed in Barmley for delivery in Barmley goes to the main sorting office and comes back?"

"No. I told you, we put it directly in Incoming and deliver it".

"So does the letter get cancelled and postmarked; does it go through the machine, or how does it work?"

"Yes, same as any other. The postmark confirms what date and time we took care of the letter".

"I guess that never happens though; I can't imagine why anyone would buy a stamp to send a letter to an address just round the corner from the post box".

"It does happen, especially with older people. If they send Christmas cards or greetings to their neighbours, for example, some people think it is bad form to deliver the letter in person, like it's a cheapskate way of doing things. They like to have the postman deliver it, even if it's just next door. In the old days, there was a separate post box for local, but there isn't the demand any more".

"You know where the package with the video for Paul Kingston was post marked? That's right, of course you do; Barmley, meaning it was posted in the post box right outside your post office. So, I'm having a little difficulty believing your version of events. Somebody posted the video in the post box, outside your post office. That's how it got into your sorting office, addressed to some guy just up the road. A few minutes or an hour or two later, you've opened it and found this video. Then you watched it. That strikes me as highly unlikely behaviour for a postmaster. Let's go through this one by one. How exactly did the package get into your hands?"

"From the post box; it would have gone straight into Incoming".

"It wasn't handed directly to you?"

"No. It has to be collected from the post box to get into the system".

"Why did you open it?"

[No response - 5 seconds]

"You opened this particular package because it was addressed to the racist, the dog shit man, is that it?"

[No response - 5 seconds]

"You were hoping to steal something from the racist, but instead of anything valuable, you found a video disk. So you watched it. You watched it and you saw the murder of a man you didn't know by another man you didn't know, and a warning that the same thing would happen to Kingston. So you copied the video and sent it to Kingston so he would know he was in danger - this racist pig, this man you despised so much who put dog shit in the post box, you tried to protect him, when you also sent the video to the Police".

"Yes. I was hoping to steal from him, because he was rich. That's why I opened it. I never hated him though, I never knew those things about him".

"You have children"?

"Yes, I have two daughters and six grandchildren, two boys and four girls".

"What ages are the grandchildren?"

"The eldest is fifteen and the youngest is two".

"Then I imagine you probably feel strongly about paedophiles".

"I, er, …"

"That's the real reason you hated Paul Kingston, isn't it? You knew all the stories; you'd heard the reports. A single man living alone in a big house. You'd seen him sneaking glances at your granddaughters, and you couldn't bear the thought of his filthy child-molesting, drug-dealing hands on those little children you love so much. You hated him so much, you wanted him dead, what with the drug dealing and the dog shit and everything. So when someone approaches you to help kill Richard Leighton, the other racist, as part of a plan to kill Kingston, a diversion if you will, you jump at it. You personally deliver a video of the killing to Paul Kingston's house, opening and resealing the package first, to make it look tampered-with, and make sure you deliver it while Kingston was out. Then you send another copy of the Leighton killing to the Police, making it look like a gang-style execution and ensuring the Police thought Kingston had been threatened with death before he was killed. You fucking heartless murdering bastard".

"No, no, it's not like that. I don't know about any of these things. I only opened the package by accident, and saw the video. It was a coincidence. Please, I don't know any of this".

"I'm trying to believe you, Mr Singh, I really am. But it's just not plausible. If you knew none of this, why did you open the package? The one addressed to Paul Kingston? Why not one addressed to, say, Mr Smith? Because Mr Smith wasn't a racist paedophile drug dealer who put dog shit in the post box, that's why".

"I opened hundreds of packages. Packages and letters. Thousands. For years. Decades".

[Pause - 10 seconds]

"Alright, there you are. I did. I'm sorry. I did".

"Oh, well, that's it then. You have an alibi. You couldn't be involved in any of this. You're free to go".

"I can go? I can go now?"

"No, you can't go now, Mr Singh, you fucking lying murdering bastard. Why did you open millions of packages for hundreds of years? How convenient - that means that Kingston's package was just one of millions. That means there is no significance to Kingston's package, since you also opened millions of others. Why did you do it? You said you wanted to steal from Kingston's package - did you steal from millions of others too?"

"Yes, that's what it was, I wanted to steal".

"We've already checked, Mr Singh, and there has never been any suspicion raised in the last twenty five years of thefts from the mail in Barmley. None at all. You're squeaky clean in that regard. You're lying. You never opened a thing; you probably packaged up the disk to Kingston yourself, you knew what was on it, probably helped make it, and were part of the plot to kill Leighton, Kingston and many others. I want to you take a polygraph test. You can refuse, but it wouldn't help your case at all. Either way, we'll get you, you lying murdering bastard. You can't run around killing innocent people, especially innocent drug dealing racist psychopaths, and expect to get away with it. Do you know what happens in prison to perverts that get their kicks making snuff movies, Mr Singh? Have you ever seen private parts sliced open end to end with a razor blade and rolled in dirt? They're going to shred you, you lousy murdering pervert, and good luck to them. Sergeant! Sergeant! Where are these lazy flat-caps? *Sergeant*! Ah - sorry to wake you, Princess, but if you're not too busy, would you be so kind as to take this vermin to the cells. We're going to charge him with conspiracy for starters. Do you have any dietary preferences?"

"But …"

"In tea - do you take sugar?"

"I don't drink tea. I'm a vegetarian. I'm having a lactose intolerance. Please help me …"

"Only bacon sandwiches and milky tea, four sugars, Sergeant. Full body search, make sure you don't miss anything. This one's dangerous; cell to himself, don't take any chances. And suicide watch; take his belt, trousers, shirt and laces. What the hell, take his fucking socks too. I need my lunch now. Then we'll get to the bottom of this".

— o —

"He's not cooperating. He's still going with the story that he knows nothing and saw the Leighton video as part of an ongoing agenda of deliberately opening and delaying postal packets during their transmission by post. He's liable for six months just for that. But we want to get him for conspiracy with a person or persons unknown at the very least. You have to get results on this operation, and this is the best shot you've got so far".

The intelligence analyst seemed to Superintendent Smith to operate in a universe of his own; a universe comprised solely of facts and records and having no regard for airy-fairy concepts like motive or opportunity or accountability.

"But what if it's true"? asked Smith. "What if he really had nothing to do with any of it? What if he really did stumble across the video and panic and pass it on? How would pursuing this line help us get Pimpinan?"

"True? What is truth anyway? I'll tell you what is true. Singh handled the video. He watched it; he duplicated it. He caused it to be delivered to Paul Kingston and Essex. He conspired. He did it secretly and knowingly, and right after that, Paul Kingston disappeared. Nothing to do with it? His filth is all over it. Right now this man is the best hope you have of a conviction coming out of Krakatoa. So who gives a shit whether or not he had anything to do with it?"

"Who *are* those guys doing the interviews? I hadn't heard any of that stuff about Kingston being a racist, or a paedophile or the dog shit thing. Is any of it true? It's the only semblance of a motive that I can see, and it's all news to me. If it's not true, there is no case".

"The truth of it is not the motive. What Singh *believes* to be true is the motive. They were prepping him for the polygraph, and I understand Singh has agreed to take the test. Thinks it will prove the truth of his story.

"Let me tell you about polygraphs. They look for imperceptible stress reactions when the subject tells a lie. Breathing, pulse, blood pressure, skin moisture, temperature. The average person cannot hide them. As well as lies, they also pick up questions that raise issues of high significance to the subject. They can only answer yes or no. Questions cannot be open; they can only be appropriate for yes or no answers. You cannot ask 'have you stopped beating your wife?' - where a yes answer would mean the subject used to beat his wife, and a no answer would mean he still beats his wife. You would have to ask 'have you ever beaten your wife?'.

"Polygraph tests are not admissible as evidence in this country, but they are gradually being referred to in court more and more. Boundaries are being tested. If you drop, in court, a bombshell of a polygraph test that shows the subject lied through his teeth, the judge may rule it inadmissible and direct the jury to disregard it, but the damage is done. The defendant is tainted in the jury's eyes.

"It's pretty easy to get a subject to fuck up his polygraph test. After the control questions, the calibration, the first question they will ask Singh will be 'have you ever been asked to take a polygraph?' Well, the answer is obviously yes, since here he is taking a test, but he will be unsure whether they mean before this one, or including this one, and will wonder whether he has misunderstood the question because it seems too obvious, and he knows that whatever he says may therefore be untrue, which will cause a spike, and he will know it. This will put him on edge and make him more nervous than he was during the calibration. He will then be asked questions like 'do you know who put dog excrement in the post box in April last year?', 'did Paul Kingston put excrement in the post box?', 'was Paul Kingston a racist?'; to all these things he will probably answer no. Each question will have high significance for him, and will have been on his mind recently, and will remind him that the questions relate to recent accusations in the affirmative, causing a stress reaction, and each no answer will cause a spike. He will be shown to be lying. Finally, he will be asked 'did you kill Paul Kingston?', and he will answer no, and this will be recorded as a truth. He will never be asked if he conspired to kill Paul Kingston, since we don't want inconvenient truthful answers getting in the way if we can't make him lie. Singh is proved to have thought Kingston was the vilest, most despicable person on God's earth. So there we have all the evidence you need to support your claim of powerful motive for conspiracy. It's called justice, and the little bastard is going down. No need to thank me".

Chapter 15 - Emma Gets An E-Mail

On Monday morning, just as he was about to enter the conference room with Special Commander Bryant and Superintendent Smith for their twice-weekly progress videoconference with the Commissioner, Commander Unwin received a cell phone call and noticed that the caller was from overseas, and decided to pick it up. It was Special Agent In Charge Gajewski, calling from San Ramon.

"I got an email from the Leadership", she said, "sent to my personal Yahoo account. I'm forwarding it to you as we speak, by secure means. You really need to give this your immediate attention; I've provided as much information as I can in the accompanying email to you. We're all over it at this end, but it's going to take time. We'll help as much as we can with source tracing and the like, but the content requires your interpretation; it may make more sense to you. Good luck, Alan, I'll speak to you soon".

Commander Unwin decided to send Special Commander Bryant into the videoconference alone to placate the Commissioner, and he and Superintendent Smith went straight to the network communications room, where they found a roomful of people waiting for them and wondering what to do next. Several of the wonderers went away as soon as Commander Unwin walked in and asked who was in charge, and he sat down with a lady with a crooked fringe who brought up two emails on two separate screens.

"I suggest you read the covering email first, since it tells you all about the background and what they're up to in America", said the lady with the crooked fringe, whose name was apparently Lona. "I'm Lona - Lona by name but not loner by nature. It's short for Palona. My Mum smoked a lot of weed in the sixties. I'm actually very gregarious really. After that you'll probably have questions I can help you with, or maybe you'll want to read the focus email, whichever you like".

Commander Unwin read the first email.

Alan,

I received this email at my Yahoo webmail account. It is undoubtedly from Pimpinan. It was send using Tor, which makes it very difficult for us to trace, unless he made any mistakes or took any shortcuts. He used the Tor browser unfortunately, so the guys say any anonymizing errors you might get from Firefox add-ons or similar are out of the picture. The email account was set up minutes before the email was sent, probably during the same browser session. It's got a .de suffix, meaning the provider saw the user as being in Germany, but that's the whole point of Tor. We are working it with all we've got and will report our findings to you as and when they arise. Meantime, we've looked at the content of the email and it means very little to us - perhaps you'll have more luck. There may be clues in the personal message to me, or this may be just an attempt at embarrassing me in the department. Anyway, it is your baby and we're just here to help - ask for whatever you need.

Best regards,

Emma

"In layman's terms, it's an anonymising system for internet usage", explained Lona before being asked, "and it works by routing all activity through a global network of servers. Each one adds another layer of encryption or decryption, until it reaches the final destination. Each server has its own IP address, but hides it from the next one, and so on, meaning you can never find where the activity originated. There are exceptions, which are the mistakes she refers to - if you download torrents from Pirate Bay, for example, it can sometimes fail to encrypt, and some add-ons like flash video downloaders do strange things sometimes if you use a standard browser, but the focus guy obviously didn't do that".

"Obviously", said Commander Unwin. "I'm none the wiser, but I'm glad you know what you're talking about".

"Think about it like an onion", said Lona, "because that's what Tor stands for - The Onion Router. Every time you succeed in peeling off a layer of an onion, all you find inside is a smaller onion. Keep peeling, and when you've finished, all you have is absolutely nothing. It keeps everything you do secret, as long as you follow the rules. Military, Police, big business - they all use it. The Americans used it to send you these two emails".

"So civilians can use it too? How does one pay for it?" asked Commander Unwin, thinking he'd seen a possibility.

"You don't. It's free, and anyone can use it by downloading software from Tor".

Commander Unwin turned his attention to the second email.

Dear Emma,

Please forgive this unsolicited intrusion, as I know you have completed your time in our little country. I would like to apologise for any distress I caused you while you were on our side of the pond. It may have appeared to you that I was stalking, but in reality it was only my good fortune that you used WiFi to send personal details over the internet during the only time I was in the vicinity. Look on it as a reminder to be more careful on public networks. Notice I did not abuse your credit card :)

I know you are now aware of my circumstances. This is to let you know that I have decided to cease my activities for a while, for personal reasons. Your ex-colleagues in Blighty are making surprisingly little progress, so I also decided to prove my sincerity by giving them one last offering in the form of the following message. Perhaps you would be kind enough to pass it on.

I did enjoy meeting you, and in a different universe, would have wished to see you again.

Best regards,

Gregory

The key to many questions is coordinated in this email in black and white; select all you need.

"What do you think, Superintendent? Anything leap out at you at first glance?"

"My first thought is that this may be another time waster. We should get as many eyes on this as we can. The body of the message seems to imply there is a clue is in the final sentence, the 'following message' after the signature line, but the final sentence implies the 'key' is in the overall email. I think we should bring this to the Team right away; get some creative analytical thinking going".

— o —

Detective Sergeant Robbins woke up and wondered whether he had missed his alarm and was late for his shift, and looked at his clock, and his heart sank as he saw it was three o'clock in the morning. This was the fifth third day in a row he had seen that ungodly hour crawl into being, and he knew he would get no more sleep before the sun came up but would be ready to fall asleep on his feet by lunchtime, and cursed the damnable insomnia which showed no sign of abating. It had started with jet-lag after he returned from Jakarta, and he hadn't been able to yet get back into his normal sleep pattern routine. Detective Sergeant Robbins resigned himself to a few more hours of dead time, and lay with his hands behind his head and his eyes wide open, and settled in to let his mind wander to what was happening in his world, and what the day would bring.

The brainstorming session in the strategic control room yesterday had been intriguing. They had each been given a printout of an email stamped 'TASK FORCE SECRET' in red and asked to collaborate to decipher the messages hidden in it. It was an email purportedly sent by Pimpinan to Gajewski now she was back in America. They were not to think about electronic aspects of the email, Superintendent Smith had said, since the technical wizards were all over it and stripping the mail down to code and analysing the metadata and reverse-engineering the routing to find even the slightest clue as to where it was sent from and how it was delivered. They were to look for clues in the wording and language used, and they had spent an hour going round in circles and getting nowhere. The one thing they did all agree on was that there was no information to be gained from the 'following message'; that one line that offered a tantalising promise but nothing tangible at all, and they had spent their time discussing possible implications in the reference to the credit card and the different universe and use of the word 'Blighty' when addressing an American. It had seemed to Detective Sergeant Robbins as though everybody had spent an hour reading 'Psychology for Dummies' and were now putting their new-found proficiency to work like experts, yet the answers remained beyond their reach. But something had triggered a little spark of familiarity inside Detective Sergeant Robbins, and he had taken his mind out of the conversations going on around him and tried to nurture the little germ of understanding into maturity. Yet the answers remained beyond his reach too. For the first time ever, they had been allowed to take the printouts away from the strategic control room to study at home.

Emails. Hidden clues. Secret messages. Playing games. Nat. It was great while it lasted, but like it always does, it fizzled and died. Detective Sergeant Robbins' mind drifted to his doomed three month romance with Nat, and how they used to email little love notes to each other at work, making them safe to open on a public screen until they were sure they were alone ... how they used to ...

And then it hit him like an express train, and the dominoes fell, and it was so, so simple. Detective Sergeant Robbins grabbed the printout from his bedside cabinet and looked at the last line again, just in case, but it fit perfectly, and he shouted "YES!" at the top of his lungs and wished someone could have been there to hear him, and called the hotline. You cannot see the message from the printout, he told them, but you can clearly see how to *find* the message from the printout, but you need the soft copy email up on the screen to do it, and I need to be there to show you. And then, while he waited for the car, Detective Sergeant Robbins planned how to reveal the secret; how to explain it to best demonstrate his detective mastery, and how to make sure Special Commander Bryant didn't steal the glory again.

— o —

The key to many questions is coordinated in this email in black and white.

Black and white. The letters are black by default; the virtual paper is white. But you can write the letters in any colour you want. Red, yellow, green. Or white. White letters on white virtual paper are completely invisible, and do not show when printed. But they are always there. That's how he and Nat exchanged intimate messages in innocuous emails. If you can find the white letters, you can read them. When no prying eyes are around. Just make sure they don't include anything that will trigger monitoring software, or anything of utmost secrecy, because white letters are not really hidden at all. You can see them, but you just don't notice them.

Select all you need.

In other words, you need 'select all'. That's how you find your white letters. Go to 'select all' with the email open, and all text becomes highlighted in blue. Including the white text, which is now clearly readable against the blue. It's so simple; it's the way school-kids communicate secrets from their parents. And Operation Krakatoa and even the FBI missed it.

— o —

The two nine-digit numbers revealed by Detective Sergeant Robbins at five thirty in the morning in front of a dozen senior officers were clearly GPS coordinates ("Get it?" asked Detective Sergeant Robbins. "The key to many questions is *coordinated* …") and the coordinated location was a house in Twyford, Berkshire. While Commander Unwin discussed with the top brass whether to hit the house hard with a team from the Firearms Unit or to try a subtler infiltration approach, the team checked the house out on Street View and Google Maps. It was a large detached bungalow with an attached outbuilding, probably a garage, both set back from the road by a front garden and a gravel driveway, and with around half an acre of rear garden. It was in a cul-de-sac comprising similar sized properties and backing on to fields. The owner was identified as a lady whose main residence was in Maidenhead. Commander Unwin's decision was made for him by the discovery on Street View of a plaque on the side of the garage door that displayed three red diamonds, and the Firearms Unit was despatched.

By nine o'clock that morning, the perimeter had been breached and the house had been declared clear. Detective Sergeant Robbins and a team of Krakatoa detectives together with the forensics team then moved in to take the house to pieces. It was a substantial property, probably built in the sixties when they still used bricks and mortar for internal walls, meaning sound proofing was of a very high standard. The house was fitted with carpets and curtains in all rooms, but was completely unfurnished other than a single mattress in one bedroom, and the large en-suite bathroom attached to that bedroom had had all the appliances removed and had been tiled in white over all surfaces except the ceiling, and was spotlessly clean. There was a solid wooden high-backed arm chair fastened to the floor with steel brackets in the middle of the room, and a single bare lightbulb overhead. The only other noticeable feature was a stainless steel drain cover in the floor, and Superintendent Smith ordered a squad to come and rip up the floor and channel into the drains to look for traces of blood and body debris. A wheeled heavy duty parallel leg workshop floor crane was found in the garage.

By late afternoon, once the house and garage had had all preliminary investigations completed, Superintendent Smith began to coordinate interviews with the neighbours and utilities services to discover more about who had been using the house and paying the bills, while Detective Sergeant Robbins and a team of dog-handlers and specialists with ground penetrating radar scoured the gardens for signs of the scent of bodies and recent disturbances in the ground. Almost the entire garden was lawned, and the borders were planted with large shrubs and bushes and poorly maintained flower beds. A large apple tree stood in the middle of the lawn at the far end away from the house, and the back boundary was a ten foot high unkempt privet hedge. Both side boundaries were delineated with substantial wood fences, six feet high. It was pretty obvious that no burying of bodies had taken place here, either recently or for many months back. Which was a bit of a mystery, thought Detective Sergeant Robbins, since this was plainly the house with the white room, where dead bodies would have been manufactured with factory regularity, and in some cases bucketfuls of body bits too big to hose down the drain would have needed disposal.

By the end of the day, the house had been barricaded into a crime scene, with a mobile forensics caravan set up at the side of the road and an operations tent erected in the front garden, and the neighbours arrived home from work and were shocked to find floodlights and press satellite vans and Police swarming all over the street and the sound of jackhammers coming from the house, and nobody professed to having any inkling that the house had been occupied for criminal purposes. Meanwhile, Detective Sergeant Robbins had found three drainage manholes covered with cast iron rectangular lids, which he had been instructed to leave unopened for now; two near the back door, and one under a bush about ten yards from the house. The excavation squad would need to plot the routing of the underground drainage system and open them up in coordination with the drain pipe opening in the morning.

— o —

The following morning, the lack of evidence of body disposal was the main focus of the investigation. Plenty of blood liftings had been discovered in the white room in grouting between the tiles, and the drains under the floor, but it was not feasible that entire bodies could have been disposed of down the six inch drainage pipe system. Then it was discovered that the manhole further down the garden was not on the overall drainage plan.

Before investigating this anomaly, Detective Sergeant Robbins decided to visit the next door neighbours' property to see whether they had a similar feature, and the layout was identical. The neighbour, a man name Stan Griffin, had inherited the house from his parents, who had bought it new in 1963. Stan said that all the houses in the street had been fitted with septic tanks, and the remote manholes were septic tank covers, but they had never been used because the local authority had reversed a decision and installed mains drainage to the street before the houses were marketed. One or two owners had dug up the empty tanks, but most people left them in situ, and they tended to come in handy for disposing of broken televisions and the like.

And that was how Detective Sergeant Robbins made the discovery that would lead to him being promoted to Detective Inspector, two years before he retired. As he lifted the airtight manhole cover with half a dozen officers looking on, knowing what he would find, he discovered he was nonetheless unprepared for the overpowering stench of death which hit him in the face like half a brick and virtually lifted him off his feet and made him contaminate the crime scene with his half digested breakfast. After they eventually dug out the thousand gallon fibre glass tank with its contents intact, laid it on its side, cut it in two lengthwise and finished piecing together the putrefying liquid jigsaw puzzle inside, they announced that they had found the remains of eleven men, but unofficially were never one hundred percent certain of the number.

Detective Inspector Robbins retired to Spain with his new wife, having never come a single inch closer to apprehending Gregory John Grigg, aka Pimpinan, and the only charge laid in respect of the eleven men in the tank and the two men nailed to the wood by the time of his retirement remained un-prosecuted forever. A postman named Singh, who had conspired with Grigg but had steadfastly refused to talk about it, was charged with a single specimen count of conspiracy to commit murder, whereupon he had collapsed and died of a heart attack on the spot and had taken his secrets to the grave.

Epilogue

Terry and I have been best friends since we were kids. He was always the brainy one with the best social skills, while I was the fastest runner, the highest climber, the best swimmer and never lost a fight. Terry thinks he's the better looking of us, but I'm not convinced. At the age of twelve, we realised that if we pooled our resources, we were formidable. School bullies avoided us, the big kids showed us respect, and even teachers thought twice before bringing us to book. We went out of our way to be nice guys, polite and gentlemanly before we understood what gentlemanly meant, and tried to make everybody learn that being nice guys wasn't a sign of weakness.

After school, Terry had a successful career developing computer systems for the Police and military, until he joined the Police as a specialist IT forensic security consultant. Even fellow computer geeks say Terry can make computer systems sing. I joined the army, and travelled the world doing what I love best - making the world a better place. It made me feel important knowing that the army would never admit my existence. I loved to work alone, with everyone depending on me. When they wanted a high profile target to disappear, or some warlord snatched from his own house from under his bodyguards' noses, they would send me.

Terry never married, but he lives with his girlfriend. Terry was my best man, and the girls got on like a house on fire on the rare occasions we all got together. And then a house on fire changed everything.

At first, Terry was the most enthusiastic. He was the one that wanted to change the world, to clean the world up, whereas I simply had this rage inside me that was out of control. They say time is a healer, but some things cannot be healed. But time makes you more level-headed; makes you see things more clearly.

Terry had access to information and chose the spots. We call them spots; we would spot a cancer and then we would operate to remove it. I did all the work, and made sure it was all attributable to me and no trace of Terry could be picked up. But I couldn't have done it alone. At first it went well, and people noticed the difference. But then Terry began to feel the project was getting too big. He got nervous, and wanted to scale back. The crunch came when they started sniffing around, rightly suspecting my fingerprint records had been tampered with. They even asked Terry to consult on Operation Krakatoa for a week; asked him how it could be done.

It amazes me that a government can train you to disappear, to live undetected, to move around freely off the radar, and then finds itself powerless to stop you doing what it's trained you to do. But I have to be careful every second of every day. Their strategy is to wait for my mistake.

Anyhow, we're done for now. It was a drop in the ocean, but it made a few lives better. Now I'm patiently waiting for two men to come out of prison, as I have some very important questions for them.

About the Author

John Cooper is a pseudonym. The author uses a pseudonym because another well-known writer exists who writes under the author's real name. John Cooper is also the author's real name, and is not an alias. Confused? All will be revealed in the unlikely event the author is ever invited onto breakfast television.

John Cooper is an Englishman whose day job is consulting for American oil companies; writing contracts for major capital projects to develop offshore oil and gas fields in the Far East. He does this under his other real name, which is not an alias either. He currently lives in Bangkok with his wife, two small children and worryingly receding hairline.

Copyright

Printed in Great Britain
by Amazon